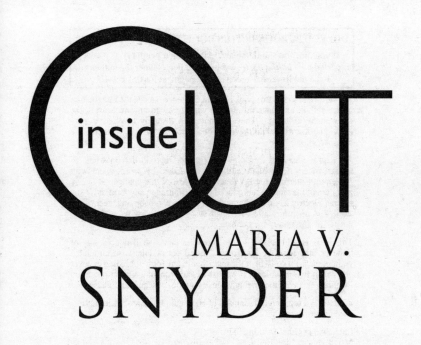

inside OUT

MARIA V. SNYDER

Published in Great Britain 2011
MIRA Books, Eton House, 18-24 Paradise Road,
Richmond, Surrey, TW9 1SR

© Maria V. Snyder 2010

ISBN 978 0 7783 0411 1

47-0111

Printed in the UK
by CPI Mackays, Chatham, ME5 8TD

To my niece, Amy Snyder, for your willingness to read my first manuscript. Your enthusiasm for my stories sparked the idea that I could write for a younger generation.

In loving memory of
my grandmother, Mary Salvatori,
and my best friend Hazel

1

A VIBRATION RIPPLED THROUGH MY BODY. I AWOKE

in semi-darkness, unsure of my location. Reaching out with
my hands, I felt smooth sides arching up and in. My fingers
touched overhead. Pipe.

A distant roar caused unease, but with sleep fogging my
mind, I couldn't quite grasp its significance. The pipe's vibrations increased as the thunder grew louder. Water. Coming
toward me. Fast.

I scrambled in the narrow space. My bare feet slipped on
the sleek surface of the pipe as I advanced toward a faint
square of bluelight emanating from the open hatch. It
seemed an impossible distance to reach.

Cogon's voice in full lecture mode echoed in my mind as
the water rushed closer. "Someday, Trella. You'll screw up
and there will be bits of you raining out of the showers."

I reached the hatch and dove headfirst through the
opening, convinced the water rushed at my heels. Landing
on the hard floor, I shot to my feet and slammed the door

shut. When I finished sealing the hatch, the whole pipe shuddered, then the vibrations calmed as the water returned to its normal flow. The metal cooled under my fingers, and I leaned my sweaty forehead against it, catching my breath.

That was close. Soft bluelight glowed all around the water-filtering machinery. Hour eighteen: I knew by the rush of water. The upper workers adhered to a strict schedule.

I checked my tool belt to make sure nothing was broken and my flashlight still worked. Then I climbed from the ductwork and made my way to level two by taking a shortcut through an air conduit. Traveling through the pipes and air shafts, I avoided seeing my fellow scrubs. But my peace and quiet ended too soon as I opened the vent, swung down and landed in the middle of a crowded corridor, scattering scrubs.

Someone knocked into me. "Watch it!"

"Come to mingle with the lowly scrubs, your highness?" A mocking bow.

Used to curses and hostile glares, I shrugged. The mass of people in the tight corridor jostled and pushed me along. Life in the lower two levels teamed with scrubs at all hours of the week. They moved from work to their barracks and back to work. We were called scrubs because rust and dust were the twin evils of Inside and must be kept at bay; however, scrubs also maintained the network of mechanical systems which kept both uppers and lowers alive.

The scrubs shoved. They frowned. They complained. I hated every one of them. Except Cog. No one hated Cog. He listened. Empathized with tales of misery. Made people smile. A rare occurrence—as rare as a person like Cogon.

I headed toward the cafeteria in Sector G2. It stayed open around the clock. As far as I could tell, Inside's length and width equaled a square with four levels. All constructed with sheet metal. Overall measurements, by my calculations—for reasons unknown Inside's exact dimensions and specifications were classified—were two thousand meters wide by two thousand meters long by twenty-five meters high. Each level was divided into nine areas.

If I drew a square with two lines across and two lines down inside it, I would end up with nine smaller squares. The first row's three squares would be labeled A, B and C, the next row D, E and F, and the last row G, H and I. With this configuration, there were four Quadrants A, C, G and I, which were Inside's corners, and five Sectors B, D, E, F and H. That was the basic map of each level. Boring, unoriginal, and predictable to say the least.

The cafeteria and dining room for the lower two levels encompassed all of Sector G2. The number two meant it was on the second level. Even a four-hundred-week-old scrub couldn't get lost. Hydroponics resided directly below in Sector G1—the lowest level—making it easy for the food growers to send vegetables to the kitchen scrubs.

The hot, musty smell of people packed together greeted me at the cafeteria's door as the noise of them slammed into me. I paused, deciding if eating was worth being in the same room with so many scrubs. My stomach growled, overruling my reluctance.

The line to get food remained perpetually long. I took a tray and waited, ignoring the stares. Most scrubs changed from their work clothes to wear the drab green off-duty jumpers before eating, but I was scheduled to scour an air duct at hour twenty. So I remained in my formfitting uniform. The slippery dark blue fabric covered every inch of skin except for my hands, feet and head. The material helped me slide through the tight heating ducts when I cleaned them. And I didn't care if I was the only person not wearing moccasins. My mocs were back at my bunk in Sector F1. With so many scrubs around to clean, the floor didn't even have a chance to become dirty.

Pushing my tray along the metal shelf, I pointed to what I wanted from three different choices. The big containers held either green-, yellow- or brown-colored slop, and they all smelled like moldy vegetables. The food was easy to prepare, easy to cook and best of all easy to reuse. I didn't even bother reading the names of the dishes. If the kitchen staff called it a casserole, a quiche, a stew or a soup, it all tasted the same. A pulpy, leafy spinach flavor dominated the other ingredients lurking in the recipe.

To be fair to the cooks, hydroponics didn't offer much in the way of variety. Mass production of the hardier vegetables had replaced diversity, and there was only so much a person can do with mutton. I didn't want to be fair, though. I just wanted something different to eat.

After being served, I found an empty seat, and let the discord of multiple conversations roll over me.

"Where've you been?" a voice asked over the din. I looked up at Cog's broad face as he pressed into a seat next to mine.

"Working," I said.

"You were supposed to be done at hour ten."

I shrugged. "Got to make sure the pipes are squeaky clean for the uppers."

"Yeah. Like it would take you that long," Cog said. "You were sleeping in the pipes again."

"Don't start."

"You're going to get hurt—"

"Who'd care? One less scrub to feed."

"Grumpy, aren't we? What's the matter, Trella? Get wet?" Cog smirked, but couldn't hold the expression for more than a second. He was soon smiling, unaffected by my mood.

"Shouldn't you be changing a fan belt or something?" I asked, trying to be nasty, but Cog ignored me, knowing it was all an act—although with any other scrub, I wouldn't be acting.

He nodded to scrubs passing our table, calling out hellos and sharing his smile.

"How's the shower head in washroom E2?" Cog asked one man.

"Much better," the man replied.

I had no interest in mundane details so I tuned out their conversation. Instead, I contemplated my only friend. Too big to fit into the pipes, Cog worked with the maintenance crew and did odd jobs. Most of it busy work, just like scrubbing. Too many idle hands had been deemed dangerous by the upper workers.

Scrubs also labored in the recycling plant, the infirmary, the care facility, hydroponics, the kitchen, the livestock yard, solid-waste facility or in the waste-water treatment plant. Most scrubs were assigned their jobs. A Care Mother noted the skills and aptitudes of each of her charges and recommended positions. My smaller size automatically matched me as a cleaning scrub. It suited me just fine.

"When's your next shift?" Cog asked.

"One hour."

"Good. Someone wants to meet you." Cog's eyes held an avid glow.

"Not another prophet. Come on, Cog, you know better."

"But this time—"

"Probably just like the last time, and the time before and the five times before that. All talk. No action, pushing false hope. You know they have to be employed by the upper officials to keep the scrubs from rioting."

"Trell, you're jaded. Besides, he asked for you by *name*. Said you were the only one who could help him." Cog seemed to think this divine calling should impress me.

"I have better things to do with my time." I picked up my tray, intent on leaving.

"Like sleeping in the pipes? Pretending you're all alone, instead of crammed in here with everyone else?"

I scowled at him. My fiercest frown, which usually resulted in some breathing room.

Cog stepped closer. "Come on. Hear the guy out."

Again, his face glowed with the conviction of a true believer. *Poor Cog,* I thought. How can he set himself up for another crushing disappointment? How can I turn him down? Especially when he was the only one who remained my friend despite my abuse. And who'd watched out for me, growing up in the care facility together.

"Okay. I'll listen, but no promises," I said. Perhaps I could expose this prophet as a fraud to keep Cog from becoming too involved.

Dumping our trays in the wash bins, we left the cafeteria. Cog led the way through the main corridors of the second level toward the stairs in Quad A2.

The narrow hallways of Inside had been constructed with studded metal walls painted white. Only Pop Cops' posters, spewing the latest propaganda, scrub schedules and the list of proper conduct could decorate common area walls on levels one and two. At least the massive bundles of greenery in every section of Inside helped break up the monotony. Although, if the plants weren't needed to clean the air, I was sure the Pop Cops would remove those, too.

I would never have had the patience to fight my way along the main paths, but Cog's thick body left a wake behind him. I followed along in this space, walking without effort and without touching anyone. A moment of peace.

We descended the wide metal steps. Cold stabbed the soles of my feet and I wished I had worn my mocs. Bare feet were useful in the air ducts, but not in the main throughways.

Cog led me to Sector B1. This prophet showed some intelligence. Sector B1 was filled with laundry machines. Rows upon rows of washers and dryers lined up like soldiers waiting for orders. The laundry was the most populated area, it had the largest number of workers, and every scrub in the lower levels came here for fresh uniforms.

Surrounded by a throng, the prophet had set himself up on an elevated dais near the break room so everyone could see him.

"…conditions are deplorable. The uppers have rooms to themselves and yet you sleep in barracks. But your suffering will not go unrewarded. You'll find peace and all the room you want Outside." The prophet's voice was strong. His words could be heard over the hiss and rattle of the machines.

I leaned over to Cog. "The wheelchair's a different touch. He'll gain the sympathy vote. What's his name?"

"Broken Man," Cog said with reverence.

I barked out a laugh. The prophet stopped speaking and focused his gray eyes on me. I stared back.

"You find something amusing?" Broken Man asked.

"Yes."

Cog stepped in front of me. "This is Trella."

The man in the wheelchair snapped his mouth shut in surprise. Obviously, I wasn't what he had expected.

"Children, I must speak with this one in private," he said.

I had to stifle another snort of disbelief. As if there was such a thing as privacy in the lower levels.

The crowd dispersed, and I was face-to-face with the latest prophet. Long blond hair, thin narrow face and no calluses on his hands. There were no blonds in the lower levels. Hair dye was a luxury reserved for the uppers only.

"Trella," he said in a deep, resonant voice.

"Look," I said. "You're more than welcome to seduce these sheep," I waved my hand at the working scrubs. "But don't sing your song of a better place to Cog. When you go back upstairs to reapply your hair dye, I don't want him left hurting."

"Trell," Cog said, shooting me a warning look.

"You don't believe me?" Broken Man asked.

"No. You're just an agent for the Pop Cops. Spewing the same bull about how our hard work will be rewarded after we're recycled. Oh, you might stick around for a hundred weeks or so, but then you'll be gone with the next shift and another 'prophet' will take your place." I cocked my head to the side, considering. "Maybe the next guy will have a missing limb. Especially if your wheelchair angle works."

Broken Man laughed, causing the nearby scrubs to glance over at us. "Cog said you would be difficult, but I think he spoke too kindly." He studied my face.

Impatient, I asked, "What do you want?"

"I need your expertise," Broken Man said.

"What expertise?"

"You know every duct, corridor, pipe, shortcut, hole and

ladder of Inside. Only you will be able to retrieve something I need."

"How did you know?"

"I've heard rumors about the Queen of the Pipes. Cogon confirmed them."

I glared at my friend. The scrubs in my Care group had given me the title and not because they admired my tendency to explore the ductwork. Just the opposite. They had teased me for my desire to spend time alone.

"Will you help me?" Broken Man asked.

"What is it?" I asked.

"You were right," he said. He leaned forward and lowered his voice. "I used to live in the upper levels."

I stepped back in alarm.

"No," he rushed to assure me, "I'm not part of the Population Control Police. What do you call them? Pop Cops? I worked as an air controller, keeping track of the air systems, making sure the filters were clean and the oxygen levels breathable." Broken Man opened his mouth wide and pointed to a large gap in his bottom back teeth. "See the space for my port?"

"Anyone can have missing teeth," I said. "I know a lady in Sector D1 who'll get rid of anything you want. Including body parts."

Broken Man rubbed a hand over his face. His long thin fingers traced a graceful line down his throat. "Look. I *have* to spout the propaganda. If I tell the scrubs Gateway exists and the Pop Cops are lying to them, the Pop Cops will recycle me."

I felt as though he'd shot a stunner at my chest. He mentioned Gateway in a matter-of-fact tone. Gateway was a myth in the lower levels. The Pop Cops insisted no physical doorway existed to Outside. But stories and rumors circulated despite their claims, and everyone liked to speculate on its location.

The Pop Cops' prophets preached that Outside could only be attained after a person's life ends. And only if the person worked hard and obeyed Inside's laws. If a scrub was worthy, his inner soul would travel to Outside while his physical body would be fed to Chomper.

Most of the scrubs believed this Pop Cop dribble. I didn't. Souls were a myth and our bodies stayed trapped Inside.

"Come again?" I asked Broken Man.

"Gateway exists and I can prove it. Before coming down here, I hid some disks in a duct above my sleeping quarters, number three-four-two-one in Sector F3. I need them and only you can retrieve them without being seen. The disks might have information on the location of Gateway."

"Might have?" He was backpedaling already.

"I didn't get a chance to look at them."

"How convenient. I'm not authorized to go above level two. There are locked air filters to keep undesirables out, and if the Pop Cops catch me, I could have an unpleasant encounter with Chomper and end up as fertilizer for hydroponics." I shivered. Inside didn't have room for many holding cells. Undesirables were simply recycled at the whim of the Pop Cops.

"Hasn't stopped you before," Cog said.

I punched him in the arm. "Shut up."

He smiled.

"Perhaps she's scared," Broken Man said.

"Not scared. Just not stupid enough to walk into a trap," I said.

"I meant that you might be scared because I'm telling the truth, and then you'd have to believe me."

"I don't have to believe anything. Especially not your lies." I turned to Cog. "Watch this one."

When I began to walk away, Broken Man called, "Going to clean air duct number seventeen?"

I stopped.

"I was in charge of the cleaning schedules before my 'accident.'"

I turned back. "Nice try, but cleaning assignments are posted all over the lower levels. See, Cog, he's grasping at air. A true prophet wouldn't have to trick someone into believing him."

"I'm sure no prophet has had to deal with Trella Garrard Sanchia before," Broken Man said.

My blood froze in my veins. Scrubs didn't worry about bloodlines; most knew nothing about their biological parents. Most didn't care. Scrubs birthed more scrubs. We mixed blood like paint. Too many colors combined, and we ended up with brown-eyed, brown-haired babies who were raised in Care groups until they were old enough to work. Me included. With my brown hair and eyes, I blended right in with the scrubs.

Only the uppers worried about bloodlines and maintaining family groups. And Population Control. They kept track of every person in Inside.

Garrard and Sanchia were two of the family names used in the upper levels.

Broken Man watched me. "That's right, Trella," he said. "Your father was from the Garrard line and your mother is a Sanchia. You were born with your father's blue eyes until they changed them." He paused a moment to let the information sink in. "You don't quite fit. Not a purebred by upper standards, but quite the thoroughbred down here."

2

"HOW DO YOU KNOW?" I ASKED.

"I told you I used to live in the upper levels. But if you want more information about your parents, you'll have to get my disks first." Broken Man leaned back in his chair with a pleased smirk.

I stepped toward him, planning to agree. A cold jab of logic halted my steps. I couldn't believe I'd almost fallen for it. Why would I care about parents who left me to be raised by scrubs?

"You spout some bull about bloodlines and think I'll get all teary eyed and desperate to find information about my parents. No deal." I grabbed Cog's arm and turned him to face me. "Stay away from this man. He's dangerous." Then I hurried to my cleaning assignment, before Cog could argue with me.

I tried not to think about Broken Man as I scrubbed the air duct, but following the circular cleaning brush with its humming vacuum was mindless work. The cleaning device looked like a hairy troll spinning and singing to himself. All

I had to do was turn him on, make sure he didn't break down and then turn him off at the end of the conduit.

Being slender and a little over one and a half meters tall made me the perfect candidate for this duty, but I also knew how to repair the troll if it broke. Thanks to Cog. He had taught me, and I was one of the few scrubs who carried a special tool belt. The black band was constructed of the same slippery material as my uniform. Each of its eight pockets contained a tool. The band held them and my flashlight snug against my waist. Regular tool belts wouldn't work in the tight air shafts. The hanging tools would bang on the metal and impede my motion.

Nothing out of the ordinary happened during my shift. I had plenty of time for the information Broken Man had told me to eat its way through the layers of my mind like acid sizzling through metal.

Devious, the way he had phrased his words. Your father was from the Garrard line. Past tense, meaning he was dead. Your mother is a Sanchia, implying she was still alive. Devious, except he had forgotten I had been raised as a scrub. Family lines meant nothing to me. Biological parents were the concern of the Pop Cops. I might have a fondness for my Care Mother (CM), but that was as far as it went. Broken Man was just trying to con me into his schemes. Give the Pop Cops a reason to recycle me.

The cleaning troll grunted as his motor strained. He had come to a bend. I gave him a little push, and the troll continued on his way. The angle of the air duct started to sharpen. I braced myself in the pipe, using my bare feet to climb behind the troll. The air shaft was one of the main trunk lines, servicing multiple levels of Inside. It cut between the levels and I could follow the troll up to level four if I could unlock the air filter between levels two and three.

Broken Man's voice tapped into my mind. Information about Gateway might be on some disks hidden on level three. Might be. Most likely not. At least I would have proof the prophet was a fake to show Cog.

During my ten-hour shift of babysitting the troll, I kept changing my mind about whether or not to check Broken Man's story. When the troll finished the last air duct on my schedule, I pulled him out and stored him in a cleaning closet.

Officially, I was off duty until hour forty. All scrubs had the same schedule. Ten hours off, ten hours on, with a break every five hours. There were no such things as vacations or holidays. Since one week equaled one hundred hours, we worked five shifts per week. Everything in Inside could be divided by the number ten. It made life simple so even the scrubs could understand. Work groups comprised ten scrubs. One CM for every ten children. Ten weeks equaled a deciweek, and a hundred weeks was called a centiweek. And so on. Although, a few old-timers called a centiweek a long year, but I had no idea what that meant.

The work shifts were also staggered so only half the scrubs worked at one time. It saved room in the barracks. I shared my bunk with another scrub I never saw. Not that I ever slept there anyway.

My shift ended on level two in Sector D, and I needed to make a decision. Below me were the rows and rows of bunks that filled Sectors D, E and F on both lower levels. From this location, it was just a matter of heading due east for two sectors, then up one level to search for Broken Man's disks.

The uppers filled their two levels of housing sectors with roomy apartments and vast suites for the important officials.

Only certain loyal scrubs had authorization to clean and maintain the upper levels, and to deliver food and laundry. Not me. I had no desire to ingratiate myself to earn the Pop Cops' trust. They rarely policed the ductwork with their sensors, believing in their filters and the passivity of the scrubs. I grinned. Except for a few of us, they were right.

Although I remembered the stories about when the Pop Cops had tried to place video cameras in the lower levels. Each and every one had disappeared. No witnesses came forward, and no evidence had been found. Eventually the cameras became another lost part of our world. Something we once had. Our computers have a whole list of things which met this criterion, but I didn't care. No sense bemoaning what was gone. A waste of time. Better to worry about what weapons the Pop Cops could use now.

It would be a challenge to search for the disks while avoiding the scrubs and Pop Cops. Like Cog had said, the threat of getting into trouble hasn't stopped me before, and I have explored all the upper level ducts more for the challenge than just to break the rules. In the end my curiosity was too great to walk away. I found an appropriate air conduit and slipped inside the tight space.

The rush of air blew past me in the active duct. Closing my eyes, I concentrated on the warm current as it caressed my face. I pulled my hair from its single long braid, and let it flow behind me, imagining for a moment that I flew.

The air shaft ended in a scrubber—a tight wire mesh impossible to bypass without unlocking and removing the cleaning filters nestled inside. This was the barrier to keep the scrubs down in their levels. I could have dismantled it and reattached the lock and filters when I returned, but the effort would eat up a lot of time.

Instead, I backtracked until I found a near-invisible hatch and opened it. Climbing from the duct, I stood on top of level two above Sector F. Pipes and wires hung down, criss-crossed and bisected the open space. I called it the Gap.

Between the levels of Inside, spaces ranged from one meter to one and a half meters high. A two-meter gap existed between the walls of the levels and the true Walls of Inside. The levels were bolted to these Walls with steel I-beams, and foam insulation had been sprayed onto them.

As far as I could tell, no one knew about the Gap. Only four near-invisible hatches offered access to it—one on each level. I had spent hundreds of hours in the shafts before I discovered them. I didn't care what the reason was for such a space around the levels, it suited me just fine.

Bluelight shone and I negotiated the obstacle course of ducts to reach the east Wall. One of the six metal dividers framing our world, it was the barrier between Inside and whatever existed beyond.

A ladder was bolted to the Wall. It stretched from the very bottom of Inside to just above level four. Using it would make climbing to the air ducts above the third level easier. Except for two problems. A two-meter space gaped between where I stood on the edge of level two and the ladder. To use the ladder, I would need to traverse the thin I-beam connecting level two to the Wall. If I slipped, I would plummet about ten meters. The drop might not kill me right away, but if I broke my legs no one would know where to find me.

Breaks in the ladder were the second problem with the

route. Someone long ago had cut off portions of the ladder as if they hoped to limit access to the upper levels. I had strung chains between the breaks, but climbing them required a great deal of upper-body strength.

No sense wasting time. A tingle of apprehension brushed my skin. I moved onto the I-beam. The beam was a little wider than my foot. Balancing on it, I placed one foot in front of the other with care. Once I mounted the ladder, I climbed until I reached the chain. Taking a deep breath, I wrapped my legs around the slender metal links and pulled myself up hand over hand to the next complete section of the ladder.

By the time I reached the next rung, sweat soaked my uniform and coated my palms. As I stretched for the bar, my fingers slipped.

I started to fall. Three wild heartbeats later, I managed to stop my descent by gripping the chain. When my body stopped swinging in midair, I grinned at the near miss. My pulse tapped a fast rhythm, matching my huffs for breath. I waited a moment before returning to the top of the chain. My second attempt to transfer to the ladder worked.

Navigating through the ductwork, I found the near-invisible hatch for level three and climbed inside the air shaft, searching for the sleeping quarters in Sector F.

Broken Man had said a duct above his rooms. Logic suggested he wouldn't use a water pipe, too messy, or an electrical conduit, no space. He had been an air controller so it stood to reason I would find the disks, if they existed, in the air shaft. *If.*

I crawled through the shaft above the rooms, counting. Small rectangles of daylight warned me when a room was occupied, and I took extra care to be quiet. Stealing glances into the quarters as I slipped by, I spotted uppers working on their computers.

I usually avoided the populated sections. One sneeze and I would be permanently assigned to the solid-waste-handling crew. The crap cleaners. Nothing like the threat of unclogging *those* pipes to keep scrubs in line.

When I reached number three-four-two-one, I peered into the darkness below. The lack of light noteworthy. Inside had two light levels. Daylight for when people were awake and working and bluelight for sleeping. Bluelight was also used for temporarily unoccupied areas where, as soon as a person entered, the daylights would turn on. In the barracks, the bluelights stayed on all the time.

Darkness in Broken Man's room meant it had been unoccupied for a long time. I shined my flashlight through the vent. The living area appeared normal. Sweeping my light on the walls of the shaft, I searched for the disks. At first, nothing caught my eye, but a strange bulge cast a slight shadow. I rubbed my fingertips over the bump and felt a slender edge.

Booby-trapped, I thought at first. Then I considered what I would do if I wanted to hide something from the Pop Cops. Either find a niche they didn't scan, tuck it behind a lead-lined piece of machinery or camouflage it.

Using my fingernails, I peeled back a thin metal sheet. Underneath was a cloth bag.

I'd been so sure Broken Man had lied, I was almost disappointed. Almost. Let's face it; if Gateway existed, I wouldn't be upset.

I shook my head. These were dangerous thoughts. They

led to hope and hope led to pain. I squelched them and focused on the contents of the bag. Four disks with rainbow rays streaked around their silver surfaces. Enthralled, I dropped the bag. It slipped through the vent and floated to the floor.

I shrugged. No big deal. Until a red light pulsed in the dark room below. Then daylight flooded the chamber as gas hissed.

Booby-trapped was right. But not the camouflage— Broken Man's rooms. Smoke filled the air shaft. I held my breath as my eyes stung and watered, blurring my vision. Pushing back, I blindly scooted away. The door banged open and a man ordered, "Halt."

Instinctively, I halted.

"Clear the gas," a female voice ordered.

A pump hummed and the gray fog around me disappeared.

Voices echoed in the chamber. Boots drummed on the floor.

"Guard the door."

"Fan out and search."

"Watch for ambush."

I wiped the tears from my eyes, eased back to the vent and peeked in. A woman stepped into my view. An intricate knot pulled her blond hair back from her face. She wore the uniform of the Population Control Police, purple with silver stripes down the outsides of the sleeves and pants. Her black weapon belt bulged to such an extreme that she looked like she wore a tire. A lieutenant commander's insignia glinted on her collar.

A lieutenant snapped to attention beside her. "No one here, sir."

"Impossible. Look again," she ordered.

He rushed off.

She scanned the room, then spotted the bag on the floor. She tipped her head back and looked directly into the vent. Every cell in my body turned to ice.

"All sectors clear, sir," another Pop Cop said.

"Get me some RATSS," she yelled. "Post guards on all air vents in Sector F3. Now!"

Her order shocked me into action. I hustled along the duct with as much speed as I could muster one-handed. The Pop Cops' Remote Access Temperature Sensitive Scanner (RATSS) would search me out through the ducts using heat-seeking technology. I had to leave Sector F3. Now. I had to find a hot spot to hide in.

As I slid through the air shaft, snatches of conversations reached me from the corridors where an alarming number of Pop Cops rushed to take up positions under the vents. I just stayed ahead of them.

"Someone sprung the trap."

"Escaping through the vents."

"Use the gas."

"Stunners only. No kill-zappers."

"Alert all sectors on level three."

My heart hammered, driving me forward on the edge of panic. With the Pop Cops in every room, I couldn't get to the near-invisible hatch. Instead, I raced toward Sector B3 where I knew of a well-placed laundry chute I could use. Impossible to climb up, laundry chutes only worked one way.

Just before I reached the chute, something bit my foot. Yelping, I twisted around. A RATSS had clamped on my toe. Damn!

Its little antennae vibrated, probably reporting my position. Imagining the information racing through the complex network of wires crisscrossing every level, I yanked my wrench from my tool belt and smashed the RATSS. After reducing it to scrap, I jerked it off my foot.

When I reached the laundry chute, I slid down two levels without having any dirty garments tossed on my head. A small bonus. I landed in a half-full bin.

The dryers hummed productively, creating one of the warmest sections of Inside. If a RATSS had followed me here, it would lose me in the heat from them and from the mass of scrubs who labored here.

I found a small crawl space behind a row of dryers and collapsed into it to catch my breath.

Questions swirled in my mind. Where to go now? I couldn't give the disks to Broken Man. He might have orchestrated this whole thing. Obviously the Pop Cops had set a trap for whoever came to collect the disks. But why not rig the vent? Maybe they hadn't known where the disks were located. That would mean Broken Man wasn't involved. So why hadn't they interrogated him before sending him down here? I hadn't wanted any trouble. Now I swam in it.

I could hide the disks on level three for the Pop Cops to find. If Broken Man wasn't a plant, then they'd known someone had come for them, but not who. Then I could walk away. Stay uninvolved. It was the safest course of action. The smartest move. The Pop Cops would have what they wanted.

Broken Man had said the disks might reveal the location of Gateway. Why risk my neck for a possibility? For something even I didn't believe in.

I just couldn't give the Pop Cops what they wanted. It rankled too much. Shoving the disks into a pocket of my belt, I hurried to find Broken Man.

Pop Cops had infested the lower level. Groups of three and four scanned the scrubs, occasionally stopping and questioning one. My skin burned where it touched the pocket concealing the disks. Trying to remain calm and invisible, I searched for Broken Man.

The dais he had used as a pulpit was empty. Cogon sat on the edge of the platform with his head in his hands.

"What happened?" I asked.

"Broken Man's gone," he said to the floor.

"Disappeared?" Figures, I thought. He was a plant and I had fallen for it like a gullible three-hundred-week-old.

"No. Taken." Cog looked up. Blood ran down his face from a gash on his forehead.

"Cog!" I ran and grabbed a towel from one of the laundry bins lining the hall. A few scrubs folded sheets nearby, appearing to ignore us, but I knew better.

"Here." I wiped Cog's eye and cheek, pressing the cloth to the cut. "Who did this to you?" Cog was a big man. No scrubs would dare fight him.

"Pop Cops," he said.

The significance of Cog's word *taken* finally sank in. My world shrank, tightening around my body until I felt like I was being crushed. Interrogation of Broken Man would lead the Pop Cops to me.

"When?" I demanded.

"Just now." Cog gestured down the hallway. "I tried to talk to them. Stop them. But…" He touched his forehead.

Figures. The Pop Cops knew a good beating was an effective way to warn a scrub. Give them trouble another time and a scrub is arrested and never seen again in the lower levels.

"How many?"

"Three to subdue me," he said with a smile, "but only one took him away. He can't do much from a wheelchair."

"You could have been fed to Chomper," I admonished him, but I was distracted.

"Could have, Trell. Doesn't mean I would have. Besides, I would have felt terrible if I didn't try to help." He sighed. "I'm talking to a wall. You don't care about anyone in this place."

An old argument. My response would be how I cared about him, and he would claim I had a funny way of showing it. But not this time. "You're right. So why do you bother with me? Why do you drag me to listen to every prophet?"

"It's called hope. It's called seeing the best in people despite the miserable conditions." He grabbed the towel from me. His shoulders sagged as he covered his face with the bloody cloth. "Maybe you're right and it's all a lie." He gestured to Broken Man's dais.

The prophet hadn't lied about the disks, but soon the Pop Cops would know about them, too. A plan raced along the circuits of my mind. "Which way did the Pop Cop take Broken Man?"

"Why?" Confusion pushed his thick eyebrows together.

"Just answer."

"Toward Quad A1. Probably going to take him up the lift to level four."

I had to hurry. "Cog, you better get to the infirmary. I need to go."

"Go where?" He glanced at the clock. "Your shift doesn't start for another two hours."

"Not your concern," I said, looking up at the ductwork. I quickened my pace, planning the best route to Quadrant A's lift.

But Cogon trailed after me. "Why do you care which way he went?"

I ignored him.

"He must be right," Cog called. His voice bright and strong again. Back to normal. "Broken Man's right about Gateway. Why else would the Pop Cops take him?"

I just shook my head.

The corridor to Quad A1 teemed with scrubs and Pop Cops, hopefully delaying progress of the Pop Cop pushing the wheelchair. When I spotted an air vent, I climbed up the metal wall. Metal rivets on the walls were the perfect size for my toes and fingers. Once inside the air duct, I scurried through the horizontal tube, using my hands and feet while sliding on my belly.

The hum of the lift set every nerve in my body afire. If they were in the elevator, I was too late. Occasionally, I slowed to peer through the air vents, trying to spot Broken Man.

I grunted with frustration. A Pop Cop wheeled Broken Man into the open lift.

3

I HAD MERE SECONDS TO RESCUE BROKEN MAN.
Good thing level one's near-invisible hatch was next to the
lift. I scrambled out of the air pipe and hunched my way over
to the shaft. The elevator's shaft was solid except for half-
meter openings at each level's Gap. If the lift passed level
one's, I would be too late.

Reaching the opening, I glanced inside. The lift remained
on level one, but the doors hissed closed. I squeezed through
and landed on the lift's roof. I held still, listening as something scraped against the doors before they shut.

"Stop," a voice ordered.

The lift began its ascent. I clutched a cable to keep from
falling. Huddled on top, I regained my balance. Risking
notice, I pried up the roof hatch just enough to see inside.

A meter below me, Broken Man slumped in his wheelchair, while a Pop Cop stood with his stunner pointed at
Cog. The big oaf must have squeezed into the elevator to
rescue his prophet, and now he was caught.

I altered my plan. Tracing wires, I found the electric feed into the elevator and fitted the white electrical wire between my rubber-handled pliers. I opened the emergency control panel on the roof, yelled, "Fire drill" and punched the stop button while cutting the wire. The lift jerked to a halt.

The occupants of the elevator were now in total darkness. I hoped Cog knew what to do. My call had warned him. As I lifted the hatch, a soft thud, a loud grunt and the unmistakable sizzle slap of the stun gun reached me.

"What's going on?" Broken Man asked with a nervous tremor in his voice.

I sucked in my breath, biting my lip.

"We need to get out of here," Cog replied.

Relief washed over me as my clenched muscles relaxed. I pulled the hatch wide open. It squeaked.

"Trella?" Cog asked.

"Hold on. I'll get a light." I fumbled for the flashlight on my belt as Broken Man repeated my name in shock.

I leaned through the open hatch, dangling upside down from my waist and held out my light. The Pop Cop lay on his side. His wide-eyed, lifeless gaze stared at nothing.

Cogon gaped at the Pop Cop's weapon in his own hand in horror. "This is a stun gun," he cried. "Why would it kill him?"

"What's the setting?" I asked.

Cog just looked at me. His eyebrows pinched together, and confusion shone in his eyes.

"The intensity." I tried again. "It's on the side."

Cog turned the weapon over. "Ten."

"That's why. It's on the maximum setting. A ten blast could easily kill an average-sized man." I still didn't see understanding in Cog's creased face. "You're twice the Pop

Cop's size. I would have set the damn thing to ten, too, if I had to incapacitate you. Look, we don't have time for this. We need to get Broken Man to a hiding place."

"Impossible," Broken Man said. "Inside has no hiding place." His face looked pale in the light.

I smiled at Broken Man's regurgitation of Pop Cop propaganda, then pulled myself back onto the roof. Using my rubber-handled pliers again, I fixed the broken wire, restored the lights and accessed the lift's controls.

"Push the button for level two," I called.

When we reached level two, I opened the back doors. A maintenance room was located adjacent to the elevator shaft.

"Cog, wheel him out and take the Pop Cop, too."

Cogon finally realized how dangerous it was to delay. Galvanized into action, he cleared everyone from the elevator.

"Leave them here, and get back on the lift," I said through the roof's hatch.

"He can't stay here. It'll be the first place they'll look," Cog said.

"I know, but he can't travel through the corridors. We'll have to camouflage him."

"How?"

"Laundry bin."

Understanding smoothed Cog's face. He delivered the laundry to the upper levels, so it wouldn't look out of place if he was seen pushing a bin.

With Cog as the sole occupant, I sent the lift back to level one, and again opened the back doors. This time the doors led to the laundry. Bins full of clean laundry filled the area by the lift. Cog grabbed one, waved to the working scrubs and pushed it into the elevator. I brought him back to level two.

"Stand in the doorway," I said. Returning the controls to the panel inside the lift, I swung down. "Help me put the hatch back on." I sat on Cog's broad shoulders and replaced the cover.

We joined Broken Man in the maintenance room as the lift resumed its regular service. The bin was full of towels. We removed them and Cog lifted Broken Man into the bin.

Before we covered him, he asked, "My wheelchair?"

"It's too big. We'll have to leave it behind," I said.

"Now what?" Cog asked as he finished arranging the towels.

"Take him down to Quad C1, but don't use this lift."

"To the Power plant?" Cog asked.

"Yes. I'll meet you there."

"What about the Pop Cop?"

"Leave him. Someone will find him."

"And the stun gun?" he asked.

"Put it back in his belt. It's too dangerous to keep." The Pop Cops would be mad enough once they discover a fallen colleague, but it would be worse if they believed one of the scrubs was armed.

Kneeling beside the prone form, Cog shoved the weapon into the Pop Cop's holder, but he paused. He closed the man's eyes and smoothed his limbs to a more comfortable position—not that the Pop Cop would care. Cog rested a large hand on the man's shoulder, bowed his head and whispered. Only the words *sorry* and *journey* were audible to me.

I suppressed the urge to hurry him, knowing Cog needed this time. When he finished, he stood and wheeled the bin from the room. I waited for a few minutes before climbing into the air shaft. I traveled to level one to assess the situation.

Walking through the corridors, I scanned faces. Level one

appeared normal. So far, the Pop Cops hadn't raised an alarm. I headed to Quad C1.

I pressed past some scrubs until I found a heating vent near the floor. After sliding inside, I replaced the vent cover and rested in the warm metal tube, catching my breath. The enormity of what I had just done slammed into me. My body shook as doubt and fear fought for control. With effort, I pushed the ugly thoughts away; I had no time for recriminations. Right now I navigated by instinct alone.

Propelled by the need to keep moving, I followed the heated air to its source. The Power plant in Quad C1 was Inside's beating heart. It pumped out electricity and heat to keep us all alive. Encompassing all of Quadrant C on the first, second, third and fourth levels, the plant's main controls were located on level four. Noise, excessive heat, dirt and fuel tanks filled level one, and hardly anyone worked in this area.

The air burned my lungs as I drew closer to the plant, forcing me to leave the vent. Sweat soaked my uniform, but a sudden chill gripped my spine when I couldn't find Cogon and Broken Man anywhere near the plant.

My name sounded in the thick air and I spun in time to see Cogon waving me over. He had hidden behind one of the fuel tanks. Broken Man was propped up in the laundry bin.

"Now what?" Cog shouted over the chugging engines.

"There's an abandoned controller's room by the fuel-intake valve." I pointed. "The door's locked, but I can open it from the inside."

Finding the air return duct crossing over the controller's quarters, I had Cogon lift me up to it. I crawled through the duct until I found a vent into the controller's room. I had discovered this small living space on one of my excursions.

Thinking it was a perfect hideaway, I had proceeded to make it my own. It hadn't taken me long to figure out why it had been empty. The intolerable noise from the plant, the oppressive heat and the fine coating of black grit covering everything had eventually driven me away despite the rarity of such a space.

As Cog wheeled Broken Man in, I cleaned the room as best as I could with the towels. Cog lifted the prophet into a chair. Dust puffed out from the cushions.

We stared at each other for a moment as the engines roared.

"We're in trouble," Cog yelled. "This isn't going to work. They'll find us."

"They'll think I killed the Pop Cop. I'll be recycled," Broken Man said.

"You were going to be recycled anyway," I said.

Broken Man jerked his head in shock.

"What did you think they would do after they interrogated you?" I asked.

"But what happened to you?" the prophet asked.

"Yeah, why are you here, Trella?"

Broken Man's nose crinkled in confusion. He was either a good actor or genuinely flustered. Drowning in trouble and still unable to trust the blond-haired man, I hesitated. Cogon stepped toward me, a mixture of fear and anger twisting his face. An expression I had never seen on Cog. There was only one scrub I cared for in this whole metal world, and he wallowed in this predicament with me.

Damn. I pulled out the disks, spreading them in my hands like a fan. Cog's mouth dropped open as though someone had slapped him.

Broken Man raked his fingers through his hair as understanding dawned. "But the Pop Cops didn't know about the disks," he said.

"Why not?" I asked.

"I used an untraceable port and covered my tracks for the file transfer. However, I wasn't as clever with my other forays into the computer system and was caught. When they questioned me before my accident and exile, they hadn't a clue about the hidden files."

He glanced around the room. "Unless they suspected."

"So the Pop Cops rigged your former quarters just in case," I said.

"Why not just pick me up and ask?" Broken Man shuddered. The Pop Cops had a gruesome reputation.

"They knew where to find you. They knew you didn't have the disks on you. Plus if they waited, they could see who you recruited to break the rules in order to help you."

"That's why you rescued him," Cog said. "You started this whole mess by getting the disks."

I bit down on my retort. In my mind, Cogon had started it when he introduced me to his prophet, but in fairness I had made the decision to retrieve the disks. "All right," I said to Broken Man. "Cog and I'll have to lay low for a while. Let's hope no one spotted Cog entering the lift. You'll have to hide here."

"The scanners?" he asked.

"The power and heat coming off those engines plays havoc with their scanners. This room hasn't been used for hundreds of weeks. Keep the door locked at all times."

Cog rubbed a hand over his face. "I could put a blind in front of the door."

"A blind?" I asked.

"It's a thin sheet of metal. The maintenance crew uses them to cover holes and dents in the walls. If you match the rivets up right, no one can tell what's behind the blind. I'll do it during my next shift," he said.

"Good. Make sure no one sees you. And when you're done, keep far away from this room. I'll take care of Broken Man."

Cog nodded, pulled out a set of earplugs from his belt and handed them to Broken Man. "I'll also bring some insulating foam to cut down the noise."

The quarters had a bathroom, but I had to make sure the water was turned on. Our shifts started in a few minutes. "Can you take care of yourself for the next shift?" I asked the prophet.

"I'll be fine for now," he replied though his eyes looked a little wild. He held his hand out. "I'll keep the disks."

"No. If they find you, they find the disks. I'll hide them," I said. I stuffed the disks back into my belt. Broken Man pulled his hand away. His expression guarded.

Cog left through the door, and I locked it behind him. "I'll be back after my shift with a few supplies."

The prophet blinked at me, but said nothing as he pushed the green foam plugs into his ears.

I climbed into the vents and found the valves to turn on the water. Then I hurried to level two to report for work.

Ten hours seemed like an eternity as my thoughts dwelled on the need to hide the disks.

After my shift, I climbed to level four. This time I didn't slip and I didn't encounter any RATSS. Ultrasonic scanners and RATSS they might have, but I knew plenty of hiding places all over Inside where the electromagnetic currents scrambled ultrasonic waves. Spots that reflected a solid wall on their scanner displays. I stayed in those hidden areas as I traveled.

In the Gap on top of level four, I had hidden a small box where I kept my valuables. It was difficult to find and dangerous to reach. Perfect for hiding Broken Man's disks.

My niche appeared untouched. Until now, I had stored only two items in this cabinet. I placed the disks next to the thread-picture of my Care Mother. Colored threads had been sewn onto a white handkerchief, and, from a distance, her face and kind eyes could be seen.

She understood my need to disappear in the pipes. Her support when Cog grew out of our group had made living bearable. I wondered what my CM would think about the trouble we were in now. Considering the problems my care mates and I had managed to cause during our stay, I imagined she would sigh with exasperation.

Imagining her frown, I smiled because, no matter how hard she had scowled, she couldn't stifle the gleam in her eyes. The gleam that said she was proud of our inventiveness. The gleam that encouraged us during lessons to think for ourselves even while she taught us the standard Pop Cop propaganda.

It must have been difficult for her, getting a new child when one of the older kids reached the age of maturity and left. Our ages had ranged from newborn to fourteen centiweeks old.

I folded the handkerchief and smoothed a few wrinkles before returning it to the cabinet. The other item in my niche was a comb decorated with pink pearls along its spine. The smooth spears pushed into my fingers as I pulled the comb through my long brown hair. With all the excitement, I had forgotten to rebraid it and it had knotted.

Thoughts of the comb wove through my mind as the comb's teeth worked at the knots in my hair. According to my CM, it had been a gift from my birth mother. My CM had kept it safe for me until I reached 1400 weeks, the age of maturity. The age when you were no longer considered a child. It was when you became a scrub and the reality of what the rest of your life would be like became suddenly and brutally apparent. The old-timers called it sweet sixteen, but there wasn't anything sweet about it.

I finished combing my hair and examined the gift, wondering which adult scrub cared enough to part with such a precious item, yet didn't care enough to contact me. Even though it was forbidden, a few mothers kept in touch with their offspring.

Damn. Every moment counted. I shoved my comb back into the cabinet. These stolen glances were a nasty habit that I needed to break. I slammed the door shut and bolted.

Never taking the same route to and from the cabinet, I snaked my way west before entering an air conduit on level four which would lead to a laundry chute I could use. The air conduit passed above an abandoned storeroom. I always shone my light down through the vent to marvel at the wasted space. A perfectly good chamber big enough to house four scrubs comfortably was being used for broken furniture.

Ghost furniture. Each time I checked, the pieces lost more of their color and texture under a coating of dust—one of the evils of Inside.

This time, when I paused a bluelight glowed, and the room appeared to be different. The couch cushions had been cleaned, revealing a brown and green geometric pattern. The mess of broken chairs had been piled in a corner. The junk on the desk in the opposite corner had been removed and an upper sat before it, working under a small lamp.

Startled, I pulled away and hit my head on the top of the shaft. The noise vibrated and the upper turned to look. With careful and slow movements, I started to cross the vent.

"Who's there?" he called.

I paused, resting my knees and most of my weight on the vent. Big mistake. The vent cover groaned and popped free. Scrabbling with my hands for purchase, I felt my legs drop, pulling my body down. The last thing I saw before hitting the floor was a black-haired man with a shocked expression.

4

AS I CRASHED TO THE FLOOR, I PULLED MY BODY INTO a protective ball. I kept a fetal position as waves of pain pulsed up and down my legs. I braced for the cry of outrage from the occupant of the room and the call for the Pop Cops.

Instead, a concerned face came into my view.

"Are you all right?" he asked. His blue eyes held a touch of awe as he stared at me with parted lips. No immediate threat.

I grunted and stretched, feeling for injuries. It wasn't the first time I had fallen, and it wouldn't be the last. My leg muscles would be sore for twenty hours or more, but otherwise no broken bones. Rising with care, I leaned on the couch as a dizzy spell washed through me.

The young man stepped back as if afraid. I suppressed a laugh; I had probably given him a real scare. Smoothing my hair, I glanced around the room. Food bowls, glasses, markers and a wipe board littered the area, suggesting the room was in use.

The tenant wore a black-and-silver jumper, indicating a

level-four resident who was in training for whatever job the Controllers had assigned him. Having never met an upper besides the Pop Cops, I had learned about them and their families from the computer's learning software in the care facility.

"Are you a…scrub?" he asked.

Oh, yes, a young one probably around fifteen hundred weeks old. Well, close to my age, but the uppers coddled their children, babying them until they were seventeen hundred weeks old.

I pointed to my work suit. "Guess."

"Oh. Yes. Well. Sorry," he said. His pale skin flushed pink.

My head cleared. He seemed in no hurry to call for help, probably didn't even know he should be reporting me. I wasn't taking any more chances; I climbed onto the couch, trying to reach the air duct. It was another meter beyond my grasp. The vent was in the middle of the ceiling, and I couldn't use the rivets to scale the side wall.

My first attempt to jump was unsuccessful. I thumped to the floor with an alarming bang.

"Stop it," he said.

His firm tone gave me pause. "Why?" I asked.

"With all the noise you're making, someone will hear you and come to investigate."

"Why do you care?" I shot back at him. "I'm the one who isn't supposed to be here. It's not like *you'll* get in trouble."

He frowned. "I don't want anyone to know about this room," he said. "It's where I come for privacy."

I couldn't help it—I laughed. "What? You have to share

a room with a brother?" I guessed. "Poor boy," I mocked. "Try sharing a barrack with three thousand others."

Fury flashed in his eyes. But I had to give him credit for controlling his temper.

"When I'm here," he said evenly, "no one can find me. No one can give me assignments. No one can harp at me about shirking my duty. No one makes me pledge loyalty to the Controllers." He stepped toward me. "And I'm not about to give it up because some scrub doesn't have the sense to be quiet."

"Well, then, it's to our mutual benefit that I disappear and we both forget about this little incident. Agreed?"

"Yes. No. Yes, but I want to know what you're doing up here."

I thought fast. "Cleaning the shaft like a good little scrub." Climbing back onto the couch, I said, "I'm finished, so I'll be returning to the lower levels where I belong. Can you give me a leg up?"

He laced his fingers together, but before I could step into his cupped hand, he pulled back.

"What? If I'm caught here, I'm in trouble."

"What's it like in the lower levels?"

"Why?"

"I'm curious."

"Go log on to the computer, look under scrubs," I said.

"I already tried. All I found was one paragraph of information. I want to know more."

"You shouldn't. Curiosity is a fatal trait in here."

He set his legs slightly apart and tucked his hands under his crossed arms.

I sighed at his stubbornness. "Imagine every space in this room filled with people. Moving from one end to the other is like swimming in a thick human tank. Constantly being jostled and pushed. Smells of scrubs invading your senses, overwhelming you to the point of nausea. Always waiting in line for food, water and for the washroom. Mind-numbing routine with change a rare event. Being battered by the noises of people eating, moving, snoring, mating and talking over the constant roar of the machinery. In the lower levels, there is no quiet place. No peace."

I drew a deep breath. My speech had come in one burst. The young man had unknowingly unleashed a deluge, which had propelled him onto the couch. Looking around the chamber, I said, "To a scrub, this room is paradise."

We stared at each other for a few heartbeats.

"No one should live like that," the man said in a quiet voice.

"Over eighteen thousand and counting do." I tried to be flippant, but my words felt heavy. A woman caught in the illegal act of terminating her pregnancy was bred until her fertility ceased. Our population bulged. Children were our future, said the Pop Cops. But why? Especially since the future looked like life crammed into every available space. None of the scrubs had a clue.

I pointed toward the duct. "I should go before I'm missed." A lie. I doubt I would ever be missed. Noted absent, charged delinquent, reprimanded but never missed.

He stood on the couch and created a step with his hands. After I had wiggled inside the air shaft, I called down my thanks.

Before I could move he said, "My name's Riley Narelle…" He paused as if embarrassed by his family names. Clearing his throat, he continued, "Ashon. Anytime you need a moment of peace, you're welcome to use my hideaway."

If he noticed the shock on my face, he didn't show it. I gave him a curt nod and hurried away, shaken by his offer. An offer that would be too dangerous for me to accept. Scrubs and uppers don't mix. Ever. The Pop Cops had specific guidelines for keeping everybody where the Pop Cops decided they belonged. Besides, we hated each other. The uppers lived in spacious quarters with their families. Their work schedules were shorter and they had more freedoms. They made the decisions and we followed.

The time I had spent at my niche and with Riley had used up most of my off hours and I needed rest. Moving through the pipes as fast as I dared, I made it to the lower level, found a comfortable shaft and fell asleep.

Empty corridors should have been my first warning. I had woken after a couple of hours to a strange hush and dropped down to level one to investigate. Pop Cops herded scrubs into the dining room. Surprised, I tried to retreat but was spotted and pulled into the flow.

Shoulders pressed against shoulders. I gagged on the overripe smell of tightly packed humans. When no more scrubs could be wedged into the room, the doors were shut and guarded by the Pop Cops. There were three "meeting" locations in the lower levels, and I guessed the Pop Cops also had our two common areas in Quads A1 and A2 filled with scrubs and sealed off just like the dining room.

I started to sweat, and not just from the excessive body heat. Standing on top of a table in the middle of the dining room was the female lieutenant commander who had ambushed Broken Man's quarters. I glanced at the clock. Hour sixty. My troubles started only twenty-five hours ago. It felt more like a week.

"Citizens of Inside, I realize this is unusual," said the LC. Her voice boomed from the speakers. "Our hundredth hour assembly isn't due for another forty hours, but we are missing a citizen."

Murmurs rippled across the scrubs. Everybody reported in at the end of each week. We all had assigned locations so we could hear the news and get updated on the rules and regulations. The Pop Cops called it an end-of-week celebration, but I knew it was just a device to keep track of the scrubs, checking for pregnancies and making sure we behaved.

"All citizens will remain in their secure locations until we find our missing person," the LC continued.

It made sense; their RATSS got confused when so many people milled about.

"We are looking for a man who calls himself the Broken Man. He uses a wheelchair, so we're most concerned he might have been injured. If any citizen has information regarding his current location or information that would lead us to him, you may be promoted to any posting of your choice."

My guts turned to metal. I couldn't move, couldn't breathe, couldn't feel. Lovers would snitch on each other with an offer like that. Cog and I were sunk. I shouldn't have gone for those damn disks. We might as well turn ourselves in. Who knows, maybe they wouldn't recycle us. Yeah, and maybe I'd be invited upstairs and given a family, a room and an interesting job. If I was going to delude myself, might as well dream big.

Oh, well. No sense wasting energy on what I shouldn't

have done. I had made my choice. I'd see it through and resign myself to whatever fate had in store for me.

Numbly, I watched as different scrubs pushed their way to talk to the LC. After two hours of waiting and sweating, the air in the room felt like a sauna and smelled like week-old dirty laundry.

The LC listened to the scrubs and inputted notes in her hand-puter until her communicator beeped. She pressed the device to her ear. Little tongues of red streaked up her cheeks as she listened. She gripped the knot of hair behind her head in a tight fist. Gesturing with curt motions, she issued orders to the other Pop Cops. They snapped to attention and marched from the room.

Turning on her microphone, she said, "Citizens, we have yet to locate the Broken Man, but we cannot keep you here any longer. Report back to your work areas or barracks. Anyone else with information is to see me at once."

The Pop Cops opened only one door to let the scrubs out. I sighed. It would be another hour for me to reach fresh air.

When I finally arrived at the door, I was directed to one of the many Pop Cops in the hallway. They registered each of us in their black census recorders that kept track of the population. The LC stood nearby. She seemed tense as she talked rapidly into her communicator.

"Name, barrack and birth week?" the male ensign asked me.

"Trella. One-one-seven. 145,487," I replied automatically. Identification was required every hundred hours. I calculated my exact age. I was 1,514 weeks old or fifteen point one four centiweeks or if I used the old-time measurement, I was seventeen point three years old.

He entered my data and waved me off. I was just about to slip past him when the LC grabbed my arm.

"Trella?"

Darts of fear raced through my shoulder and stabbed my heart. My thoughts scrambled as I stared at her violet eyes and angular features. I used all my energy to nod, keeping my face calm.

"Come with me," she ordered.

She still had a firm grip on my arm; I had no choice but to accompany her along the corridor. Once we were far enough away from the noise of the Pop Cops, she stopped and released me. I glanced around, considering escape. The array of weapons hanging from her belt kept my feet planted.

"My sources tell me you spoke with the Broken Man around hour nineteen this week. Is this correct?" she asked.

Not trusting my voice, I nodded again. Those little laundry weasels. Scrubs complained about the Pop Cops and how they hated them and weren't to be trusted, yet the first chance a scrub had to ingratiate themselves, they jumped. Granted, the offer was stellar, but I knew I'd never squeal on my fellow scrubs.

"Then why didn't you come tell me?" she demanded.

"It didn't seem important."

A condescending smile twisted her lips. "*I'll* decide what's important. Tell me what you and—" she consulted her data screen "—Cogon talked about with Broken Man."

Damn. She knew about Cog. Did they have him? I worried. It was common knowledge Cog had a weakness for the prophet-of-the-week so I went from there. "Cogon wanted me to meet this Broken Man. He said this new prophet had proof Gateway existed."

I shrugged. "Cog's my friend. I met the prophet in the laundry. He started spouting some crazy crap about using meditation to transport yourself through Gateway to Outside. Yet he didn't have a shred of proof."

"Yes. You scrubs seem to have a fascination with Gateway despite the facts." The LC shook her head. "Go on."

"I told Cog to stay away from him, that he could get in trouble. Then I reported to my work shift." I shrugged again, hoping to appear nonchalant.

She studied my face. I feigned innocence.

"Have you talked to Broken Man or seen him since hour nineteen?"

"No."

"If you hear anything or see anything, you're to report it to me immediately. Understand?"

"Yes, Lieutenant Commander…?"

"Karla Trava. Report to your workstation."

"Yes, sir." I walked away. I felt her gaze drilling holes into my back. The desire to run, to jump into one of the ducts and hide pushed at my muscles. Instead, I kept a steady rhythm and only looked back as I turned the corner. Lieutenant Commander Karla met my glance with a thoughtful and lethal squint.

5

ONCE I WAS OUT OF LIEUTENANT COMMANDER KARLA'S
toxic sight, I sighed with relief. It was short-lived. I had
gotten off easy. Too easy. I had the feeling I was now in LC
Karla's crosshairs. A dangerous position to say the least.

The Pop Cops tended to be cocky in their dealings with
the scrubs. Yes, they arrested and recycled without any
backlash, but they seldom jumped to conclusions. They
watched. They waited. They knew they could find a scrub
without much effort, and they enjoyed seeing who else the
bad scrub could draw into trouble.

That's why I had always thought the prophets were Pop
Cop spies. The prophets preached about Outside and the
final reward for enduring the horrible living conditions just
to see who believed and who remained a skeptic. The
skeptics seem to vanish as if the Pop Cops sanded them out
of the masses like rust spots, removing the defective genes
from the general population.

I had been wrong about Broken Man being a spy. The Pop

Cops wouldn't be searching so hard for him if he were one of theirs. And now the Pop Cops had learned a person could disappear in the lower levels, which meant their flippant attitudes would change.

Instinctively, I knew LC Karla wouldn't give up her search for Broken Man. So I was screwed and destined to become fertilizer for hydroponics. What could I even hope to gain from this situation? I doubted finding Gateway would make everything rosy.

Longing for Outside to be a real place welled up from the tight corner of my heart where I had squashed it. The type of longing that could overwhelm me and reduce me to a mental case, chanting "a million weeks, a million weeks," as I dashed through the plain hallways of Inside. Hallways so empty of character that if the sector and floor level hadn't been painted on every wall, people would be lost for weeks and no one would miss them. Scrubs as empty of character as the walls. Because we all knew that hope and longing and desire were deadly to our peace of mind.

My involvement with this search for Gateway was to prove it didn't exist. To show my heart it was wrong to long for change, forcing it to accept my life and focus my energies on finding the small joys Inside might have to offer. Joys that Cogon had already found. And yet, he had always been drawn to the prophets, seeking their stories about the rewards given for good deeds.

Unwanted thoughts swirled in my mind. The time spent at the assembly in the dining room followed by the interrogation by LC Karla had run well into my hour sixty to seventy shift. Five hours remained.

Forget it. I looped back to the dining room, hoping Karla

and her goons were gone. A few Pop Cops lingered nearby—normal for this area.

As I stood in line for food, I could feel the tension pouring off the other scrubs. Taking a bowl of the leafy green slop, I found an empty chair. The meal failed to improve the mood of the room. When I stood, a scrub pushed me aside and sat in my seat. Typical.

Only the vision of Broken Man starving made me return to the food line. After a half-hour wait, I filled another bowl with the spinach casserole. By the time I reached the tables, most of the scrubs I had sat with were gone. I threaded my way through the dining room, pretending to search for a seat. Once I reached the back, I checked to see if any Pop Cops had noticed me, then slipped out the door. Taking food from the dining room was not uncommon, but since the Pop Cops searched for Broken Man, I knew carrying a bowl of food would draw immediate suspicion.

Sliding into the nearest heating vent, I pushed the casserole ahead of me as I crawled through the duct. The warm air flowing across my skin turned hotter as I drew closer to his room, but I stayed in the vent. The risk of being spotted outside his door was too great.

"Trella! Where the hell have you been?" Broken Man demanded as soon as I poked my head through the heating vent.

I didn't answer him. Dripping with sweat, I rolled from the shaft and onto the ground.

Broken Man lay sprawled on the floor. Black streaks of grit striped his clothes.

"What happened?" I asked.

"You were gone so long, I had to use the bathroom."

A man-sized, clean track on the floor from the chair to

the bathroom. His present position made it clear getting into a chair was harder than sliding out.

I stood and helped him back into his seat. My assurance to Cogon that I would take care of Broken Man's needs seemed foolhardy once I fully realized his physical limitations.

I handed him the food. As Broken Man shoveled the casserole, I realized the ear-aching noise of the Power plant was muted. Foam had been sprayed onto the walls, and, when I opened the door, a sheet of metal covered the entrance.

When he finished his meal, I took his bowl. The rank aroma of stale sweat filled my nose, and I coughed to cover my expression. From the way he wrinkled his face, I could tell I didn't smell any better. Funny how people can stand their own stink, but not others. I explained to him what had happened since Cog had been here.

"The Lieutenant Commander was quite upset about your disappearance," I said. "Do you know her?"

"Lieutenant Commander?" Broken Man tapped his spoon against his lower lip. "Which one?"

I blanched for a moment, envisioning an army of LCs patrolling the lower levels like clones. "Said her name was Trava."

He huffed. "Trava is a family name. Almost all the Pop Cops are Travas."

"Oh. Karla Trava. Why doesn't she have another family name?"

"Travas don't take on any other names. Not even the children who are born to a Trava and another family member. In fact, if you mate with a Trava you are then registered as a Trava." He considered. "Unfortunately, I know Karla. You never did ask for more information about your biological parents."

"I've been a little busy," I said, my words laced with sarcasm. "Besides, you fed me a line of bull just to get me to help you."

"Believe what you will, but watch out for this LC. She's intelligent, cunning and intuitive. Her family is not only in charge of the Pop Cops, but work closely with the Controllers, as well. She's well connected to all the powerful people."

"Why worry about the Controllers? Aren't they just in charge of the uppers?"

"They tell the Travas what to do. And the Travas make all the decisions for Inside. Every admiral is a Trava, and every time an upper links with the computer, a Trava knows. Every mechanical system running Inside has a Trava at the switch."

"That's the way it's always been. Why do you make it sound as if it's wrong?"

"It hasn't always been this way. You scrubs know nothing of what goes on in the upper levels. Exactly what the Trava family wants."

I really didn't care what the uppers did or didn't do. My throat burned from the heat and dust, and my short nap hadn't been enough to fully revive me. "I need more sleep before my next shift."

"I need more food," Broken Man said. "I did some exploring. There's a kitchen here, but no electricity."

"I'll turn on the juice, but it may take me a while to get you other supplies. I'll see what I can do."

Broken Man nodded even as he frowned at me. "I should get a few hours of sleep, too."

I helped him into bed and felt a twinge of guilt as the black dust puffed from the mattress, causing him to choke. It would probably be another twenty hours before I could bring him food and help him shower.

The bedroom and bathroom were two small squares adjacent to each other. Both led out to the living area, another square which bordered the equally tiny kitchen. Inside was divided into rectangles and squares. The designers had to have been obsessive-compulsives, and I cursed them for their lack of imagination. Again.

Grabbing a couple of drinking glasses from the kitchen, I filled one with water. I set the glasses on the night table beside the bed. When Broken Man peered in confusion at the empty glass, I told him it was for urinating into so he wouldn't have to drag himself to the bathroom. His face muscles drooped in sad understanding as I waved goodbye.

Reconnecting the electricity to the small apartment proved arduous. If I hadn't been tired, it would have taken me half the time to find the connectors.

Finally, I found a quiet place to sleep in one of the heating shafts. As I drifted off, an odd thought touched my mind. Why was Inside always heated?

I awoke at hour seventy-nine. Clocks had been installed in every room and corridor of Inside so scrubs couldn't use the excuse of not knowing the time. I had an hour until my next shift so I headed toward one of Sector F1's washrooms. Peeling off my sweat-stiffened uniform, I stood under the shower's warm water. Once I dried off and put on a clean uniform, I checked my tool belt, making sure all my tools were in the right spots and that my flashlight still worked. I never felt properly dressed until the familiar weight of my belt settled on my hips.

I fought my way through the corridors to my scheduled air shaft. On the way, I encountered Cog. He scraped paint chips from one of the corridor walls. Patches of rust sprinkled the metal. Another of Inside's evils, rust was not tolerated and repainting remained a constant chore.

Glad to see him, I touched his arm. His honey-brown eyes slid in my direction. Tight lines of worry streaked across his sweaty face. Cog pulled the scraper from the wall.

"What's going on?" he whispered. "Is everything okay with—you know?"

I nodded. "He's fine."

Cog pointed with his nose toward the two Pop Cops who hovered at the end of the hall. "They're watching me."

"What happened?" I asked.

Cogon winced. "The Pop Cops escorted me to their office for questioning about my little skirmish before they arrested Broken Man."

I studied his face in concern but didn't see any bruises. Understanding my look, Cog touched his ribs and winced again. This time in pain.

"They said I was their best suspect. They threatened to recycle me just for defending my prophet. Told me I might as well confess to killing their colleague, and tell them where Broken Man was hiding." Cog clamped his teeth together as defiance flashed in his eyes. "I'd confess to murder, but I won't give him up."

"Why? You could negotiate and tell them where he is in exchange for not being fed to Chomper."

He stared at me as if I had spoken gibberish. "He's important, Trell. He can find Gateway."

"He *might* have a location. Big difference, and one not worth being recycled for."

"He knows. I can feel it."

I huffed in annoyance. "Come on, Cog. You're an intelligent man. How can you believe in Gateway without proof?"

"The disks—"

"Could be part of the ruse."

He smiled. "Then why did you risk punishment to get them?"

"To prove Broken Man wrong."

"Then go ahead, prove us wrong." His confidence turned smug and he watched my expression with a knowing grin. "You can't resist a challenge. It got you into all kinds of trouble in the care facility."

"We're not in the care facility anymore." I tapped his bruised ribs, emphasizing my point. "The stakes are higher."

"So is the reward."

I shook my head. We had lapsed into the same old argument with no ending and we had talked too long. The Pop Cops headed our way. Their continued interest in Cogon meant he remained their primary suspect.

"Why did they let you go?" I asked.

"Two scrubs came forward while I was being questioned and claimed they saw Broken Man wrestle the Pop Cop for his weapon before the elevator doors closed."

My breath locked in surprise. After a moment I asked, "Did you get their names?"

"Not yet. But I will."

"Keep playing innocent," I whispered to him as the Pop Cops came within earshot. Then in a louder voice I said, "And my cleaning device has been making weird noises."

"I'll let maintenance know," Cog replied.

"Thanks." I walked away.

Another twist. I sighed. Why would two people lie? Especially when the right information could make their lives a lot easier.

The questions would have to wait while I dealt with my supervisor. She paced the hallway in front of my cleaning troll's storage area. A red cuff clenched in her long-fingered hands. She frowned at it.

"Trella," she said with a snarl. "Going to show up for work this shift?"

I braced myself. What rotten luck. The supervisors checked to make sure each scrub assigned to them was at the proper work location about once a week. My bad luck to have her looking for me during my last shift. At least I hoped it was bad luck and not the directive of a certain lieutenant commander.

"Where were you?" she asked.

"Special assembly." I glanced at the cuff. If she snapped it around my wrist, I would have to report to the Pop Cops for discipline. They would probably assign me to work in waste handling during my off hours. When I completed the punishment, the cuff would be removed. Until then, everyone would know I was in trouble.

She hissed in exasperation. "The assembly lasted two hours. You were missing for eight." She pulled the cuff open.

"It took me almost two hours to get out of the dining room, and then I had to wait to speak with Lieutenant Commander Karla."

The LC's name elicited the desired effect. Her hand paused in midair and she shot me a white-faced look. Usually only ensigns and lieutenants policed the lower levels. LCs were as rare as a change in routine, and all the scrubs knew to keep their distance.

"Oh, well, in that case." She lowered her arm, probably

assuming time spent with a Pop Cop lieutenant commander was worse than working in waste handling.

I never thought I would use fear of the Pop Cops to my advantage, but I knew my supervisor wouldn't check my story with the LC. Watching me pull out my cleaning troll and heft it into the air shaft, she stayed until I had climbed into the shaft to begin my shift.

While I followed my troll through the air ducts for the next ten hours, I planned the best way to gather supplies for Broken Man. My choices were limited. The only time I could take enough food from the kitchen to stock Broken Man's refrigerator was when everyone was at the hundred-hour assembly. Problem was, my presence was required, too.

When the buzzer sounded for the assembly, I dutifully reported to the dining room and stood in line.

"Name, barrack and birth week?" the Pop Cop asked without even looking up.

I repeated my stats.

"Health changes?"

"No."

"Blood test." He pointed toward another Pop Cop.

Waiting in this line, I held my arms close to my stomach as a Pop Cop drew blood from a scrub's wrist using a device we had nicknamed the vampire box after reading one of those mythical stories in the computer. The stories we had been allowed to access chronicled myths and legends of strange creatures like vampires and ghosts. They also mentioned things and animals we have never seen. When questioned, my Care Mother explained those items were no longer available.

I shuffled forward in line, dreading my turn. After you insert your arm in the vamp box, two prongs jabbed into the skin and sucked a couple drops of blood out through a tube and into a chamber where it was analyzed in an instant.

The Pop Cops checked for illegal substances, pregnancy and other health markers the scrubs didn't really care about. Blood tests were done at random hundred-hour assemblies, but they were never more than six weeks apart. The Pop Cops had them scheduled in advance and, for a price, you could find out when the next test would be. A scrub named Jacy had a whole network of informers, and he always knew when the Pop Cops planned tests and inspections.

The next scrub to be checked was a woman. The ensign running the analyzer grabbed her arm. Before the woman could react, he clamped a bright yellow bracelet on her wrist. She was pregnant. Shock, fear and surprise warred on her face as she tried to cope with this new information.

"Eight week checkups required," the ensign droned. "Schedule with the infirmary."

The woman was waved on. She staggered toward the dining room with her other hand gripping the irremovable bracelet. Now the entire population of scrubs would know she was with child. She'd work her shifts until she gave birth, spend a week in the infirmary, hand her baby over to the care facility and then return to work. It felt more like a breeding program than a miracle of life. One of the many reasons I would never have a child.

I took my turn with the vamp box and wove my way through the dining room toward the kitchen, finding a seat as close to the kitchen doors as possible. LC Karla stood on one of the tables. A fire burned in her eyes as she barked orders to the Pop Cops around her. I wondered why she chose this location instead of the other two meeting areas. Perhaps she enjoyed standing on the table. Yeah, right, just like I enjoyed these assemblies.

Another buzz sounded, signaling all scrubs were in their designated locations.

Karla addressed the crowd. "Citizens, welcome to the end of the week celebration. Now begins week number 147,002."

An old scrub sitting next to me chanted. "A million weeks! A million weeks! A million weeks!"

Another scrub leaned over to him and said, "Hush, old man, you'll be lucky to see another two weeks. No one cares about the millionth week. We won't be here."

His companion laughed. "Just think," said the second man, "in another seven thousand weeks or so, everyone in this room will be gone and there will be a whole new generation forced to listen to the same crap."

They chuckled together as the old scrub squinted at them. In the minds of the scrubs, the millionth week had been blown to mythical proportions. Some prophesied that on week one million, our fuel and air would run out, ending all our lives. Others claimed we all go Outside. But when you considered the average life span of a citizen was sixty to seventy centiweeks, and there would be roughly a hundred and twenty-two generations of scrubs before the millionth week, it was hard to get too concerned.

With a gnarled finger, the old scrub tapped the man who had hushed him. "Laugh all you want, but the millionth week isn't the end. It's the beginning."

"…Broken Man." Karla Trava's voice cut through the buzz of voices around me. My attention snapped back to her.

"Information is still needed. You will be rewarded for any tips that lead us to him." She stopped for a heartbeat. "But don't lie to me." Her tone turned deadly. She gestured. Two Pop Cops pulled a scrub forward. Karla yanked the poor guy up to the tabletop by his collar. He swayed on weak legs and his face was a mask of fear. His hands trembled. Silence blanketed the dining room.

Karla patted her weapon belt, looking as if she debated. With a blur of motion, her kill-zapper jumped into her hand. She pressed the nozzle to the scrub's chest.

"This," she said, "is what I do to liars." A crackle built to a crescendo as the man jerked and twitched.

When the lieutenant commander pulled the weapon away, the man dropped to the floor with an echoing thud.

6

THE SOUND OF THE SCRUB HITTING THE FLOOR BURNED
into my mind like the kill-zapper had burned into the man's
chest. I shook in my chair, feeling hot and short of breath.
It didn't take much imagination to envision myself an arm's
length away from LC Karla with a kill-zapper at my breast.

She stepped off the table and let the usual ensign read the
weekly announcements. The ensign stumbled over his
words, probably thrown by the unnatural silence in the room.

Little by little, whispered conversation spread, and the
ensign's voice evened out. My plans to collect food during
the assembly took on a higher level of danger. Karla Trava
had raised the stakes.

Even so, I couldn't let Broken Man starve. Time was
running out. I faked a coughing fit. My seatmates glanced
at me in annoyance. I sputtered and choked for a while then
stood and headed for the kitchen doors, hoping anyone who
was interested would assume I sought a drink.

As soon as the doors closed, I bolted to the refrigerators.

Grabbing cheese, sheep's milk and containers of vegetable casseroles, I piled them on one of the stainless-steel counters. I shut the refrigerator and sprinted to the freezer, tossing a few hunks of frozen mutton onto my pile. With panic fueling my actions, I leapt up on the counter next to the food. Right above my head was a vent to an air duct. I opened it and loaded the shaft with the provisions. Careful not to block the airflow, I shoved and stuffed until my breath came in puffs.

When finished, I replaced the vent cover, hopped down and filled a glass with water. I slipped back into the dining room, covering my gasps for air with the drink as I reclaimed my seat. None of the scrubs gave me a glance, and I hoped no one suspected.

When the signal sounded to end the assembly, I filed out with the rest of the scrubs. The line of people bulged sideways. Even though the scrub's body had been removed, everyone avoided the spot where he had fallen.

As I passed Karla, she pressed her lips together and cocked her head to one side. I dropped my gaze and tried to look as inconspicuous as possible, which only resulted in her calling out to me.

"Trella, come here," she ordered.

I stepped out of line. My heart jumped in my chest. "Yes, Lieutenant Commander?"

"Feeling better?"

"Excuse me?"

"Your cough. I hope you're not getting a virus."

Her concern was frightening. "No, sir," I said, my mind roiling. "I just must have swallowed something wrong."

"Oh, yes, I understand," she said with an even flat tone.

"I find myself having to swallow wrong things all the time. They leave a bitter taste. Makes me choke. Churns my stomach."

I had no answer. My mind buzzed with warning signals.

She studied me for an eternal minute, then said, "Hour zero. Time to report to your station for your next shift. Air duct twenty-two, I believe."

"Yes, sir," I managed to squeak out. I joined the flow of scrubs to the hallway, not daring to look back at the LC. She had been reading my file. She knew all about me, and she wanted me to know. Damn.

An interesting fact about air duct number twenty-two was it crossed right above the kitchen, and eventually, if you followed it far enough, it passed right on top of Broken Man's hideout.

Once I reached my cleaning station, I hefted the troll into the air shaft. Then I raided a maintenance closet for extra supplies. Crawling behind the troll, I built a crude skid. I kept glancing behind me, checking to see if LC Karla had sent a couple of RATSS to spy on me.

When the troll reached my stash of food, I shut it down while I rigged the skid up to it. I peered through the vent. The kitchen bustled with activity. Scrubs filled containers and chopped vegetables. Two ensigns strolled through the chaos. They were probably keeping track of the knives, counting in their heads to make sure a scrub didn't steal one and attack the Pop Cops.

No sign of Karla. My relief surprised me. Subconsciously I must have been expecting her to ambush me;

to reach through the vent and cry "Gotcha!" before she kill-zapped me.

With that awful image in mind, I loaded the food onto the pallet as fast as I could, then restarted the cleaning troll. The troll's engine strained with the extra weight. I had to smile when I flipped open one of the control panels on the side of the troll and turned a tiny thumbscrew. Cogon had shown me how to increase the machine's throttle, so it could move faster. An increase of speed meant I would finish my work sooner, and would have more time off—provided no one caught me.

The troll lurched forward as the engine roared. Its speed stayed the same, but it had no trouble pulling the skid.

Paranoia made me keep checking for RATSS, but the troll and I reached Broken Man's rooms without incident. I popped the vent off and swung down, dropping to the floor.

"Hello, Trella," he said.

I spun. He sat in a corner of the living room. I smelled him from here. He was ripe.

"I don't have a lot of time," I said. Pulling a chair under the open vent, I used it to reach the food.

"Here, let me help." Broken Man sprawled on the floor and used his arms to drag himself across the room. He wriggled into a sitting position and held his hand to me.

I handed the supplies to him, and he made a pile next to his legs. When the skid was empty, I hopped off the chair and carted the food into the kitchen.

"Hungry?" I asked from the kitchen.

"Very."

I brought him a spoon, and he dug into one of the yellow

vegetable casseroles. When everything was put away, I stepped onto the chair again.

"I'll be back after my shift with fresh clothes," I called. He waved his spoon in goodbye. I climbed into the duct, turned the troll on and completed the air shaft.

When I finished my assigned ducts, I headed to the washroom. Fresh laundered uniforms and clothes were always stacked in large canvas bins on wheels. Empty bins were then used for dirty garments.

I collected a bunch of clothes, linens and soap and bundled everything together with a towel. At my next stop I added some cleaning supplies, hoping to reduce the black dust coating every surface of Broken Man's rooms.

He had returned to the corner when I plopped down with my bundle. I showed him what I had brought. He smiled in relief, but I cringed over the black grit between his teeth.

"Shower?" I asked.

"Please."

I hesitated for an awkward moment. How to go about this? Fortunately, he had thought ahead. Poor man, he had hours alone with nothing to do, and I didn't think to bring him anything to occupy him.

"Get a chair from the kitchen and put it in the shower," he said. He set a businesslike tone as he gave me instructions.

As I placed the seat under the nozzle, he pulled himself into the bathroom and began to undress. His short commands only faltered when I tugged off his pants and underwear and hoisted him into the chair. I turned on the water and gave him the soap and the washcloth, leaving him to wash himself in private.

As I cleaned the dust, I wondered how he had gotten the long jagged scar stretched across his lower back. Shorter scars marked his arms and torso. His withered legs had flopped when I had moved him. I stopped wiping for a second to try to envision his life before the accident. One insight I did have while helping him into the shower. He was a natural blond, and I should probably apologize for the harsh comment I had made when I first met him about going back to the upper levels to have his hair dyed.

When I checked on Broken Man, he had turned the water off and sat dripping. I handed him a towel and assisted in drying and dressing. I debated how to move him. Despite my smaller size, all the time I'd spent climbing through the ducts and pipes had strengthened my muscles. Not wanting him to drag his clean clothes over the floor, I wrapped his arms around my neck, pulled his weight onto my back and in a hunched-over shuffle managed to get him into the chair in the living room.

"Thanks," he said as he combed his fingers through wet hair.

"Food?" I asked.

He nodded. I brought him a bowl.

As he ate, he pointed to one of the walls where a rippled pattern was the only notable feature.

"See that? I bet it's a computer terminal. I couldn't reach it from the floor. Can you lift it?"

I studied the pattern. It consisted of horizontal sheets of metal about two-centimeters wide connected like a curtain. A dent at the bottom allowed my fingers to slide under.

"That's it," he said.

I pulled it up, then stepped back in alarm as the metal curtain disappeared under the wall with a rolling sound.

Behind the sheet were a flat computer screen and a console of buttons and plugs.

"Yes!" Broken Man said. For the first time since we had rescued him, his face glowed with excitement. "Help me get closer."

I pushed his chair next to the wall. He reached out to touch a button.

"Wait," I said in alarm. "If you turn it on won't the Controllers know about it?"

"No. It's only when you hook up to the internal system. The basic public system for the scrubs doesn't require a port. Besides, I just want to see if it works."

He pressed a series of switches. His hands moved with a practiced grace. The computer screen brightened, and the symbol for Inside appeared. Typically unimaginative, the symbol looked like a cube with a capital *I* on the front panel. As the children in the care facility would say, "Boring." Little did they know the activities and schooling in the CF would be the most interesting part of their lives. I shook my head of the gloomy thoughts as Broken Man changed the image on the screen.

After a while he said, "It's still connected to the main system. We could access my disks from here."

"Which would lead the Controllers right to us?" I asked, again afraid this seemed too easy. Too convenient. It made sense the upper worker who used to live here had a computer hookup, but that it still worked was suspect.

"Yes it would. Except I have a program to reroute the tracking software, so the Controllers would be led to another computer station on level four."

"You know it works?"

"Well…" Broken Man rubbed his back, considering. "Obviously my original program had a few flaws, but I had found another more effective program hidden in the system. I copied it onto my disks. Unfortunately I was caught before I could use it." The memory of pain spread across his face. His blue eyes squinted into the past.

"Who created the other program?" I asked.

"The security on it was too good to crack. But I believe it was probably a member of the Garrard family."

"Garrard?"

"They are unhappy with the status quo. All the major families were upset with the Trava takeover, but in time they grew complacent and believed there was nothing they could do to restore the original balance of power."

"Hold on. The Trava takeover?" I asked. "The Travas have always been in charge."

"No, they haven't. The Travas want the scrubs to believe that, and they're hoping eventually, with enough generations born, the uppers will forget they ever had a say in the running of Inside. But I've uncovered the truth. All nine families at one point had an equal vote. Each family elected one of their members to be a part of Committee. This Committee made decisions and supervised the various mechanical systems of Inside." Broken Man frowned. "Each family had a specialty—air systems, waste water, electrical— which turned into a major disadvantage."

"Why?"

"The Travas' specialty was security and only they had access to the stunners and kill-zappers."

"Oh."

Broken Man met my gaze. The wrinkles on his face

deepened as if he alone shouldered all the responsibly in letting the Travas dominate. I guessed he was around forty-five centiweeks old.

"There was a group of uppers who tried to regain control of a few systems, but they failed," he said.

"Would the group be willing to help us if you actually find Gateway?" I asked.

"No." Broken Man fiddled with the computer. "The consequences of getting caught are too great for the uppers."

It had been a hypothetical question. I planned to prove there was no Gateway. Prove to Cog that the people of Inside had been sealed off from Outside.

Besides the Pop Cops' insistence of a purely spiritual final resting place for the good people, the rumors surrounding Outside ranged from wild guesses to tales of horror. I knew *something* had to be beyond our walls. And whether this place was Outside or something else, speculation ran rampant.

A few scrubs claimed it was a vast wasteland, others a magical kingdom where fairies flew through the air, a number declared water surrounded us and a couple maintenance scrubs thought our own garbage was piled around us. We reused and recycled everything, but a small portion of pure waste disappeared through a flushing system the Controllers maintained. Cog had tried to use that fact in his argument about Gateway.

All the rumors didn't sway me. I didn't care. Why worry or speculate about an inaccessible place? We were trapped in Inside until we ceased to exist and Chomper turned our bodies into fertilizer. End of story.

I concentrated on Broken Man's statement about getting no

help from the upper families. It fit—uppers wouldn't risk themselves and their cushy life for a bunch of scrubs. Although, I couldn't help thinking about Riley in his hideout on level four.

His family names seemed important to him—a source of pride. How did he feel about the Travas controlling our world? Maybe Riley and a few uppers would like to see life altered? I grimaced. Sappy bull. I was getting soft, letting hope grow a centimeter. Snip. Snip. I mentally cut it back.

"If the computer works, all I need to do is retrieve your disks and you can access them? Right?" I asked.

Broken Man bit his lip and said nothing.

"What's wrong? I thought you have a gap in your mouth for the port."

"I have the gap." He paused. "Problem is…I don't have my teeth."

"What?"

"They're not real teeth. We just call them that. They're needed to access the internal computer network. They're designed so the Pop Cops can keep track of who is in the network and restrict access to the computer system by pulling an upper's port."

I sank to the floor. Rubbing my face in my hands, I said, "Now you tell me."

7

NOTHING MORE I COULD DO. THE END. THE POP COPS
had Broken Man's port. Without his port, he couldn't access
his disks and the information. No information meant no
proof or disproof of Gateway's existence.

"Lieutenant Commander Karla has my port," Broken
Man said.

I stared at him. Was he serious? "You want me to ask her
for it back?"

"Think, Trella. She doesn't know about the disks. Pulling
my teeth is standard procedure. She would have sent it to
computer ops to check what I've been accessing in the
system, and they would have returned it with their report."
Sudden understanding lit his gray eyes. "The report! I should
have known. A few of the files I'd viewed probably made
Karla suspicious and she set a trap in my room. If only I heard
about you before she rigged my quarters."

His comment reminded me of how I had gotten involved.

Cog knew I couldn't resist a challenge. "If Cog hadn't told you about me, we wouldn't be here now."

He shook his head. "Your reputation as Queen of the Pipes intrigued me first."

"Yeah, but Cog was the only person who knows what I'm really capable of. And he's too quick to trust, he falls for any line and is too eager to get involved."

"The opposite of you?"

"Of course. I'm not the one getting my hopes dashed every time a new prophet arrives."

"Yet here you are."

In trouble with no solution in sight. "A moment of weakness and an excellent lesson on what *not* to do in the future. Provided I even *have* a future."

"From what I've seen in the lower levels, do you really want to live the rest of your life in these conditions?" he asked.

The standard scrub reply was to shrug and say there was nothing I could do about it or to regurgitate the Pop Cop line about a better afterlife. But I had the opportunity to actually prove or disprove the theory about Gateway and Outside. If I wanted to risk my life. Was being alive enough for me? Could I really walk away without trying?

Broken Man could see the answer in my eyes. "Karla's office is on level four, Sector—"

"A. I know. It's the only area I avoid." Last thing I needed was for the Pop Cops to catch me in an air duct above their offices and holding cells. I enjoyed a challenge, but I wasn't crazy. And I limited my time spent in the Gap above four to trips to my box.

Contemplating the theft of his port from the lieutenant commander, I crossed over from rational to insane. "Do you know what type of security measures are installed in her office?"

"The door's always locked, but I'm guessing you're not going to use it." He smiled. "Probably the usual motion sensors."

LC Karla knew someone had used the pipes to get the disks. Would she rig the air ducts above her office with sensors? Broken Man had said she was smart, so I assumed she had. But did she know about the Gap above the ductwork? I needed to do a reconnaissance mission to her office. It would require a great deal of planning.

"How do I know which port is yours?" I asked.

"There's an identification number etched into the bottom." Broken Man recited his number and I committed it to memory.

"I need to eat before my next shift. Hopefully I'll think of a way to bypass the LC's security measures."

Various scenarios ran through my mind as I returned to the main corridor of level two. No brilliant ideas had formed by the time I shuffled through the cafeteria line and sought a free seat. And consuming the casserole of the day failed to ignite any exceptional plans.

The only way I could enter Karla's office would be to find the wires for the motion detectors and disable them without setting them off. It would be time consuming and danger-ous. The probability of missing a sensor would be high.

The noise in the room rose to an uncomfortable level. I grabbed my tray, intent on leaving, but two scrubs stood right behind me. A young man and woman. They both had the same nose—a distinctly petite feature with a perfect shape. Combined with their matching oval faces and light greenish-brown eyes, I knew they were related. They wore the drab-gray and shapeless overalls of the recycling-plant workers.

Pitching his voice so the sound cut through the din, the man said, "We want in."

I stepped aside so he could claim my seat.

He shook his head. "We want to help you."

"With what?" Confused, I glanced at each one.

She gestured to the table. Two more seats were empty. The scrubs sat and she pulled me back down.

I yanked my arm away. "Who do you—"

"I'm Anne-Jade and he's my brother, Logan. We want to help you find Gateway."

Stunned, I gaped at them a moment. "But, I'm not—"

"Save it for the Pop Cops," Logan said. "We know what you've been up to. We saw you with Cogon before he entered the lift. Saw the lift stop and Cogon leave the elevator's maintenance room with the laundry bin. It wasn't hard to figure out."

They hadn't told Karla, which meant a bribe. "What do you really want?"

"To help," Anne-Jade said. Her lips pressed into a thin line, drawing her oval face into a serious expression.

"Why? You could get recycled."

She swept her hand out, indicating the mass of people. "This is intolerable. I'd rather be recycled than to continue to live as livestock."

Instinct kicked in. Too many people increased the chances of getting caught. Besides, I couldn't trust them and I preferred to work alone. "Sorry, no. I can't get anyone else involved."

"We're already involved," Logan said. "Who do you think covered for Cogon?"

I scrambled for a reply. "Look, I'm thankful you saved Cog, but I really don't know how you can help right now, and—"

"Listen." Logan held up a metal wind-up toy near his ear then handed it to me.

"What—"

Logan gestured for me to listen to the toy. Not happy, I brought it close and almost dropped it when Broken Man's voice whispered in my ear. He talked about Gateway and the disks, and I heard my own harsh reply. I stared at the little mouse murmuring in my hand. Its metal key turning. "How?"

Logan grinned. "Voice transmitting device sewn onto Broken Man's shirt. This—" he picked up the mouse "—records and replays the conversation." He held the device in the palm of his right hand, acting indifferent to the incredible danger he had placed us all in.

Realization finally clicked, and my bad situation turned downright rotten. I groaned. "You're Tech Nos."

Working in the recycling quadrant, Tech Nos "rescued" certain discarded items from the upper levels. They played around with the illegal technology—illegal for scrubs to have—and made it better. The Pop Cops hunted and killed these Tech Nos as fast as they would disease-carrying vermin. It was amazing Logan and Anne-Jade were still alive.

"How do you…where do you…" I couldn't finish. The recycling-plant workers were monitored, their bunks searched on a regular basis.

"We're allowed to make toys and different supplies from the metal waste." Logan twisted the key. "Most of our toys are delivered to the uppers for their children, but we keep a few *special* ones."

With space at a premium, scrubs owned few possessions. "Where?"

"Here and there. A few stay with us. This little guy is my favorite right now, and if a Pop Cop asks about it, I just say I'm doing safety testing on it before sending it to the uppers."

Impressive and scary. "How much did you hear?"

"The conversation you had with Broken Man and Cog," Anne-Jade said, "and the rescue. But wherever you have hidden him, we can't get a signal."

At least they didn't know about the port. "I still don't think you can help me."

"We're assuming you're going to need to enter a few secure locations in search of Gateway. We have *other* gadgets," Anne-Jade said.

When I didn't respond, she huffed in frustration. "How did you plan to get past the motion detectors?"

"With creative wiring."

"No need. We've built an invisibility device," Logan said with pride.

I couldn't mask my disbelief. "You can make me invisible?"

"To the sensors. When you turn on our Not-There Machine, the sensors won't detect your presence."

Passion shone from Logan's eyes, but I wasn't a sucker. "You two are either working for the Pop Cops or delusional." I stood to go.

"This isn't proof enough?" Logan held the toy mouse up.

"Yes. Proof you're working with the Pop Cops."

Logan opened his mouth to speak, but Anne-Jade shot him a look. "Fine," she said. "Think what you want, but you owe us one for covering for Cog."

"I don't—"

She ignored me. "In the supply closet in Sector H1 is a small cleaning device."

"Anne-Jade, if she doesn't trust us, we shouldn't trust her," Logan said.

She frowned at him. "Someone has to take the first step." Returning her attention to me, she said, "Do you know the one?"

"Zippy?" He was a quarter of the size of the regular trolls, and made to fit into tight pipes.

"*You* have names for the cleaning devices, and you call *us* delusional?" She tapped her chest to emphasize her point. "If you hold down its…Zippy's on button for ten seconds, it not only cleans dirt, but will suck up all evidence of your presence in a place where you shouldn't be."

I'd heard more believable fairy tales. "How can Zippy suck up the evidence?"

Logan perked up. "Motion detectors emit pulses—"

"She doesn't need to hear a bunch of technical mumbo jumbo," Anne-Jade snapped at him. "It comes down to trust, Trella. You take Zippy out for a spin, and then let us know what else we can do to help you."

They wove through the crowded cafeteria, taking their "toy" with them. The harsh clamor of multiple voices seemed louder than before. I suffered the noise as long as I could before leaving the room and reporting for my next work shift.

My thoughts replayed the encounter with the Tech Nos. If I was found associating with them or using illegal technology, I would be kill-zapped in an instant. I didn't doubt I would be caught. I just wanted to… What? Find Gateway first?

I chided myself for such mushy thoughts. The end result

would probably be exposing the whole endeavor as a hoax. Instead of wasting time, I concentrated on the next task, letting no emotions cloud my judgment. If Zippy worked, then it would make retrieving Broken Man's port a whole lot easier. And if it didn't? Then I hoped I could outrun the Pop Cops again.

During my shift, I planned how best to approach LC Karla's office. I overrode the speed control on the cleaning troll and increased the pace. If I finished all my scheduled ducts early, I could sleep for a few hours before sneaking to level four.

"What do you want to know?" Jacy asked in a low voice. The scrub leaned against a column of bunks, appearing relaxed, but tension rolled off him. Two of his buddies hovered nearby. They kept watch, ensuring our conversation wouldn't be overheard by the Pop Cops. Bluelight lit the scrubs' barrack in Sector D1, and the snores and heavy breathing of sleeping scrubs filled the room. The musty smell of dirty socks mixed with sleep-breath, creating a rank odor. No wonder I slept in the pipes.

"I need to know Lieutenant Commander Karla's schedule," I said.

We were in a poorly lit corner. Rows and rows of bunks, reaching from top to bottom filled the room. Three beds per column. One meter of headroom per bed. The wooden dividers between them contained two drawers. One for the possessions of the first shift scrub who slept there and the other for the second's.

Right now the row we occupied was half-empty. Most scrubs had finished their shift at hour thirty and were in the cafeteria.

"Why do you need her schedule?" Jacy's dark brown bangs hung over his eyes. He studied me through the gaps.

"Doesn't matter."

"Yes, it does." He straightened.

He had grown since our time together in the care facility. I tilted my head to meet his gaze. If he tried one of his old tricks, I already knew the location of the closest ceiling vent. The design of the bunks made it easy for me to scale them if I needed to escape.

"Lieutenant Commander Karla's been causing a lot of trouble for us. I don't want to upset her any further. In fact, she asked me about you."

A stream of cold fear shot down my back. Jacy dealt with information. His group of five always knew where the Pop Cops were. They warned their clients of surprise inspections and raids. Even though the scrubs worked hard, they found time to engage in a number of illegal activities.

"What did you tell her?"

"I had a kill–zapper at my chest so my memories are a little fuzzy. Perhaps if you tell me why the LC's interested in you, it'll help me remember."

His expression remained guarded and I guessed the bastard already knew but wanted to confirm his suspicions.

"You'll live longer if you don't know." Ha. I managed to surprise him. "Are you going to tell me Karla's schedule or not?"

"And what do I receive in exchange?"

Typical scrub. Nothing without a price. "I'll act as a lookout for you. One time only."

He laughed. "I have a ton of people willing to watch for us."

"From air duct seventy-two?"

His smirk died. "You can get in there without an upper's help?"

I nodded. Number seventy-two crossed over a few highly sensitive areas, including the Control Center and Pop Cop headquarters. The uppers didn't want a disgruntled scrub near them. The two scrubs allowed in the shaft always had a Pop Cop escort.

Energized, he paced. "Can you install a microphone in seventy-two for me instead?"

"A mic is illegal. How did you—?" Tech Nos. I didn't need to know more. "You want me to put it where the cleaning trolls won't suck it up?"

"Yes!"

I considered. "It's more dangerous than acting as lookout. It's worth two requests—Karla's schedule and what you told her about me."

"Deal."

His response was too quick. I should have negotiated for more.

"I'll have her agenda in an hour." His posture relaxed, but concern lingered in his eyes. "I told the LC the truth."

My stomach felt as if I had fallen off a pipe. "And?"

He huffed. "Same old Trella, giving nothing away. Not even for your fellow care mate."

"The mate who bullied and tormented me? I guess you would find it odd I don't hold any fond feelings from our time together."

He waved my comment away. "You were cold from the start. We had to bully and torment you just to get a reaction from you." Jacy bent close and lowered his voice. "I told her all about it. How you escape into the ducts to be alone. No friends. No interest in associating with your fellow scrubs. But I neglected to inform her about your Queen of the Pipes title."

"Why? It's just a taunt." Even Broken Man had heard about it.

"Really? You spend hours in the pipes. You must know every nook and cranny of Inside. If I searched for a missing prophet and had exhausted every known area, I would turn to the Queen of the Pipes for guidance." He paused, giving me time to understand. "She already suspects you're involved, telling her about your title would give her a reason to arrest you."

"But you could have earned a better post."

He shrugged. "I did it for old time's sake. Besides, if you're hiding Broken Man, that means you actually *care* for another person and there's hope for you yet. Meet me here in one hour." He strode away with his friends at his heels.

I spent the time sifting through all Jacy's comments. He had been wrong about me. I'd had friends in the care facility after Cog left. Before I was picked on and teased—the victim of multiple pranks and nasty rumors. At least one or two girls. I just couldn't remember their names.

When I matched LC Karla's work schedule to mine, I found I would have a single two-hour window between hours thirty-eight and forty to search her office.

The heating ducts would be my best bet to enter Karla's office. Low to the ground, the vents opened into every room in Inside. Although they were small, Zippy and I just fit. They also snaked between the rooms. One of the drawbacks to using the heating system was that there were no connections between levels. Since the Power plant spanned all four levels, each level had its very own network of ducts. The other limitation was the heating system couldn't be accessed from the Gap.

I needed to ascend to the fourth level, then enter the heating system. Aiming for the abandoned storeroom, I hoped Riley wouldn't be there. As I moved through the air shafts with Zippy tied to my tool belt, my thoughts turned to the young upper I had surprised.

Riley's comments replayed in my mind. He used the storeroom to escape assignments and avoid having to pledge loyalty to the Travas. Perhaps his life wasn't as easy as I had thought.

I slowed when I reached my destination. Peering through the air vent, I scanned the room below with care. The furniture had been rearranged again, but no one was there. The green and brown couch was now located right below the hole, and a metal stepladder leaned against the side wall. Riley must have moved it for me. I smiled, but then dismissed the notion. An upper caring about a scrub? No way. And I wouldn't let myself believe it. Stick with the plan, I chanted under my breath.

Hanging from the air duct, I dropped onto the couch. I waited a moment. When no one rushed into the room, I slipped into the tight heating vent. Pressing Zippy's on button, I counted to ten. He hummed and chugged along the duct as I pulled myself by my elbows and pushed with my feet.

I hoped any noise I made would be dismissed as the regular cleaning. Even if he didn't work, having Zippy along would help my cover if I was caught.

By the time we drew near LC's Karla's office, sweat soaked my uniform and my arms ached. Switching Zippy to Neutral, I examined the room through the vent's cover.

From my limited vantage point, a large desk dominated the space. I counted three computer monitors. On the wall opposite the vent hung a variety of weapons and handcuffs. My heart stuttered for a few beats, before settling into a fast pace.

Again, I waited and listened for sound. LC Karla was supposed to be off duty, but Jacy had warned me the schedule wasn't completely reliable.

I wiped slick hands on my uniform, unscrewed the cover and pulled it slowly into the vent. According to Broken Man, the Pop Cops motion sensors would be in the four corners of the room for maximum coverage.

Nothing else left to do, I pushed Zippy through the opening and held my breath, preparing to flee. He rolled a couple feet and stopped. His hum transformed into a low chug. When the alarm failed to sound and no Pop Cops burst through the door, I eased from the vent.

I searched the desk and opened all the drawers as fast as possible. Karla's office also contained a long worktable, a couch and a bench with chains and cuffs. A sudden vision of me secured to the bench while the LC questioned me jumped into my mind.

Shelves filled with RATSSs decorated another wall. I ignored their mechanical stare, yet prepared to dive back into the heating vent if one moved.

My desperation increased. No sign of Broken Man's port anywhere. Closing my eyes for a moment, I drew in a few deep breaths. Think. Where would you put his port? I scanned the room once more. A gray closet in the corner drew my attention.

My joy when the closet's door swung wide disappeared in a heartbeat. A metal mesh gate covered shelves filled with various items—evidence, probably—and was locked. A small keypad had been installed on the lock's outer plate. None of the tools in my belt would be able to bypass the bolt. I would need a code to open the gate.

The third shelf down held a row of ports. Broken Man's must be among them, sitting mere inches from me. So close.

"Don't move," a voice ordered from behind.

8

I CLOSED MY EYES AS A HOT FLUSH OF TERROR LIQUEFIED
my muscles for an instant.

"Put your hands where I can see them. Slowly," he ordered,
but his voice squeaked a bit. Either from nerves or youth.

Perhaps I could talk my way out of this. I moved my hands
to the side.

"Turn around. Slow."

I faced him. My surprise transformed into suspicion. "Did
you follow me?"

Riley lowered the stun gun. "No, I— What are *you*
doing here?"

"I could ask *you* the same thing. Unless you're Lieutenant
Commander Karla's assistant? Why didn't you tell me you're
a Pop Cop?" My bold response seemed to have the desired
effect as Riley struggled to answer questions I had no au-
thority to ask.

"I'm not.... I monitor the electrical system." He gestured

to his headset. "There was an electrical drain coming from here. I came to investigate."

"All right then. Investigate." I swept my hand, indicating the room. "I'm finished cleaning the ducts." Picking up Zippy, I headed toward the open vent. The little troll was hot.

"Wait." Riley stepped into the room, closing the door behind him. He still held the gun, but he aimed it at the floor. "You're not cleared to be on this level." He glanced at the open evidence closet. "Why are you here?"

I dodged the question. "How do you know I'm not cleared?"

"I checked."

"But you don't know my name." And unlikely to find it.

"I pulled up the approved list. Assuming your birth week is close to mine, I only found one scrub under sixteen hundred weeks old, but I forget *his* name."

"I'm on special assignment this week. The records haven't been updated yet." The heat from Zippy grew intolerable. I dropped him by the vent and crouched to enter the duct.

"Stop or I'll stun you."

I looked over my shoulder. He pointed his gun at me. By the intensity radiating from his blue eyes, I knew he was serious. And he seemed taller than before. Why hadn't I noticed his muscular build?

"You're not going to tell me why you're here, right?"

"Right," I said.

He sidestepped to the closet, keeping his weapon trained on me. A quick glance at the shelves, then his focus returned. I met his gaze. He squinted as if his thoughts raced.

"There are weapons and devices free for the taking, but

you stood here. You want a port. Except you wouldn't be able to use it. No scrub can."

Riley was smarter than I had thought. Too smart.

Hoping to throw him off, I said, "I was just curious, seeing what would be important enough to be locked away. I stopped in here to fix my cleaning device." Zippy's hum increased and small tendrils of smoke reached for the ceiling. Good boy.

"No. I've been learning about the lower levels. Being caught in the upper levels is bad enough, but to be found in Karla's office...to risk your life... Wait. Something big is going on in the lower levels. Someone can't be found." His eyes unfocused as he followed the logic.

No time left. I spun Zippy. The metal burned my hand.

He snapped his fingers. "You want Domotor's port!"

I switched Zippy off and raised my arm, triggering the motion sensors. A shrill clang pierced the air. Distracted by the noise, Riley sought the source. Without hesitation, I shoved Zippy into the vent and followed the troll, pushing him as fast as possible through the narrow space despite the heat searing my fingertips.

"Listen!" Riley shouted after me.

An odd request. I craned my neck to look back. His hand grabbed the vent's cover and slammed it closed. After a few moments, the alarm cut off in midclang. Damn. I wanted the noise to mask my retreat. As I debated how much sound I was willing to risk, the rumble of many feet and the crash of a door reached me.

Reinforcements. Crap.

I had managed to crawl three meters from the vent. All the Pop Cops had to do was send one of Karla's RATSS after me and I would be caught in no time.

"What's going on here?" Karla demanded.

Her voice stopped my heart and I wondered, if she kill-zapped me, would it resume beating?

"Sensor malfunction, Lieutenant Commander," Riley said.

"But the alarm—"

"My fault. I accidentally triggered it while repairing the device. I apologize for any inconvenience to you, sir."

"Inconvenience! *Your* accident disrupted our meeting and woke every off-duty officer on level four. You'll have to be reported. Name?"

"Riley Narelle Ashon." His voice remained calm. Impressive, considering how terrifying Karla's scrutiny could be.

"Narelle? What are you doing monitoring security systems?"

Good question. Only the Trava family had access to the security network.

"I'm with electrical, sir. When the device malfunctioned it sent a spike through my workstation and I came to investigate. I thought I could fix the sensor, sir."

"You thought wrong. What's your birth week?"

"It's 145,414, sir."

Ha. He was only seventy-three weeks older than me.

"You're just out of training. How did you get assigned electrical?"

"It was my choice, sir."

"Your choice? Oh. Top of your class. Well you obviously need more training. Report to Commander Vinco Trava for extra duty."

Extra duty meant the dreaded red cuff and hard physical labor in the lower levels. The uppers were probably assigned a boring or mindless task nobody else wanted to do.

"Yes, sir," Riley snapped.

After a few seconds of quiet, it dawned on me. Riley hadn't reported me again. Even faced with a punishment, he still kept quiet. A strange sensation rolled through me—relief mixed with… I couldn't name it. Odd.

"You're dismissed, Mr. Ashon. Lieutenant Arno, your unit can return to their stations, but I want you to stay," she ordered.

The shuffle of feet faded and the door clicked shut. I decided to wait. No sense alerting Karla to my presence. I wondered how long I would be stuck here.

"Where were we, Arno?" Karla asked.

"Discussing the situation below," Arno said.

"Anything?"

"No. No one is talking. The scrubs are terrified. They're ratting out their friends. We've uncovered more illegal activities this week than in the past thirty weeks. Caught a woman who was raising her own children. A whole family unit."

"That's new. What did Vinco do?"

"The kids were too old for the care facility. They would remember a mother and might band together. He sent them to Chomper, and the woman was assigned to the *sheep* breeders."

He reported the demise of three children in a bored voice. Enraged, I wanted to strangle him.

"Harsh." A hitch cracked her voice, but then she continued speaking without emotion. "But appropriate. It would be dangerous if the scrubs formed loyalties." She paused. "You've increased the pressure to find Domotor and still no results?"

"Yes, sir."

Domotor? Riley had mentioned his name, too.

"Cogon's our best suspect, but he's had dozens of scrubs vouch for him." She paused.

Dozens? Wow. I knew he was well liked, but didn't think so many would risk their lives for him.

"He knows something, I can feel it," Karla said. "What about our informers? Have they heard any rumors?"

"No. Everyone's keeping quiet. No speculation. No gossip. It's as if Domotor never existed. Usually when a prophet disappears, there are rumblings of unease and talk of martyrs. This time nothing."

Domotor must be Broken Man's real name.

"What about the young girl…Trella?"

All of a sudden it felt as if the air shaft tightened around my body. I struggled to draw a breath.

"I had a few of my men ask about her," Arno said. "Keeps to herself. No absences. No reprimands on her record. No friends except Cogon."

"There's an interesting connection. Arrest them both. Perhaps Cogon will be more informative if we threaten Trella's life and vice versa. Put them each into an interrogation room. Inform Commander Vinco when they're there."

"Yes, sir."

I had to warn Cog. He needed to disappear. But where could I hide the big man? With Broken Man? No. Cog had sealed his door.

Arno left the office, but Karla remained. No more time. Risking capture, I slid through the vent, pushing Zippy ahead. Cooler to the touch, the little troll had worked. I wondered if Logan and Anne-Jade had invented a device to open locks. I bit down on a laugh. I would be lucky to survive the next ten hours let alone make another attempt to steal Broken Man's port.

I reached Riley's storeroom. No sounds, but I paused for a few precious minutes before opening the vent's cover. The place was empty. However, the ladder had been set up underneath the air shaft, and a wipe board rested on the couch. A note for me written on the surface.

It read "I've covered for you, now it's your turn. Meet me here at hour fifty-eight."

I erased the message with a corner of my sleeve. By hour fifty-eight, I would either be in custody or on the lam. It was doubtful I could meet him. A tweak of disappointment surprised me. I repeated my mantra. Never trust the uppers, the Pop Cops or the scrubs. It all boiled down to survival.

As I climbed the ladder I wondered, was survival enough?

"Shouldn't you be in an air shaft working?" Cog asked. He was elbow deep in a piece of machinery in the Waste Handling Plant. Black goo smeared his coveralls and dripped onto the floor. A fetid stench fogged the air.

"The Pop Cops are coming to arrest you and me."

He ceased tugging. "How do you know?"

"Overheard Lieutenant Commander Karla. They're going to threaten to recycle me if you don't tell them about Broken Man. You need to hide. Now."

Instead of pulling his arms out, he resumed his work.

"Cog!"

"Hush a minute. I need to think."

"I thought it out. We both hide and then…"

"What? We live like fugitives for the rest of our days?

Or do we find Gateway and leave? Do you believe in Gateway, Trella?"

"I believe something is going on in the upper levels. I believe the Pop Cops are lying to us."

"No kidding. You need to answer my question. Do you believe in Gateway?"

"It doesn't matter. We need to get you somewhere safe first and then we'll worry about the next step."

Cogon grunted and pulled a wad of black cloth. "Contraband." He unrolled the mass and a bottle fell. "Flushed through the waste system during a Pop Cop raid."

"Cog!" My panic increased. He acted so casual.

"It does matter if you believe or not."

"Why?"

"Because there is nowhere for me to hide. They'll find me pretty quick and keep searching for you. I'm going to let them arrest me, and I'm going to confess to killing the Pop Cop on my own and clear your name. And I'm going to eventually tell them I hid Broken Man, sending them to various hiding spots. And when they don't find him, I'll confess to killing him, too, and dumping his body in a number of tanks and feeding bits of him to machines. Hopefully they'll investigate each and every claim."

I stared at Cog as my body numbed with horror.

"See, Trell? It does matter. Because for me to endure, I need to know you believe in Gateway and know you're searching for it. To know I am helping by keeping the Pop Cops occupied while you find it."

"But you'll be fed to Chomper!"

"I don't have a problem with that."

"But I do."

"It's not your decision."

"You think finding Gateway is more important than your life?" I asked him.

"Yes."

"Why? Aren't you happy with the status quo? You smile at everyone. You have a ton of friends."

He held up his filthy foul-smelling hands. "This *is* the rest of my life. Nothing is going to change unless *we* do something. I've been waiting for the right circumstances. This is it."

One of the maintenance scrubs hustled over. "Cog, a group of Pop Cops are looking for you. Want us to distract them?"

"No thanks. Go back to work." Cogon met my gaze. An unanswered question still hovered between us.

"I don't know if I believe in Gateway or not. But I won't stop searching for it until I prove beyond a doubt it does or doesn't exist. Will that help you?"

Shouts and loud voices reached us.

He smiled. "Yes. Now, shoo." He waved me toward the heating vent. "Won't help my story if you're found in here with me."

"What about the maintenance scrub?"

"He'll cover for me."

I raced for the vent and scrambled through. The Pop Cops must have been prepared for a fight. Surprise laced their voices when Cog agreed to go with them. Sure enough, the other scrub never mentioned me. He could have used the information in exchange for a better position. Proof of Cog's uniqueness.

Lying in the warm duct, I felt truly alone for the first time in a long while.

★ ★ ★

If Cog was going to sacrifice himself, the least I could do was report to my work shift and pretend nothing had happened. Catching up on the three hours I'd missed, I toggled the troll to move faster, reminding me of Cog.

We had been care mates. My earliest memories involved a confusing array of new faces, being upset and longing. Even though Cog was two hundred and sixty-eight weeks older than me, he befriended me. Life in the noisy and chaotic facility was bearable with him. Then Cog had his fourteenth centiweek celebration and "graduated" from the care unit, leaving me.

I had known he would go, but I hadn't been prepared for the devastation inside me. He visited and he was reachable, but his new life and friends kept him busy. The change from having him as my almost constant companion to seeing him for an hour every two weeks left me distraught and an easy target.

My other mates didn't understand. Life in the pipes was preferable to being taunted by everyone. Once I had my celebration, I left the facility and Cog found me. I vowed not to get too close to him or anybody, fearing the return of pain. But Cog just wouldn't give up. And now he was gone again.

I let the waves of anguish pound in my chest. Abandoned and alone. I rode my emotions as I would surf in a water pipe, allowing the force of the liquid to take control.

Eventually, I fought for control and won. I shoved the sadness deep within me, locked it down and focused on the present. My shift was over.

The cleaning troll slowed as it neared a turn. Access to a maintenance area was a few meters ahead. When we reached the area's door, I stopped the troll and slid the panel wide. Wrestling with the awkward device, I stored the troll in a cleaning cabinet for the next scrub.

As I debated whether or not to travel through the pipes or main corridors, the door opened. Three Pop Cops entered the small room.

My heart desired immediate action, screaming for my legs to run. Logic forced my body to ignore the panicked commands. I gave the newcomers space and stepped closer to the access panel, planning to escape through the air shaft if needed.

A lieutenant eyed my work suit and bare feet. "Finishing your shift?" I recognized his voice from Karla's office. Lieutenant Arno.

"Yes, sir." I kept the quaver from my voice.

"You're under arrest."

The quaver dropped into my stomach. "Why, sir?"

"For lying to Lieutenant Commander Karla," He snapped.

"Lying, sir?" Cog wouldn't have given in so fast. Unless… My thoughts shied away from how horrible it would have to be for Cog to tell her about me.

"We know you're involved with Broken Man's disappearance despite what you said. You *will* tell us where he is." His tone left little doubt.

The Pop Cop on his left pulled a pair of handcuffs from his belt. I gauged the distance to the panel, but hesitated. Running was the action of a guilty person and I—well, I was guilty, but I trusted Cog. It seemed too soon.

One of Arno's gadgets beeped. He grabbed the black communicator. "Yes?"

The Pop Cops waited as he listened.

"Are you sure?" He shot me a nasty look. "All right. I'll be there." Replacing the device, he reported to his companions, "Looks like the little scrub is clean." Then to me he said, "Your friend Cogon just confessed to killing my officer by himself. You're free to go...for now."

He strode from the room with the Pop Cops a step behind. When the door clicked shut, I sagged against the wall, letting the metal cool my hot skin. I didn't linger long. My next shift started in ten hours and I had a promise to keep.

After a meal and a few hours of sleep, I aimed for Broken Man's hideout. I hadn't visited in over thirty hours, but at least he had enough food. When I slipped into the room, he sat at the computer terminal, looking well groomed for a man in hiding.

He smiled with relief. "Thank air you haven't been caught."

"Not yet."

He sobered. "Will Cogon tell them where I am?"

"How do you know about Cog?" I glanced around. Was someone else coming here? The place appeared to be clean.

"The computer. I can access general information. When I saw Cogon's shifts had been reassigned, I assumed he was arrested."

"He was. But don't worry about Cog ratting you out. He can be stubborn when he wants." I explained Cog's sacrifice to Broken Man.

He closed his eyes and pressed his hand over them. "A martyr. He will be remembered."

My throat felt as if Zippy had lodged there. I swallowed, and focused on the ground. Broken Man's chair legs had wheels. "Where did you get the chair?" I demanded.

He wiped his eyes and squinted at me. "Chair?"

"The wheels?"

"Oh. I made it. I found an old toolbox and a broken cart. With nothing else to do, I had plenty of time to rig this up." He straightened in his chair, grinning slightly. "In fact, I've gotten pretty good at helping myself. I can take a shower and pull myself into a chair. I guess my muscles are getting stronger." His posture wilted a bit. "Trella, will you do me a favor?"

I stiffened. What more could he want? "Depends."

"If you are caught, tell the Pop Cops where I am."

"Why?"

"I'd rather be kill-zapped than starve until I expire."

Good point. "I'll make sure someone knows where to find you, *Domotor,*" I promised.

His defeated attitude changed into surprise. "How do you know my name?"

I related my adventures in LC Karla's office. "Riley knows I wanted your port. We'll have to find a way to access the computer without it."

"Impossible." He stared into the distance for a few moments. "What are the boy's family names?"

"Narelle Ashon. Why?"

"He's Jacob's boy." He peered at me. "You never asked me about your family."

"The family *you* invented so I would help you?"

"I didn't—"

"Doesn't matter. Even if you were serious, from what I read of the *real* uppers, no real family would abandon their child in the lower levels, so I have no desire to know anything about them."

He put his hands up in defeat. "All right. Have it your way. We still need my port, though. Any ideas?"

"I make another attempt." How remained the problem. Zippy worked but would tip Riley off again, and the lock was impossible to pop. Unless the Tech Nos had another useful device.

"Do it when Riley's on shift."

"Why?"

"He covered for you before and might do it again. Hopefully he's sympathetic to our cause."

Broken Man's words reminded me of Riley's note. He asked me to meet him. And to trust him. I did owe Riley one, and would meet him at hour fifty-eight. But trusting him was out of the question.

9

THE RECYCLING PLANT OCCUPIED THE ENTIRE 11 quadrant. Piles of discarded and broken items littered the space. Scrubs sorted the heaps of trash into smaller loads. Other scrubs moved around the plant's machinery, feeding metal into the blast furnace, glass pieces into the kiln and thread into the looms. And, beyond the equipment, another set of workers crafted goods from the melted glass, from the sheets of metal and the bolts of cloth.

I wore the shapeless coveralls of the workers, blending in with ease. A few Pop Cops wandered around, and I practiced my cover story in my mind just in case.

Heat from the machines thickened the air, and a film of fine grit formed on my clothes and skin. A hot metallic smell dominated. I pushed through the noise and activity, looking for Logan and Anne-Jade.

The reason thick-soled boots were required for this area crunched under my feet, and I skirted piles of kitchen utensils and torn clothing. Nothing was wasted. Everything was recycled and reused. Human waste and food traveled to the waste-handling system to be turned into fertilizer for hydroponics. Water looped through the water-treatment plant and air blasted through a series of tanks and scrubbers.

Even people contributed when their life ended. Their lifeless bodies were sent to Chomper's Lair—a room next to the solid-waste facility—to be transformed into…I wasn't sure. Wild rumors and creative speculation circulated about the place. Not many scrubs were allowed in there—well, not alive anyway. A few called the room the Final Gateway.

My thoughts drifted to Cog. When a well-loved person died, scrubs would line the corridors to Chomper's Lair to pay their respects. I yanked my morose thoughts away. They distracted from my mission.

Anne-Jade and Logan sorted a number of small circuit boards. I joined them. Anne-Jade shot me an annoyed look, but Logan smiled in welcome. In order to appear to be working, I moved items around.

"What are you doing here?" Anne-Jade asked. The words hissed.

"I need your help."

She scanned the Pop Cops nearby. "Couldn't you wait until our shift is over at sixty?"

"No, I work the even shifts."

Logan leaned close. "Did Zippy help you?"

"Sort of."

They waited, and I explained about the power drain being noticeable to the electrical systems manager.

"That *is* a problem. We will have to install a—"

"Not now." Anne-Jade's long golden hair swung as she shook her head in exasperation. "What do you need?" she asked me.

"I could use a new-and-improved Zippy and something to open locks."

"Zippy's it for now. If I had some time…" Logan stared into the distance, probably reassembling Zippy in his head.

"How much time?"

He shrugged. "A week."

"Too long." I considered. Since I knew where to find Broken Man's port, I could reduce my time spent in Karla's office and be gone by the time the spike registered. "What about the lock?"

Logan flashed me a bright smile. He pulled a narrow timer from his pocket and handed it to me. "I thought you would need this. Place it below the keypad and press the button. Instead of the time, the display will show the code for the lock in about three to four seconds."

I marveled at the device. "How?"

"Do you really want to know?" Anne-Jade asked.

"No. This is wonderful."

"Anything else?"

I hesitated. Broken Man had said it was impossible, but, with these two, impossible could be possible. "Do you have a device to access the uppers' computer network?"

Anne-Jade and Logan exchanged a glance. Once again, she scanned the room before asking, "Like a port?"

I nodded.

Another significant look flashed between them. "That's the *ultimate* goal of a Tech No," Logan said. "I managed to hack into the uppers' computer system about as far as I can go without one. All I need is a port to open the door, then I would *own* the system. Own it!"

"Has anyone achieved that goal?" I asked, wondering just how many Tech Nos there were.

"No, but…" He sought Anne-Jade's permission. She waved him on, despite the strain lined on her face.

Logan stepped close to me. "But, we're almost there."

"How soon?"

"Twenty weeks, maybe more."

Too late to help me. "Any chance you could speed it up?"

Anne-Jade turned on me. "No. Crafting these devices takes an immense effort. And it's just us. You're looking at the entire Tech Nos. The Pop Cops have decimated our group, and the only reason we're still alive is because we move slow and proceed with the utmost care. So far, we have out-smarted the uppers." Twin circles of red spread on her cheeks.

"We know we'll be found out eventually," Logan added. His tone remained flat as if he discussed a routine event. "We just want to impart the maximum damage before we're fed to Chomper."

With Zippy leading the way, I crawled through the air shaft on level four. The trip here felt routine. Bad sign. Before Broken Man, I had limited my trips into the upper levels to once every five or ten weeks. Now I popped up here every off-shift.

I turned Zippy off as we neared Riley's room. No sense alerting him to our presence even if hour fifty-eight was only minutes away. Peering through the vent, I searched for Pop Cops.

Riley sat on the edge of the couch. After a moment he

stood, glanced at the clock, smoothed his shirt and adjusted his headset. Nervous or bored, I couldn't tell for sure. The Pop Cops could be waiting in the corridor for Riley's signal. And why would he be wearing his headset?

Now or never. I reached the vent above the couch and removed the cover. Riley jumped at the sound. I suppressed a grimace. He was nervous. Because of a trap or because of me? At least he wasn't armed.

I dropped Zippy onto the couch and climbed down the ladder. Keeping my feet on the lowest rung, I prepared to bolt at any sign of trouble.

"I thought you wouldn't come," Riley said.

He appeared older. No longer in training, he wore a plain gray shirt and black pants. Fresh scratches marred his cheek and neck, and his left sleeve was torn and bloody.

"What happened?" I asked, gesturing to his arm.

A wry smile twisted his lips. "Extra duty with Commander Vinco. The commander delights in knife fighting and uses his unarmed *helpers* for target practice."

I couldn't resist. "Unarmed?"

Impishness lit his face. "So far, I've managed to survive the duty, much to his annoyance." He rubbed his shoulder as the humor faded from his expression. "But he's getting creative, which is not the reason you're here." He stared at me for a moment.

Warmth flushed through me. I imagined I was quite the sight. Wisps of brown hair had sprung from my braid long ago and clung to my sweaty face. Stains and tears marked my one-piece cleaning uniform, which felt rather tight all of a sudden. Bare feet roughened with calluses completed the picture. I don't know why I cared about my appearance. I hadn't before.

"Aren't you going to come down?" Riley pointed to the couch.

"I'll stay here."

"You still don't trust me even after I covered for you?"

No sense sugarcoating it. "Yep."

"Then *why* are you here?"

"I owe you one."

"Wonderful," he muttered. He crossed his arms and frowned. "You might as well go then. I can't help you if you don't trust me." Riley turned to leave.

Not the reaction I expected. "Help me with what?"

He paused. "Getting Domotor's port."

"Why?"

Riley faced me with a challenge in his blue eyes. So used to the various shades of brown in the lower levels, the color still amazed me.

"If you want to know why, then have a seat." He swept his arm wide.

Curiosity was a lethal trait. Scrubs learned in the care facility not to ask too many questions or challenge what you were taught. To accept and agree meant more privileges, fewer punishments and a decent work assignment. A few had learned this lesson quicker than others. A few still hadn't accepted it.

My Care Mother followed the Pop Cops' rules, but she lacked the inner conviction. She punished because she had to, not because she agreed with the rules. If one of us found a loophole, she honored it and applauded our inventiveness.

Unfortunately, my talents in creative explanations had been limited. And the faded scars crisscrossing my body reminded me I should squelch all curiosity. But should didn't mean I would. I settled on the couch next to Zippy.

Riley pointed to the little cleaning troll. "Is that what you used to keep the motion detectors silent?"

"I'm not answering anything until you tell me why you want to help me."

He swallowed his first comment, drew a deep breath and said, "After meeting you the first time, I searched for more information about life in the lower levels. My interest triggered a warning. Good thing I was still in training, the warning was sent to my trainer who's also my father instead of the Controllers." He touched his left arm. Blood still welled from a number of cuts.

"What happens when the Controllers are alerted?"

A wince flashed across his face. "You don't want to know."

"Yes, I do. You're an upper. How bad can it be?"

He paused. "Interesting. The ignorance goes both ways." Balanced on the couch's armrest, his gaze slid past my shoulder. "Makes sense, though. The Trava family wouldn't want uppers and lowers to unite." Riley's focus returned to me.

"Nor would we. You uppers think we're filthy livestock bred for one purpose. To work."

"I see the propaganda has worked. You believe the Pop Cops."

I jumped to my feet. "I'm not like those sheep. I don't listen to all that bull."

"Really?" He raised one eyebrow in a mocking sneer. "Where did you acquire your vast knowledge of life in the upper levels?"

"In the care facility."

"Which is run by the Pop Cops." Smugness replaced his scorn.

I preferred the sneer. "So your purpose in inviting me here was to prove I'm an ignorant scrub?"

"No." The word ground out as if it originated deep within him. He held up both hands in a stopping motion. "I'm trying to understand why you automatically assumed I'm a spoiled brat. And I wanted you to think about where you've gotten your information. It's either from the Pop Cops or from the computer system, which is run by the Controllers. Both can't be trusted."

"Gee, thanks for that little nugget of advice. I wonder how I survived all these weeks without it." I headed to the ladder. What a waste of time.

"Wait." He grabbed my arm.

I yanked a screwdriver from my tool belt. He let go.

"Please listen," he said to my back. "This isn't going the way I thought it would. When my father asked why I was so interested in the scrubs, I told him—"

I rounded on him. "I knew this was a trap! Is your father waiting outside with a troop of Pop Cops?"

"No." This time the word growled. Riley's hands shook as if he fought to keep from grabbing me again. "I told him I wanted to help the scrubs, to do something…anything to ease their horrid living conditions."

"Really?" Disbelief tainted my voice.

"Yes." He practically shouted the word.

"Why?"

"Because of what you told me when you…er…visited last week. Before you dropped in, I thought scrubs were…" His arms moved in a vague all-encompassing gesture. "Were like your little device there, but bigger. We're taught nothing more about scrubs than they clean and work. We're threatened to be exiled to the lower levels if we do anything really bad. It's implied that if we survived, the rest of our weeks would be filled with hard physical labor." He held a hand up, stopping me from contradicting him. "Look. There are no pictures in our training computers. Truthfully, I hadn't really thought about who lives in the lower levels at all. But there you stood, a real human being. My age, with…" He dropped his arms, slapping his hands against his legs. "Never mind, you wouldn't believe me. My father said there was nothing I could do to help. He was right until Domotor went missing and I caught you in LC Karla's office."

"Caught?" I feigned innocence—all I could manage. His speech rolled around in my mind, and I couldn't quite grasp the significance. "Don't you mean found?"

"No. Caught. You didn't see the petrified look on your face when you turned around. It was gone in an instant, but I'll never forget it." He smiled at the memory.

He *could* smile. *He* wouldn't be fed to Chomper if caught. "Is there a point to all this? My work shift starts in an hour."

"My father had told me about a few uppers who'd tried and failed to circumvent various security systems in the computer network long ago. Domotor was rumored to be trying again before his accident and banishment to the lower levels. When you showed up looking for Domotor's port, I guessed you know where he is and you're helping him."

"Why would I care if Broken Man is trying to bypass computer systems?"

Riley stepped closer. "If the other upper families regain control of Inside, then we can make life in the lower levels better."

I studied his expression for signs of deceit. Broken Man had said the upper families wouldn't want to help. Or did he tell me that so I would focus all my energy on finding Gateway? Riley seemed sincere and he already knew most of it. How much worse could it be for him to know?

"You're right. I'm here to fetch Broken…Domotor's port."

"You'll let me help?"

He managed to downplay his triumph. Impressive. I nodded.

"I'm monitoring the electrical usage for level four during the next shift. I can't disable the motion sensors because it would be recorded, but I can hide the spike from your device." He glanced at the little cleaning troll. "Smoke was coming out of it before. Will it work?"

"Yes." Logan had repaired Zippy before I left.

"Good. I wasn't able to find the code for the lock. How do you plan to get into the evidence closet?"

"I have another…ah…device."

He raised his eyebrows, inviting me to elaborate.

"It's better you don't know."

"As long as it works fast," he said. He slid his hand into a pocket.

I tensed, but relaxed when he withdrew a port. He handed it to me.

"What's this for?" I examined the white interface. The size and shape mimicked three molars in a row, but underneath a square-shaped metal piece stuck out. Small numbers had been etched into the metal box. It was hollow except for a line of copper pins. I guessed the bottom piece was inserted into a person's jawbone to anchor the port.

"To exchange for Domotor's. An empty spot will alert LC Karla. Do you know his ID number?"

"Yes, but what about the LC? She's also scheduled to work the next shift."

"All the high-ranking officers have a meeting in the Control Room at hour sixty. It lasts about an hour. She's usually there."

"Usually?"

"Wait to enter her office until a few minutes past sixty. The computer lists the whereabouts of important people so if there's ever an emergency they can be contacted. If she's not listed in the meeting room, I'll flash the lights in her office to let you know."

"Do you always know where she is?"

"No. I only have second degree security clearance. The hour sixty meeting and its attendees are general knowledge."

General knowledge to the uppers. The scrubs hadn't a clue, and what we did know was doubtful. So much for reporting to my shift on time.

"Get in position now," Riley said. "I don't want to open the door until you're hidden from sight. Just in case someone is out in the hall."

"How come you're the only one who uses this room?"

"It's hard to find and has been forgotten. I doubt anyone is outside, but it never hurts to be too careful."

I agreed with him, being extra careful should be our motto. Turning away so Riley couldn't see my smirk—our motto, like we were a gang—I opened the heating vent and slipped inside, taking Zippy with me.

Riley crouched down to help replace the cover. But before setting it in place, he touched my arm. This time I didn't flinch as the heat from his hand sizzled in my blood. I met his gaze.

"Be careful," he said.

Cog constantly told me to be careful, but Riley's voice sounded different. I wondered if it was fear or genuine concern.

"You, too," I said.

He nodded then replaced the vent's cover. Rolling Zippy ahead of me, I slid through the tight space toward Karla's office, but my mind reviewed the strange conversation with Riley as I traveled. Could the Controllers be as bad as the Pop Cops? It was hard to imagine and yet I couldn't shake the image of blood dripping from his arm, nor could I forget the warmth that still lingered on my skin from his touch.

I reached Karla's office and slowed. Creeping toward her vent, I listened for any noise. The soft bluelight shone through the vent cover, signaling an empty room. My body was so used to the ten-hour system, I felt rather than knew when it was hour sixty. I hoped my supervisor wasn't looking for me.

The glow remained steady. After a few minutes, I removed the vent's cover. Another couple passed before I turned Zippy on and pushed him out. When the alarm failed to sound, I hurried over to the gray evidence closet. Opening the doors, I pulled out Logan's device and placed it under the keypad, pressing the button.

It hummed and a series of numbers filled the small screen. Typing in the code, I braced for an alarm, but the bolt slid back. I exchanged the fake port for Broken Man's, checked the ID numbers twice, then relocked the closet.

The room's daylights flashed a few times. I grabbed Zippy and dove into the vent. Voices sounded beyond the office door. The vent cover stuck in the hole. I tugged on it as the pings of someone entering a code rang. It jerked free. I placed it over the vent as the door opened.

"Alarm off," Lieutenant Commander Karla said.

Daylights swept over the blue glow, trapping me and illuminating a frowning Karla. I couldn't ever recall seeing the woman smile.

"This had *better* be important," she said to the lieutenant following her into the room.

"Our detainee just gave us a clue to Domotor's location. I need your permission to assign a search team," the lieutenant said.

"Has he implicated anyone else?"

"No, sir."

"Hard to believe he managed to hide a physically disabled man without help." Frustration tainted her voice.

"He's strong and has a high pain tolerance, sir."

My heart stumbled. Only one way to discover how much pain a person could tolerate.

Karla grunted. "But he's too big to fit in the air shafts. Another scrub had to be involved."

"But we have no real evidence, sir. That cloth bag could have been blown down to the floor. It's light enough to have been sucked up by the return air."

"No. I know a scrub was there, and I'll find out who was in the air shaft," she vowed. "No *scrub* gets away from me."

"What about the search team, sir?"

"Take team four and report back to me immediately. Understand?"

"Yes, sir." The lieutenant strode from the room.

The LC scowled at his retreating form. She stood gazing at the door as if lost in thought then left her office, pausing only to reactivate the alarms.

I waited a few minutes to ensure she was gone. The need

to act pulsed in my body. Cogon suffered while I wasted time. I headed toward Riley's room with reckless speed. Even knowing Riley wouldn't be there, disappointment still jabbed me when I reached the place. I hid Zippy under the couch and hurried to Domotor's room. My shift be damned. Cogon would not suffer in vain.

10

I HELD DOMOTOR'S PORT BETWEEN MY FINGER AND thumb, flourishing the unit.

The prophet pumped a fist in the air and grinned. "Good work!"

"How long to get the information?"

"It'll take about forty to fifty hours," Domotor said.

I groaned aloud.

"If I'm not careful, I'll alert the system to my presence and we'll be discovered." He studied my face. "Trella, get a few hours' sleep. You look terrible."

I ignored his remark, but thought about Riley's comment about circumventing computer systems. "Are you going to tell me your real agenda?"

He fidgeted in his chair. The ecstatic expression faded and wariness touched his eyes. I hadn't given him the device.

"Are you really seeking Gateway's location? Or was that my incentive for retrieving the disks and your port?"

"It's complicated," he said.

"Meaning a dumb scrub wouldn't be able to understand?" My hand fisted around his port.

"No." He pushed the hair from his eyes. The long blond strands hung loose. "Meaning you don't know enough about the upper levels to realize that even if we find Gateway, we might not be able to unlock it without gaining control of key computer systems."

"Do you even believe Gateway exists?"

"Yes, I do." His gaze remained steady.

Damn. Either he was a good liar or he told the truth. "How do you gain control of the systems?"

"Through the computer network, but I need to find out who the real Controllers are."

"You mean which Travas?"

"No. All the upper families think the admiral, vice admiral and captain, who are all Travas, are the Controllers. But I found a command flow chart in a forgotten file that put the Controllers above the admiral."

"Then who are the Controllers?"

"No one knows. Not even the Travas. But I've overheard them speculating, and they believe the Controllers live Outside and send instructions through the computer. Sort of a divine influence."

Shock rolled through me. The thought of people or even a divine being dictating what we did Inside from Outside was hard to grasp.

"Just because the Travas believe it doesn't mean it is true."

"Do they know what is Outside?"

"No. No one does. It's all speculation. A few Travas think the divine presence lives in the computer network. Others think the computer itself has become intelligent." He shrugged. "Knowledge of before was erased from the computer system thousands of weeks ago. Something has to be beyond our walls. The Controllers must know."

I mulled over the information. "Gateway could just be a computer link to the Controllers, and not a physical exit."

"It's possible. And you're holding our only chance to find out."

I unfurled my fingers. His port rested in my palm. Cog's life in exchange for this. No turning back now. I would stay the course until the end.

He snatched his port as a hungry man would grab food. Relief washed the worry from Domotor's expression. He inspected the device and then inserted it into the gap on the right side of his lower jaw. I wheeled him over to the computer.

"Get some rest," he said half-distracted. "You're welcome to use my bed."

A few hours remained in my shift, and I needed to put in an appearance. But I entered the kitchen first to inventory his food. Not much left. A few lonely bowls of casserole occupied the small refrigerator. More than thirty hours remained to the next assembly, and I doubted I could cough my way into the kitchen again. The prospect of standing in line multiple times for extra food seemed daunting.

I straightened the dishes and checked his bedroom. The clicks and taps from the keyboard followed me. His sheets hung to the floor and his blanket was a balled-up wad. Must be hard to make a bed when you couldn't use your legs.

Pulling everything off, I remade the bed with clean linens. A mistake. The fresh sheets called to me. My body ached. My thoughts pushed through a numb fog. A sense of loss pressed between my shoulder blades. I settled on the edge of the bed and rested my head in my hands.

What had I expected? Give Domotor his port and voilà! Directions to Gateway would appear in a matter of minutes. Huffing in tired amusement, I admitted that, yes, I had been expecting instantaneous results despite all my efforts to believe Gateway didn't exist and to not get my hopes up. I guess a part of me really desired a true exit to Outside. Now the possibility of a computer Gateway instead of a physical Gateway sucked all hope away.

I should be happy. Domotor's discoveries would prove me right. Yet the possibility of the Controllers not living with us or even being a person caused a finger of fear to brush my spine.

Morbid thoughts circled and conversations replayed in my mind. To escape them, I laid down. I would rest a few minutes.

"Lousy son-of-a-Trava!" Domotor's curses woke me from a dreamless sleep. Hours and not minutes had passed. So much for my shift. I hoped my supervisor hadn't checked on me. I stretched and padded to the living area.

Domotor scowled at the computer monitor. He punched a few keys then slammed his fist on the table.

"What's the matter?" I asked.

"New security systems have been installed."

"And?"

"I might not be able to get around them." He typed a few words. "The program is…odd. The Controllers aren't usually this…creative. They stick to what they know and what has worked."

"Perhaps your earlier forays into the system alarmed them?"

"Possible. But this other program should work. It's just complicated." His attention returned to the screen.

I left him to his work and showered. My stomach growled with urgent need and I resigned myself to spending the next five hours gathering food for me and Domotor.

He grunted when I said goodbye. I traveled through the heating vents until I reached one of the main hallways. The scrubs traveling through the corridor ignored me. No curses. No taunts. I joined the flow and aimed for the cafeteria in Quad G2.

Standing in line, I noticed the stiffness of the people around me. It was well known I didn't like them and they didn't like me. They called me Queen of the Pipes, believing I thought I was better than them. Used to glares and sneers, I now had scrubs avoiding eye contact. Different. And the ones who met my gaze, nodded. A few smiled in encouragement. Stranger still was the muted hum in the room. Pop Cops patrolled the aisles between tables, and a mist of fear hung in the humid sweat-scented air. Yet a sense of purpose emanated as if no matter how afraid they were, the scrubs were determined to endure the Pop Cops' scrutiny.

I pushed my tray along the metal track and pointed to a vegetable casserole. The scrub spooned a ladle-full into a bowl then added in a second scoop. I glanced at the man in surprise.

"There's a clog in the kitchen's air shaft," he said. "Can you clean it out for us?"

It took me a moment to realize he was talking to me. "Report it to the kitchen manager."

He stared at me. "I did. She said to have *someone* check the shaft at hour eighty." He returned to filling bowls and the press of the scrubs waiting behind me propelled me toward the tables.

Odd. The whole exchange worried me. The scrubs couldn't know about me. Could they? No. They'd rat me out in an instant. I shoveled the food into my mouth, but didn't taste a thing.

There had been plenty of chances for scrubs to gain favor by implicating me. Yet here I sat with a double portion. Enough for Domotor and me. Instead of standing in line again, I stored the leftover food and checked the cleaning schedule.

My next shift started at hour eighty. Air shaft twenty-two was the first job listed on my sheet. Twenty-two crossed over the scrubs' kitchen. I licked my dry lips. The man had said there was a clog. Could it be an ambush? No. Why go to all that trouble? A simple anonymous note to the lieutenant commander would do the trick.

Something was going on. I searched for Jacy. He held court in his corner of the barracks. A tone signaled the end of a shift. I hung back, waiting for the crowd to thin. He spotted me and soon the scrubs hurried away.

After scanning the barracks, he pulled two round disks from his pocket and handed them to me. "The listening devices," he said.

I remembered my deal to plant them in air shaft seventy-two. The metal felt cold in my hands. About a quarter inch thick, the silver circles fit within my palm. An inner circle of gold-colored mesh coated the one side, and a black magnet clung to the other.

"Stick them close to the vents. They won't come loose even when the cleaning trolls go through," Jacy explained. "Put one in the Pop Cops HQ and the other over the Control Room."

I hid them in my tool belt. "I have another question."

"Goody. I have more listening devices."

"Not that type of question. At least I think the answer wouldn't be worth anything."

He brushed away his hair, revealing his dark eyes. "Now, I'm intrigued."

"I just want to know the latest gossip, what rumors are circulating."

Jacy studied my face. "You never cared before. Why now?"

"The lower levels feel…odd."

"With twice as many Pop Cops patrolling, people are scared and nervous."

"I get that, but…" How to word my questions without giving too much away? "But they have the chance to…make their life better, and I don't know why they don't take it."

"You should know why. Do you really need me to spell it out for you?"

I nodded.

He shook his head. "It'll cost you two more devices."

Figures. "Only if it isn't some bull."

"It's not. This is serious." He stepped toward me and lowered his voice. "Despite what you think, scrubs aren't stupid. We put it together. One missing prophet, Cogon arrested for hiding him and LC Karla asking questions about you." He held up three fingers. "If we rat you out to the Pop Cops, then the prophet is found and you and Cog are recycled." His fingers curled in and formed a zero with his thumb. "We're left with nothing. No hope, Trella, is worse than fear. Right now, we hope you're up to something that will benefit us all."

All feeling drained from my body. Logic leaked from my brain and panic filled the empty space. "And if I'm not?"

"No one will believe you. See we know something big is going on. Big enough to cause the Queen of the Pipes to come down from above and mingle with her fellow scrubs."

"But…but…" My vision turned to static. I drew in a few breaths. The air smelled musty and damp with a hint of body odor. "But what if I fail?"

"Doesn't matter."

"What?"

He gave me a sad smile. "It's the *effort*, not the results that matter."

Coming from the man who was all about getting something in exchange for his information and services, I didn't believe him. The scrubs were either holding out for a better offer from the Pop Cops or waiting for me to perform a miracle for them. Sheep don't risk their necks for other sheep.

Yet my conviction faltered when I discovered what clogged the air shaft above the kitchen a few minutes past hour eighty. Food containers filled the duct. Enough food to feed me and Domotor for weeks.

I peered through the vent and watched the bustle of the kitchen scrubs. Pop Cops also kept an eye on them, but they had still managed to hide food despite the danger.

They counted on me. Again panic threatened to overwhelm me. If nothing changed in the lower levels, the scrubs would be disappointed and upset for risking the little comforts they had.

Shoving the confused terror into a deep corner of my mind, I concentrated on the task at hand—getting the food to Domotor's hideout. With my makeshift skid and the troll's help, I transported all the containers to the air shaft over his quarters then continued to work my shift.

The hours crept by. Each time I changed air ducts, I kept expecting to be arrested. When I encountered the first RATSS, I almost screamed. The thing focused its antennae on me.

"Name and birth week," a mechanical voice ordered.

I answered.

"Noted. Continue working," it said.

It drove away and my heart resumed beating. I was questioned by two more RATSS in two other shafts.

By the time hour ninety arrived, my muscles were so tight I could have climbed a vertical shaft without breaking a sweat. Grateful to be done, I returned the cleaning troll to his closet.

"There you are," my supervisor said. Her eyebrows pinched together with annoyance and a red cuff hung from her fingers.

I bit down on a sarcastic reply. No sense upsetting her further.

"I waited for you at the end of your last shift, but you never showed. Where were you?"

My thoughts raced. "My cleaning device broke in the shaft and I had to repair it. Took me an extra hour to finish." I hoped she hadn't waited an hour.

She tapped the red cuff on her thigh. I kept my face neutral.

"Next time, leave it behind and check to see if I'm waiting. I've got Pop Cops breathing down my neck. They want to know if anyone misses a shift."

"Yes, sir." Calling her sir always mollified her.

As expected, her expression smoothed. "I wanted to let you know there will be a lot of RATSS in the pipes. The Pop Cops believe there's evidence hidden in one of the air ducts." She huffed in disbelief. "We're *supposed* to work around them. Just try not to break any of the RATSS during your next shift."

"Yes, sir."

She checked my name off her list and left to find the next scrub. I waited for my pulse to calm before sliding into the heating ducts and heading toward Domotor's room. The air shafts wouldn't be safe for me to travel in for a while. And I hoped the RATSS hadn't discovered the cache of food above Domotor's hideout.

I entered his quarters through the vent. Domotor was slumped over his keyboard sleeping. Wasting no time, I transported the food containers from the air shaft to the refrigerator and freezer.

When I finished, Domotor straightened a bit in his chair, but he rested his forehead in the palm of his hand. His hair covered his expression.

Not able to wait anymore, I asked, "Any progress?"

His reply was muffled so I stepped closer and touched his shoulder. He dropped his arm and met my gaze. Hollowness lurked in his eyes.

"What happened?" I asked.

"We're done."

11

I UNDERSTOOD THE LOOK OF DEFEAT IN HIS FACE, BUT not the reason for it.

"What happened?" I asked.

"I hit a wall. The security system has been enhanced and I couldn't bypass it."

I ignored the tightness gripping my throat. "Is there another way?" The question squeaked out.

"No."

"There has to be." A whisper, all I could manage. My body felt as if it were trapped in a metal compactor.

"There isn't." He rubbed a hand over his cheek as he stared into the distance. A combination of emotions crossed his face, but they moved too fast for me to decipher. "Unless…I follow Cog's example and reveal myself to the Travas. They'll know I have my port and where I am, but I could find the information we need before they get to me."

I searched his expression. He was committed to sacrificing

himself. Good to know. "You said 'could find,' does that mean the information is there to retrieve or you think it might be?"

"The information is there, but I can't guarantee I'll access it before the Controllers sever my link."

Too big a risk right now. I thought about the problem. Even though I knew nothing about the computer and its security, I remembered a comment Logan had made about the uppers' computer system.

"Wait until I return before you attempt to retrieve the information. I need to check a few things and report for the hundred-hour assembly."

He agreed to wait and I hurried off. I had much to do in the hours remaining before assembly.

"Sure can," Logan said. A delighted smile spread across his face.

"No," Anne-Jade said at almost the same time.

Once again I had donned the shapeless overalls of the recycling-plant workers and joined the Tech Nos in sorting through a pile of clothing. We pulled buttons and cut zippers from the ruined garments before feeding them into Shredder. The device had a more technical name for how it recycled the threads, but the scrubs nicknamed everything.

"No as in he can't do it?" I asked Anne-Jade.

"No as in I won't let him. It's too dangerous. He'll be caught."

"We're going to be discovered anyway. Might as well go out with style," Logan said.

She scowled as Logan pouted, but by the tight set to Anne-Jade's shoulders I knew she wouldn't change her mind. A Pop Cop sauntered by and we concentrated on our work.

Her reaction didn't make sense. They had covered for Cog and told me about Zippy. Why was this different? I ran a tattered shirt through my fingers. The steady plink of buttons dropping into a bucket and clack of zippers kept time with my thoughts.

The answer was right in front of me in the movement of their hands. They worked as one, progressing through the pile of clothes without any signs of communication. Anne-Jade wasn't afraid he would be recycled, but that he would be recycled without her. They were a matched set.

I used logic. "If he doesn't help, Broken Man will go after the information anyway. He'll be arrested and interrogated, which will lead the Pop Cops to me and I'll lead them to you." I suppressed a shudder. The pain would have to be horrible for me to rat on them.

"Are you threatening me?" Anne-Jade thrust her scissors in my direction.

"No. I'm just stating the facts. We've come too far to back off now. If Broken Man's efforts fail, then you and Logan will be recycled without causing any damage."

Her arm dropped and she returned to cutting zippers. "When do you need him?"

"Right after assembly is over. Logan, meet me in the hallway outside the care facility."

He flashed me a grin, but Anne-Jade kept her eyes on her work, ripping threads and seams with more force than needed. The sound of tearing cloth followed me as I left the plant.

I had a few more bits of unfinished business. Jacy's listening devices needed to be installed. Air duct number seventy-two was located above the fourth level. It didn't cross over Riley's room. In fact, it supplied air to two areas only. The main control room in Quad G4 and the Pop Cops headquarters and holding cells in Quad A4. Extra filters had been installed and a few special scrubbers.

Remembering the gas hissing from the canisters in Domotor's room, I guessed the extra precautions kept an enemy from sending airborne poisons through the vents.

The known ways into seventy-two were either through the vents in the actual rooms or at the air source. Since I doubted LC Karla would let me use her office to climb into the duct, I headed to the air plant in Quad I4. I could cut a hole into the shaft from the Gap, but the ducts weren't labeled and the effort to figure it out would consume more time than I had available.

I wore the air workers' plain white jumper, tucking my hair under the bump cap. The air filters and scrubbers were cleaned on a regular schedule. Between shifts only a few scrubs lingered to keep an eye on the equipment. I strode to a two-meter-high rectangular box as if I had an urgent purpose. A large air shaft entered the side of the container and another exited the other end. No one questioned me as I climbed the ladder to the top of the container and the access ports that allowed the scrubs to remove the filters, clean them and return them.

Lowering myself, I squeezed through the rows of filters. Soft and made of a cloth mesh, the bags trapped the dust particles in the air. A strong current pushed through the chamber. I tried hard not to damage the filters as I swam through them. On the intake side of the container, I climbed into the oversized trunk air shaft and followed it up to one of its branches—air shaft seventy-two.

Working my way through air filters and wire security

screens, I reached the Pop Cops headquarters and placed a microphone near a vent.

I couldn't resist making a side trip to the holding cells. Risky, yes, but there could be a way to rescue Cog, I rationalized. When the covers on the vents turned into solid bars, I knew I had reached my destination. Slowing, I moved with care. Only a slight whisper of fabric sounded.

Harsh daylight streamed from below. Armed Pop Cops occupied the room. Desks and chairs with handcuffs littered the space, appearing to be a processing area for the inmates. Double doors festooned with locks filled the back wall.

Farther along the shaft the light changed into a muted yellow. The smells of sweat, blood and fear created an acidic stew. Taking shallow breaths, I peered into the dank cells. Black bars caged tiny areas only big enough for a bed and toilet. Although, calling the metal slab a bed was being generous. Three cells lined each side of the room with a short corridor between them. Cog was the sole occupant.

His bulk filled the slab and his feet dangled off the end. In the sickly half light the raw and bleeding bruises on his face resembled rotten meat. His eyes were swollen shut and his breath rattled. I rested my forehead on the duct for a moment, trying to see past the fog of horror and guilt clouding my vision. Pressure built inside my skull and chest as if I would explode. I fought to muffle my sobs.

My fault. Retrieving those disks had been a lark. I didn't believe in Gateway, didn't care about the prophet. One mistake, letting the cover slip through my fingers, and Cog… I wanted to shy away from the vision, but I forced myself to face the image of Chomper crushing and pulping Cogon's lifeless body, and to hear the sound of splintering bones and the wet smack of bodily fluids. I let the consequence of my actions burn into my mind.

No way to change the past, I could only hope to affect the future before I met the same fate. For Cogon, and in Logan's words, I would inflict the maximum damage.

"Cog?" I whispered. When he didn't stir, I cupped my hands around my mouth and called louder. After the fourth try, he moved his head.

"Trella?" His voice rasped like a rusty hinge. "You caught?" He struggled to sit up with frantic haste.

"No. I'm in the air shaft above you."

He relaxed, resuming his prone position. "Good, 'cause I can't break those bars to the duct to help you escape. So don't get caught."

"How are you—"

He waved his hands in a pushing motion. "No worries. Did you find Gateway yet?"

Despite being beaten his confident tone astounded me. I squashed the honest reply between my molars and hedged. "Not yet."

"How soon?"

"Don't know."

"I hope I'm alive when it's opened. Just to see the look on the lieutenant commander's face."

My jaw ached as the Chomper vision flashed. "Cog, can I bring you anything?"

"No, but you can do something for me."

"Name it."

A harsh bark erupted from him, and, at first, I worried he was choking but then realized he was laughing. Between

gasps he said, "And I…had…to *beg* you…to see Broken…
Man. Wish…you were this…cooperative before."

"Cogon," I warned.

"Whew. Back to your old…self. I need you to plant
Broken Man's clothes to help my alibi. Obviously, the Pop
Cops haven't found him and they think he's moved to
another hiding place. But after the next—" he drew in a
deep breath "—next round of torture, I'm going to
confess to killing him and I need evidence. I'm going to
tell them I shoved his clothes into the space behind storage
closet two-two-one in the care facility. Do you know
where it is?"

I smiled at the memory of Cogon showing me his hidey
hole. "The one where you hid your…what did you call them?"

"Spirits."

"Now I remember. So called because they burned on the
way down and floated right to your head, making you feel
as light as a ghost."

"And you believed me, too."

"Did not."

"Did, too. You used to follow me around the common
room, making sure I didn't turn into a ghost."

"You have it all wrong. *You* followed *me*. And I'm the one
who kept *you* from getting into trouble."

"Me? Who covered for *you* when you went exploring?
Me. That's who! And I'm still protecting you."

The dagger of truth popped the warm bubble of memories.
Cold reality rushed in, shocking me into the present.

A bang echoed through the cells, and a wedge of daylight
sliced the yellow glow.

"Who're you talking to, scrub?" a man asked.

"The rats," Cog said.

The man's harsh laughter grated on my nerves. "Did they respond?"

"No."

"I'm not surprised. Rats wouldn't demean themselves by interacting with a low-life scrub."

"*You're* talking to me, Vinco. Does that make you worse than a rat?"

Vinco growled. "That's *Commander* Vinco, scrub. Since you're in such a chatty mood… Porter bring me my knife!"

There was a muttered reply. I strained to see Commander Vinco. I wanted to put a face to the man who hurt both Riley and Cog.

"Damn assembly. My *knife* will be talking to you on my next shift," Vinco said.

The white light shrank then disappeared with the slamming of the doors.

"Trella?" Cog pitched his voice low.

"Still here."

"You shouldn't be. Get going before you're marked tardy for assembly."

"But I need to hide Broken Man's stuff for you."

"You have time. The Pop Cops won't be looking for it until hour twelve."

His matter-of-fact tone about the exact time had an ominous ring. A cold unease crept up my spine. "How can you be so sure?"

"Vinco's next shift starts at hour ten. I can take a beating and I can endure most pain. But two hours of Vinco's knife is all I can bear."

★ ★ ★

The bell rang for the hundred-hour assembly as I climbed from the bag-filter's chamber. Damn. No time to change the stained and sweat-soaked uniform. I raced to my assembly station—the cafeteria—and ended up last in the short line. Only three scrubs between me and LC Karla. She leaned against a table, watching the check-in process. I wondered why she was here again.

My voice didn't waver when I repeated my stats, but my heart beat a faster rhythm when Karla eyed my work suit with a contemplative purse on her lips. I tried to sidle past her.

"Running late?" she asked.

"Sorry, sir." I stepped toward the dining room.

She blocked my way. "You weren't scheduled to work. What have you been doing during your off time?"

Her stare could have frozen the warmest heart. I blinked. Caught by surprise, my mind blanked.

"Hey, Trella," another scrub called. An older man with short gray hair and a stooped posture, he had gone through check-in just before me. "Thanks for helping with that clogged drain. Without your little hands, I don't know what we would have done."

"Anytime," I said, waving.

Karla snatched my hand and inspected my short fingernails.

"No dirt under your nails?" She waited.

"I washed my hands, sir. They were in raw sewage."

She dropped my hand as if I were contagious and gestured for me to join the scrubs assembled in the cafeteria. I stood next to the man who had covered for me. As Karla pushed her way to the front, I leaned close and whispered my thanks.

"Anytime," he said, winking.

LC Karla climbed onto a table to address the crowd. "Citizens, welcome to the end-of-the-week celebration. Now begins week number 147,003." She scanned the scrubs. "I have good news. We have caught the man responsible for my officer's untimely recycling, and we will find Broken Man soon. However, if you know of anyone who may have helped hide Broken Man, you are to tell me immediately. Rewards for accurate information may result in promotion to the upper levels."

Absolute silence filled the room. All moisture evaporated from my mouth and gushed from my pores. I couldn't help glancing at the man beside me. Why didn't he raise his hand and tell the LC about lying for me? He didn't move. No one did.

LC Karla's body stiffened and she shook as if waves of pure anger pulsed off her. She glared at the crowd. "Fine, then you *all* will be interrogated. One at a time."

She relinquished her tabletop position to the ensign on duty. As he read the weekly announcements, murmurs circled the room. But the whispers held a timbre of outrage.

The man leaned over. "She's made a mistake." He met my gaze. "Whatever you're up to, do it quick. I think you'll be first on her interrogation list."

I listened to the rest of the ensign's message without hearing a word he said. My thoughts tumbled in circles, ending at the same point. I stifled the desire to jump on a tabletop and shout to the scrubs, "Don't get your hopes up!"

When the assembly was over, I bolted into the kitchen. Karla stood at the exit and I didn't want to remind her about me. If she caught me later, I could say I had needed to start my cleaning shift. True to a point.

No Pop Cops had arrived yet, and the kitchen scrubs took my presence in stride, preparing food for the next meal. I could reach the air vent above the countertop, but would have difficulty getting inside. Scanning the kitchen, I searched for a stool to stand on.

A thud sounded behind me and I turned. On the counter rested a stepladder. The type with only a few rungs and used to reach into high cabinets. Without delay, I climbed on the counter and up the ladder.

"Thanks!" I called as I pulled myself into the air shaft. The ladder was gone by the time I closed the vent's cover. I traveled through the shaft to the hallway outside the care facility in Sector H2. Once there, I glanced down. A stream of scrubs heading toward their work assignments flowed below me. I waited a few minutes then dropped down on the stragglers.

No curses. No taunts. I could get used to it. Although if I failed to help the scrubs, the verbal abuse would resume. I laughed. If I failed, the scrubs would be the least of my worries.

Logan paced the hallway, biting a nail. I scanned the hallway to make sure no Pop Cops lingered nearby. He stopped when he saw me. I pulled his hand down.

"Try not to look so nervous," I said. "How do you manage to work on Zippy and the other technology without giving yourself away?"

"Anne-Jade. She has nerves of glass. It has to be pretty hot for her to melt."

"We'll be out of sight soon." I guided him to a small door near the care facility. Taking his decoder from my tool belt, I whispered, "Keep an eye out." Then I placed the device near the door's lock, pressing the button.

"Anne-Jade? What are you doing here?" Logan asked.

I looked over my shoulder. Barefooted, Anne-Jade wore a skintight dark blue work uniform. Her thick hair had been wrestled into a single braid.

"I need Trella's birth week and barrack number," she said.

"Why?" Logan asked.

"Good idea," I said, rattling off my stats. "I'm supposed to be in—"

"Shaft one eleven. Got it." She hurried off.

I reviewed my cleaning schedule in my mind—two water pipes and a bunch of air ducts on level one. Nothing too challenging for her.

The decoder had finished. I unlocked the door and pulled Logan into a small storage room filled with stacks of linen diapers. Closing the door, I switched on my light. Situated under the shelves was a heating vent. My fellow scrubs didn't bat an eye when I wormed into the heating system, but Logan's presence would draw unwanted attention. I had thought ahead, remembering this closet. However I had failed to find a solution for missing my shift, hoping we would be done in time for me finish it. But Anne-Jade figured it out.

"Oh," Logan said. His puzzled expression smoothed. "She's pretending to be you so the Pop Cops won't be suspicious. Smart!"

"So are you," I said.

"Not that kind of smart."

"There's another kind?"

"Oh, yeah. I know the tech stuff, but she's the one who disguises it. The Pop Cops walk by our stuff all the time and don't know it's there. She's the one who figures out what we can take from the recycling plant and when. She's the one who insisted we not tell the other Tech Nos about us."

"That is smart," I agreed. Pulling the vent cover down, I pointed. "Follow me, it's not far. Close the vent when you're through, and keep quiet. Voices carry in there."

He nodded and then gnawed on a fingernail. I squirmed into the vent and moved ahead to give Logan room. My sore forearms protested. From all the time spent in the ducts, I would develop calluses on my elbows and wrists. How would I explain them to LC Karla?

The trip to Domotor's room took twice as long as usual. Logan's slight build fit into the shaft, but his arm muscles weren't used to pulling his weight. When we finally entered the hideout, Domotor woke with a jerk. He had been sleeping on the couch. He pushed himself into a sitting position and studied Logan in alarm.

"I hope he is one of the 'few things' you needed to check on. And not a Pop Cop in disguise?" he asked me.

"Yes. Logan's here to see if he can help with the computer system."

"Unless he's a technological wizard, he—"

Logan spotted the computer and wasted no time. He settled before the monitor. I helped Domotor into his chair and wheeled him closer to Logan.

The Tech No squealed in delight. His fingers flew over the keyboard. "You have a port!" He grinned.

"Yes, but you can't—"

"I know stealth mode. I'll be like a ghost. What are you trying to do?"

Domotor launched into technical double-talk. Logan's eyes lit with the challenge. The prophet nodded and made impressed noises as they worked. I settled on the couch. My desire to interrupt to inquire about clothes for Cog's ruse warred with my desire for sleep. I tried to remember the last time I slept. The effort needed to calculate proved too much for my exhausted brain, so I rested my head on the couch's arm.

"… need an upper computer to access the data," Logan said.

I sat up and rubbed my eyes. The vision of Logan and Domotor peering at me with twin concerned expressions failed to dissipate.

"What happened?" I asked.

"We figured out where the information is," Domotor said. His demeanor didn't match his words. "But…"

"It can only be accessed from a computer on the upper levels." He gave me a few seconds to let the news sink in. "Can you get Logan to level four?"

"Doesn't he need a port?" I asked.

"Not anymore." Logan smiled with smug satisfaction. "I set up my own account; all I need is a password and the right connection."

"Why won't it work here?"

Logan tried to describe the inhibitor function on a lower-level computer. I lost him after the second word.

Domotor thankfully interrupted. "Five minutes is all he would need. Can you do it, Trell?"

Could I? Crawling through heating vents was easier than climbing to another level. I doubted Logan had the upper-body strength needed to pull himself up the chains. Unless… We could ride on top of the lift. But where would we find an unoccupied computer and, if we did find one, then how long would it remain unoccupied?

"I need a few hours to think about it."

"Perhaps Riley could help," Domotor said. "I'm sure he would know where to find a computer."

"I don't think we should involve him," I said.

"Who's Riley?" Logan asked.

"It's better you don't know." Too many knew about us already. Our chances of getting caught increased with each new person. Maximum damage, I chanted in my mind.

"He's proven himself trustworthy. This is too important to leave to chance," Domotor said.

I grumbled even though he was right.

"We'd better go. I don't want to be late for my shift," Logan said.

His words reminded me to ask Domotor about his clothes.

"Sure, take what you need."

When I returned from his room with the pants and shirt he had worn the day we had rescued him, Logan grabbed the shirt. He jerked off the top button. I remembered the microphone.

"Don't want to lose this," he said, then handed me the disks. "We don't need these, though."

I looked at Domotor. He avoided my gaze and shifted in his chair as if searching for a more comfortable position. Waiting, I tapped the disks—the irresistible bait that lured me on this fool's errand—against my legs.

Eventually, he gave me a sheepish grin. "The programs on them are worthless *now*. If I could have used them *before* I was caught, they would have worked."

"But they can help Cog," Logan said.

They would delay the inevitable. I pushed those morbid thoughts away. "It's better than nothing."

★ ★ ★

Hour ten and Logan had reported to his shift on time, the clothes and disks had been hidden in the storage closet and I had to figure a way to get Logan to level four. I stopped by the laundry room. All the clothes for Inside were washed here. Scrubs rolled big white canvas bins to transport piles of clean and dirty garments. Bins also stood under the chutes to collect the uniforms and clothes from the upper levels.

Along the left side wall rested stacks of clean uniforms for the scrubs. Each pile was specific to a different work area and was sorted by size. The blue color of the pipe scrubs seemed bright compared to the rest. Laundry and kitchen scrubs wore the same white uniform.

Stealing scrubs' clothes was easy. A steady stream of people headed to and away from the stacks and no one cared if you picked up one or a hundred. The uppers' clothes, though, were placed in marked bins—one per family. Pop Cops kept a close watch over them.

After a circuit around the room, I left knowing I would be unable to borrow a few uppers' garments from the bins. However, if I wasn't picky, I could intercept a few items as they traveled down the chutes.

I rigged a net in one of the shafts. Clogs in the chutes were rare, but not unheard of. Hopefully, I'd catch a Logan-sized disguise.

My next problem would be harder to solve. Climbing to Riley's room on level four, I reviewed my options for finding a computer terminal. I could spy on one of the upper's suites. Keeping track of their comings and goings, I could determine when the suite would be empty. But how long would it take? And, working my own shifts, I would only have half the picture.

Bluelight shone through the vent into Riley's room. When I was certain it was empty, I dropped through the vent and onto the couch. The daylights turned on automatically and I jumped to my feet in surprise—it had never happened before.

I found the tiny motion detector. Its sensor was aimed at the couch, and the simple device had been wired to the light switch. Everything else appeared to be the same. The ladder leaned against a side wall, and the furniture remained in place. A moment passed and nothing happened. I checked under the couch. Zippy looked undisturbed in his hiding spot.

I relaxed. Riley had spent time fixing the place up. Wandering around the room, I found a few of his possessions. A broken keyboard with a tangle of wires streaming from under it, a chewed marker, a wipe board with a technical diagram of circuits drawn on it and a stuffed sheep. Not made with the skin of a real sheep, but the wool was genuinely fuzzy and soft, and the rest had been constructed of cloth. A child's toy. And from its worn and threadbare appearance, I knew it was well loved.

I picked the sheep up and stroked its wool. The care facility had few toys for the children to share. Most of our time in the facility had been spent training for our future jobs. Cleaning trolls instead of dolls, and engines to take apart and repair. The Care Mothers evaluated us and decided our careers based on our aptitudes.

The memory of Cog racing Jacy to see who could rebuild an engine first caused me to smile. Cog loved to get his hands dirty and he probably would have gotten the maintenance job even if he hadn't grown so big. My tendency to explore the ducts also made my Care Mother's job easy in placing me. I didn't have the patience to be a Care Mother or a gardener for hydroponics.

Computer time had dominated our learning hours. Teaching stories to read, mathematics to learn, our society's customs and expectations, and a basic knowledge of the physical machinery and how our world worked had all been the main focus of learning. According to Riley, the information we learned had been Pop Cop propaganda. I wondered just how much was accurate.

A click sounded behind me. I spun, reaching for my tool belt. Riley slipped into the room and closed the door without making any more noise. He wore his headset and work uniform.

He raised an eyebrow at my defensive posture. "I see you found Sheepy."

"Sheepy?" I replaced the toy. "That's not a very original name."

He shrugged. "I was three hundred weeks old when I got him and his mother as a present."

"What's her name?"

He grinned. "Mama Sheepy."

I laughed.

"You *do* know how to smile and laugh," he said. "I was beginning to worry."

Sobering, I searched his expression. "Worry about what?"

"That you had no joy in your heart."

What an odd statement. "What do you mean?" I demanded.

"I put myself at considerable risk helping you and it's good to know you can…that you're not…that you have…" He slapped his hands to his face and then dropped them as if in surrender. "I always say the wrong thing around you. Look, can we start over?"

"Over?"

"Yes. Over. Wipe the board clean."

"But I would have to go back to hating you and not trusting you," I said.

"Oh, well don't do that." He paused and chewed his lip. "Does that mean you like and trust me now?"

"I don't hate you."

"Trust?"

"The debate is ongoing."

"You're giving me squat. You know that, don't you?"

I suppressed a grin, but couldn't keep a straight face. "Yes."

He shook his head. "Okay. We won't wipe the board clean, but how about we ignore all our previous misconceptions and biases about each other and start as two regular people who *don't* hate each other. Agreed?"

"Agreed."

"Great. Hi, I'm Riley Narelle Ashon and this is Sheepy Narelle Ashon." He picked up his stuff toy and waved the sheep's paw at me. Then he held out his hand to me. "And you are…?"

I grasped his hand, marveling at the feel of his smooth skin. "Trella Garrard Sanchia."

12

THE NAME HAD POPPED FROM MY MOUTH WITHOUT
thought. I was sure Riley's shocked expression mirrored my
own. He let go of my hand.

"How do you know?" he asked, recovering faster than I did.

I waved a hand as if I could erase my words from the air.
No luck. They hung in the thick silence between us. I pulled
my uniform away from my chest. The fabric peeled off my
sweaty skin. Why was this room so hot?

He squinted at me, his demeanor stiff and cold. "Are
you a spy?"

"No. Domotor told me the names, but I don't care."

"I see." His tone implied otherwise.

"Look. I'm just a stupid scrub. Domotor wanted me to
help him and he offered to give me information on my
birth parents as a bribe. Except I don't care who they are or
why they abandoned me in the lower levels. I'm helping him
for my friend Cog. End of discussion."

Understanding lit his eyes and another emotion softened

his posture. When I realized he pitied me, I crossed my arms over my chest to keep myself from punching Riley in the face.

"Since we already did a partial board–ectomy, let's just move on. What do you say, Sheepy?" Riley pressed his nose against the sheep's as if communicating with the stuffed toy telepathically. He pursed his lips and nodded. "Sheepy says he's hungry." He quirked a smile at me. "Sorry. Oh… wait." Once again, Riley stared at his toy. "Sheepy also says he doesn't believe you're a stupid scrub. In fact, he thinks you're quite smart and if you say otherwise, he'll bite you on the leg."

Amused, I huffed in mock outrage. "Tell Sheepy that if he bites me on the leg, I'll send Zippy after him."

"Zippy?"

"My little cleaning troll. He has a nasty habit of shredding dust bunnies."

He laughed. "Sheepy's not going to back down. He meant what he said." All humor evaporated from Riley. He pressed fingers into his right temple, wincing in pain. "My break's over. I need to return to my station." He met my gaze. "Did you come here for a reason?"

"Yes. I need help…" How should I phrase the request?

"Name it."

I stared at him. He used the exact same words I had when talking to Cog. Did he overhear us?

"What? Did you expect me to say no?" His confusion seemed genuine.

"I…"

"I have to go."

I told him about needing a computer, but didn't mention Logan's name. "Preferably one located in an isolated area."

"I'll see what I can do, and let you know during my next shift." He strode to the door.

"How?"

He paused with his hand on the knob. "Come to our room, I'll try and schedule my break time to coincide with your visit again, but you might have to wait a bit."

"You knew I was here?"

"Yes."

"How?"

He gave me a mischievous smile. "Sheepy told me."

On my way back to level two, I checked to see what I had netted in the laundry chute. A couple shirts, three pants, a handful of undergarments and a Pop Cop's uniform. I debated about the uniform as I sent the rest down. It could be a great disguise, but it also could be trouble. Did the Pop Cops keep track of their uniforms? Did they all recognize each other by sight? If a person wore a white kitchen uniform, I wouldn't know if they were scrub or spy. Postponing my decision, I rerigged the net and left the uniform within its black web.

I stopped at the cafeteria, pushing my way through the miasma of so many people gathered together. When I reached the serving scrub who had mentioned the clogged air shaft, I paused.

"Your problem is fixed," I said.

He nodded.

"Thanks."

He made eye contact and resumed filling the bowls with food. But he squared his shoulders, stood a little straighter and the barest hint of a smile settled on his face. The image of his smile hovered in my mind. Even though we had a limited variety of food, the kitchen scrubs worked hard to cook meals for the rest of us.

Cogon had always thanked the servers, calling them by name as he moved through the line. I remembered being annoyed and impatient with him as he held up the rest of us who waited. Considering Cog's present situation, I regretted every harsh word I'd said to him.

I fought my way around filled tables, searching for a seat. Jacy and his buddies occupied an entire table. When I glanced back at them, Jacy patted the vacant seat next to him. Funny. There hadn't been an empty one there a second before.

Understanding the hint didn't mean I would take the hint, I hesitated, but couldn't produce a good reason to avoid him. I sat next to him.

"The microphones are working well. Thanks," Jacy said.

"No problem." I shoved a spoonful of green bean casserole into my mouth.

"We've already gotten a few nuggets of useful intelligence. Do you think you could install a few more?" His casual tone didn't match the intensity in his eyes.

"Where?"

"Over the Control Room and in the lifts."

"Monitoring Pop Cops not enough?"

His gaze slid over the mass of scrubs. I copied him, trying to see the people through his viewpoint. Clusters of miserable expressions dominated, but a few smiles and a couple of laughing faces stood out from the crowd.

"No. Not enough at all," he said. "Can you do it?"

"Sure." I ate a few more scoops of casserole. When I realized I hadn't even tasted the food, I slowed down and made a conscious effort to savor it. Not bad. Did the cooks change the recipe?

"What do you want in return?" he asked.

Interesting question. He dealt in information. "How about you tell me if you hear anything I would consider important through those microphones?"

"Deal. In fact, I'll start now. I heard Cog confessed to killing Broken Man and dismembering him." Jacy watched my expression. "Gruesome, I agree. And despite the evidence the Pop Cops found, I don't believe Cog is capable of harming anyone." He gestured to the scrubs around us. "And neither do they. *If* Cog killed the Pop Cop, we all know it had to be an accident."

He waited, but I wasn't going to confirm nor deny his theory.

"Cog has taken the blame for everything. However, Lieutenant Commander Karla knows Cog is too big to fit into the air shaft above Broken Man's room, and she's determined to find the scrub who started this whole mess." Jacy stared at me. "And do you know what Cogon did then?"

Icy fingers of dread clutched my heart. "No."

"He saved your ass. Again. He told Karla that Roddie was in the air shaft."

Roddie? I spun the name around my mind, but failed to recognize him. "A friend of Cog's?"

"You don't know who he is?" Jacy's face creased as if he smelled a rotten stench.

"Should I?"

"You damn well should! He was the man who Karla killzapped at assembly 147,002. He was recycled because of you and you don't even know his name!"

Stunned, I lost the ability to even form a reply. He was right—when he…Roddie had been kill-zapped, all I had worried about was my own skin. Karla had claimed he lied to her, but I didn't know why he had lied.

Jacy answered my question before I could voice it. "Roddie told LC Karla Broken Man hid in the recycling plant to help Cog. When the Pop Cops discovered the ruse…well you know what Karla did. But Cog told Karla she had been too hasty in kill-zapping Roddie and he was in on the plan from the beginning." Jacy leaned closer to me. "Karla didn't want to believe the explanation. Too easy, she said. But her boss ordered her to close the case. So you…" He jabbed me in the shoulder with a stiff finger. "You are clear. Unless you do something stupid, you're no longer a suspect."

He grabbed his tray and stood. "I hope you're worth the effort. I hope you manage to do something with all of this, because as a human being, you're worthless." Walking away with his cronies in tow, Jacy didn't look back.

The seats at the table remained empty as I moved the food around my plate, building heaps and creating designs out of the cold vestiges of my casserole. The bell sounded for the new work shift, jarring me from my morbid thoughts.

I hurried to my assigned ducts and went through the motions. Insert cleaning troll, turn on and follow. Turn off troll, remove and lug to the next shaft. Gratitude to Cog for taking the heat off me warred with Jacy's admonishments. Worthless might be the right word for me. Events had spun beyond my control. I relied on Logan and Riley to reach the next step.

I dragged the troll to the cleaning closet when my shift

ended. Every muscle in my body ached and my head felt as
if it were stuffed with wet towels. I wanted to find a warm
spot and sleep, but Riley worked the odd-hour shift and I
needed to climb to our room.

Our room. I stifled a laugh. Riley's name, not mine for
where we met. The trip was a hard slog. Bluelight from the
room shone through the vents and, after checking for
ambushes, I dropped to the couch. White daylights switched
on. My tired brain connected the dots and linked the motion
sensor with Riley's precognitive knowledge of my arrival.
Too bad. I liked his explanation better.

After scanning the room, the only change of note was the
presence of Mama Sheepy. A twin of Sheepy except for her
larger size. He rested in the space under her belly and
between her legs, protected and safe. Mama Sheepy's wool
was flat in the middle as if she had been used as a pillow. An
image of a young Riley with his black hair mussed, sleeping
on Mama while clutching Sheepy formed in my head. I
braced for a stab of jealousy, but I couldn't produce the
emotion. Instead, I kept the pleasant image in my mind as I
carried the sheep family to the couch.

Squirming into a comfortable position, I waited for
Riley. I played with the sheep. Not caring that I had lost
it and gone soft. Not caring about Gateway. Not caring
about what might happen the rest of the week. I enjoyed
the moment.

"Trella."

His voice pierced the bubble of my dream. Cold reality
replaced the feelings of warmth and safety. I blinked awake.
Luckily Riley hovered over me and not a Pop Cop. Falling

asleep up here was deadly. I wanted to blame the couch, but knew my erratic snatches of sleep were to blame.

He straightened with a smile on his face. "Sheepy told me to let you alone, but I only have thirty minutes."

His stuffed toys were still clutched in my hands. I sat and placed them on the cushion next to me. Riley settled on the opposite end. I smoothed my hair and wondered how long he had been here before waking me.

"I've been searching for a computer terminal, but every one up here is either in constant use or located in a populated area. The only option left is for you to use the terminal in my room." He held up a hand, stopping my protests. "My father works even shifts. You can come during the next one."

"What about the rest of your family?"

An odd half-flinch creased his face for a second. "He's all I have, so no problem there."

"What happens if the Controllers find out we used your computer?"

"As long as you don't use my port, there is no way to prove I'm involved."

"It's still a big risk."

"So is this." Riley gestured to me and him.

"Good point." I considered his offer. "Where is your suite located?"

"Sector E4."

I waited for the number, but he stared at the wall as if making mental calculations. "What's your—"

"Are you going to tell me why you need access to the computer?"

"No."

"You still don't trust me." He stated it as a matter of fact, but his arm muscles bulged as he pressed his palms into his legs.

I looked at Sheepy and his mother lying between us. The information about the uppers circled in my mind. Coddled, pampered and privileged had been the line. Yet it missed the mark with Riley. "I trust you."

"Then why won't you confide in me?"

"Partly for damage control and for selfish reasons."

"We're not accepting cryptic and vague answers right now. More detail, please."

"We?" I asked.

He pointed to the sheep. I couldn't help smiling. Such a stupid little toy, yet I admitted he filled the missing gaps deep within me. Picking up Sheepy, I held him close to my face. He was easier to talk to than Riley. "Damage control is to minimize the number of people who could expose this whole adventure. The selfish reasons are mine. Eventually, I'll be caught and fed to Chomper. I'm hoping to cause a lot of trouble before then, and I hope I can convince the Pop Cops you were just a dupe. Someone I used and who didn't know what was going on. I'm already responsible for sending one person to Chomper and another…" I swallowed as a shudder of guilt and horror swept through me. "It's only a matter of time before he is sent. Don't you see, Sheepy? I don't want anyone else to be recycled because of me."

Silence stretched, but I kept my gaze on the sheep, avoiding Riley's expression. I couldn't face his censure.

"I didn't know you were a Trava," Riley said.

"What?" I glanced at him. His eyebrows hovered midway between his eyes and hairline in almost thoughtful surprise.

"The Trava family decides who is fed to Chomper. I hadn't realized you were a part of them."

"That's too easy. I can't blame them. The Travas set the rules and carry out the punishments. My actions caused another to break the rules."

"Oh. So you forced this person?"

"No, but—"

"But what? I'm trying to understand how you're responsible. Is the blame all yours? My father told me the Travas aren't supposed to be setting the rules—that it should be a Committee of all the families. The rules themselves are suspect. And there is also a thing called free will. I had a choice back in Karla's office. You never asked me not to tell. I decided to help you instead. Are you responsible for my extra duty? No. I am."

"You can twist the argument any way."

"Exactly. You can shoulder all the blame and become a martyr. Provided anyone knows what or who you're martyring for. Or you can accept that some things are important enough to fight for and realize there will be sacrifices along the way." He peered into my eyes. "I've assumed this is one of those important fights. An effort to regain some of the freedoms we all lost. I'm well aware of the danger, but am still committed to helping you. You trust me and I need to trust you. So let's take it to the next step. Tell me why you need access to an upper computer."

I debated. If I told him about Gateway, he might think I was delusional. Yet he risked his life for me. "We're hoping to find a way to circumvent the Controllers' security measures in the network so we can access a few files and retrieve critical information."

"Which information?"

"About how the various mechanical systems are set up and how to alter them without letting the Controllers know." So I omitted a few facts. At least I wasn't lying.

He relaxed. "See? That wasn't so hard." He stood and pulled a stack of clothes from underneath the couch. "I've borrowed a training uniform for you." Riley gestured for me to stand and held the uniform against me. "Looks like it will fit."

His knuckles touched my shoulders and a ripple of warmth spread through my body.

Riley continued to study me. He tossed the uniform over one arm and reached for my hair. More than a few strands had escaped my braid. He smoothed them next to my face. "Leave your hair down. It makes you look younger." His fingers brushed my jaw.

I suppress the sudden desire to press his hand against my cheek. "Younger?"

"You're supposed to be a student."

"We'll be in your suite. Are you expecting visitors?"

"No. But there's a chance someone might come, and I'd have a harder time explaining why two scrubs were in my room."

"Good point."

As he rummaged through the pile of clothes, I tugged the rest of my hair from the braid. Combing my fingers through it, I separated it into three sections.

"Don't," Riley said.

"Why?"

He didn't answer. He pushed my hands away and drew my hair over my shoulders. Stepping back, he cocked his head as if contemplating. "You look so stern and serious with your hair tied back." He gestured. "That's more like the

Trella I first met. But it's not quite…right." He mussed up my hair, pulling a few strands over my face. "Ah-ha! Perfect!"

I shot him a withering look.

His smile widened. "Even better. It's like I've been transported back in time."

"Ha. Ha. Funny," I said in a flat tone. Sweeping the hair from my face, I tucked it behind my ears. "Do you have a disguise for my companion?" I asked, trying to return to the point of my visit.

"I didn't know who you were bringing along, so I found a basic coverall worn by the maintenance workers. It's one-size-fits-all and we're used to seeing the crew with rolled up sleeves and pant legs."

He handed me the clothes. The fabric on the student's garment had the same coarse and durable weave as the jumpers worn by the lower kids in the care facility.

A pained expression crossed his face. "Break's over. I'm in three-six-ninety-five in Sector E4. Will you be able to find it?"

"Yes."

"When?"

I calculated how much time I needed to find Logan and lead him to level four. I hoped Anne-Jade would cover my shift again. "Around hour forty-two."

"See you then." He slipped from the room.

I waited a moment just in case an upper saw him leaving the room and investigated. Diving behind the couch probably wouldn't be the best hiding place, but it was better than being caught halfway inside the air duct. After enough time elapsed, I set the ladder under the vent. But before I climbed, I snuggled Sheepy back in his protective spot under Mama Sheepy.

★ ★ ★

On my way to find Logan, one of Jacy's guys bumped into me. He slipped me two listening devices without a word and ambled on his way. Laughter echoed through the hallways and people lingered in small groups, talking. The tension in the lower levels had eased.

After a few moments, I realized why. The number of Pop Cops patrolling the area had dropped to normal. As I hurried to Logan's barrack, scrubs tried to catch my gaze. A few smiled at me with hope shining in their eyes and others cocked an eyebrow with a questioning look.

For the first time, I was the center of attention. Everyone watched me as if I were a bomb. Would I explode and cause a disaster or would I pop and cause a miracle? The pressure of their stares squeezed my chest until my lungs wheezed with the effort to draw a breath.

Pop Cop spies still worked among us. It amazed me that they hadn't discovered my involvement. Perhaps Karla waited for me to make a mistake. Right now she had no evidence I was involved in Broken Man's disappearance, but if she stalked me for a few weeks, she would eventually catch me breaking the rules. Hard to believe, but breathing became more difficult, and I wished for simpler weeks. My lonely life in the pipes seemed a distant and pleasant memory.

I met Logan and Anne-Jade as they entered the barrack. Odd-hour shifts had finished and even would begin soon.

Logan's light brown eyes sparkled. "Time to play?"

Anne-Jade shot him a sour look.

"Meet me in corridor A2-5 in one hour," I told him. "Anne-Jade, can you cover my shift?"

"Sure." She met my gaze. "Please don't let anything happen to him."

"I'll try." My throat felt hot and dry.

"Hey," Logan said. "I'm a grown man. I can take care of myself."

"Are you kidding?" Anne-Jade shot back. "If it wasn't for me, you'd be late for everything. Too busy playing with your toys."

I left. The sounds of their mock argument followed me from the barracks. One of Jacy's men waited in the hallway. He fell into step beside me.

"Boss wants to see you," he said.

"When?"

"Now."

"I can't. My shift's starting. Tell him I'll stop by later."

He wrapped his strong fingers around my right elbow. "You'll see him now." He pulled me along.

I squawked in protest, but he stared straight ahead. Twice my size, I knew I couldn't pry his grip off, but I could jab him with a screwdriver. My left hand closed on the tool.

"I wouldn't do it," he said. "It would…annoy me."

Interesting choice of words. I rationalized my cowardice and decided to wait. After all, there was no sense making a scene.

Jacy held court in his corner of Sector D1's barrack. At least six unhappy expressions turned to me as my companion delivered me to his boss. My worry switched from annoying the man clamped on my elbow to Jacy's livid face.

"I knew it would happen eventually," Jacy said. The muscles along his arms quivered and his eyes held a wild shine. "I just wasn't…prepared." He swallowed and his anger eased a bit.

"What happened?" I braced for the answer.

"I want to blame you, but I can't." He looked away.

My guard's fingers dug into my skin and I yelped.

Jacy's attention snapped back to me. This time grief lined his eyes. "Cogon's been scheduled for execution."

13

HIS WORDS SLICED THROUGH MY HEART, CUTTING IT
into little pathetic pieces. I understood how he could feel
unprepared. The knowledge that the Pop Cops would
recycle Cog had been trapped deep within me and ignored.
I planned to deal with it later or, better yet, hoped it would
disappear altogether.

"When?" I asked.

"Hour ninety-nine. They plan to walk him down to
Chomper's Lair and kill-zap him there." Outrage filled Jacy's
voice. "They figured it would be easier than lugging his
body down there. The timing is so Lieutenant Commander
Karla can use his execution to lecture us during the
hundred-hour assembly on the consequences of disobeying
the Pop Cops."

I did the math. Fifty-eight hours left.

"If what you're doing can help Cog, you'd better do it
quick," Jacy said.

"I can't do anything with a broken arm."

He nodded and the big guy released my elbow. I rubbed the joint and turned away.

"Trella," Jacy called.

"What?" I almost growled at him.

"Let me know if you need anything. Anything at all."

It was a generous offer, considering the last time we conversed he had called me worthless. "Got it."

With my emotions spinning, I hurried to meet Logan. I walked right past my turn and had to stop. Distractions would be dangerous, and all our efforts would be for nothing if we were caught before accessing the computer. I squashed my fear and worries into a small metal box and dropped in the shattered remains of my heart for good measure. Locked with an obnoxiously big lock, I pushed the container into a far corner of my thoughts.

Focused and almost robotic, I marched toward corridor A2-5. Logan fidgeted and paced, trying to appear nonchalant, but failing miserably. At least he wasn't chewing his nails.

I led him to the door of the maintenance room next to Quad A's lift. While he watched the hall, I opened the door's lock. Memories of Cog and I hiding Broken Man in a laundry bin in this room threatened to overwhelm me. I clamped down on the feeling. No emotions allowed. We slipped inside and locked the door.

Pushing the air vent open, I pulled out a bundle. "Here, put this on." I handed Logan the coveralls Riley had given me. While he dressed, I donned the student's uniform. The black jumper with silver piping along the pants and sleeves sagged around my waist, but I cinched it tight with the belt.

When he was ready, I climbed into the air shaft and helped Logan inside.

"It's bigger than the heating vent," he said.

"Sounds still carry, and I'm about to show you a place only I know about. You can't tell anyone. Not even Anne-Jade. Promise me?"

"Ooh. Sounds like fun. Of course, I promise."

I slid through the shaft, stopped under the near-invisible hatch and pushed it open. Logan pressed a hand to his mouth to smother his cry of surprise. Turning on my light, I climbed into the meter-and-a-half-high space and moved aside so Logan could join me. He stared at his surroundings while I closed the hatch.

"What is this place?" he asked in a whisper.

I shrugged. "I call it the Gap. There's one between each level."

"Wow. What's it used for?"

I gestured around. "Space for the pipes and wires. I think everyone's forgotten about it. I can only get in here through one near invisible hatch on each level. Come on, but crawl quietly." I hurried toward the lift. The easiest way to get Logan up to the fourth level was by riding on top of the lift.

A meter-high metal barrier divided the Gap from where the lift cut through the four floors of Inside. From the inside of the lift, it appeared the shaft was solid, but each level had a half-meter opening into the Gap. I pulled my extendable mirror from my tool belt. Shining the light in the shaft, I used the mirror. The lift was on the third level.

"When the lift comes down to our level, we don't have much time but we need to quietly move onto the roof and stay there until we reach the top," I said.

"What happens at the top?" Logan bit his thumbnail.

"We climb into the Gap before the lift descends."

Logan stared, and nibbled on his nails. If he were a computer, he would be making the rumbling crunching noise that meant it was calculating.

"Once we're on, do we have to wait until an upper wants to go to level four?" he asked.

"No. Once it's down, there are override controls on the roof."

Logan shivered as we waited. "It's cold here. I wonder why there is all this extra room. Does the Gap run the entire length of Inside?"

I explained how each level was connected by steel I-beams to the Wall.

"How about under the lower level, is there a Gap there?" he asked.

"Yes. All the levels are surrounded by Gaps."

"What's beyond the Gaps on the sides?"

"The Walls of Inside."

He considered. "What do the Walls feel like?"

"There're covered with insulating foam."

"I meant temperature. Hot or cold?"

"Oh. The foam's room temperature, but the few places where there isn't foam, it's ice-cold."

He grinned. "Have you pressed your ear to it?"

I admitted I tried to listen for sounds from the other side. "I heard nothing besides the Hum." Produced by the machinery, the Hum was a constant background noise. It seemed like Inside's breath, and most scrubs no longer noticed the Hum.

"Too bad."

Eventually the lift passed with a chilly blast of air. We scrambled over the barrier, but landed with care on the lift's roof. I pressed the override button for the fourth level. I didn't think it would concern the occupants too much. The Pop Cops always complained about the lift's odd quirks.

Voices reached us from below, but they were indistinguishable. I put a finger to my lips as Logan's eyes flew wide when the lift ascended. It moved fast and in a handful of seconds we reached the top. I waved Logan on. In his haste, he fell with a grunt and a bang over the barrier into the fourth-level Gap.

We halted, listening for sounds of discovery. Nothing but the hiss of the lift's door shutting. I grabbed the edge of the barrier and pulled until my hips rested on it. The lift dropped away, leaving my legs dangling. Logan scooted back and I joined him on solid ground.

After taking a moment to recover, I led him through the maze of pipes and ductwork to the hatch. Finding the hatches the first time had been difficult. I'd spent hours exploring each Gap for the near-invisible hatch. Grinning, I remembered how disappointed I had been when I found the last one. The search had provided me with a challenge unlike my prior week-to-week pointless existence.

When we reached it, I whispered in Logan's ear, "No talking, no sounds at all from now on. Got it?"

"Yes."

The fourth-level hatch opened into air duct number fifteen, which crossed over the giant water storage tanks in Sector H4 before cutting through the uppers' rooms in Sector E4. I counted the suites, but then realized I didn't need to as I felt Riley's impatience through his air vent before seeing his worried face staring at the ceiling.

Under the vent, he had a stepladder set up on a table. Removing the cover, I slid my legs out. "Feet first," I said to Logan before lowering myself down.

Riley hurried to put the ladder away after Logan had reached the floor. We stood in the middle of a small living area. Couch, two chairs and one low table decorated the room. The two men eyed each other.

"It's safer if I don't introduce you," I said into the uncomfortable silence.

"He's a scrub," Riley said.

"So?" I shot back.

"He doesn't have a port and can't access the computer network."

Logan smirked. "Don't need a port. Where's your terminal?"

Riley failed to look reassured but opened a metal curtain just like the one in Broken Man's hideout. He pulled over one of the chairs and gestured for Logan to take a seat.

"What about your port?" I asked. "If you're too close—"

"Took it out and put it in a metal box." Riley rubbed his right jaw as if he were unused to having it missing.

Logan wasted no time. His fingers flew over the keyboard. "This is going to take a while. I have to distract the Controllers and take a circuitous route in. Don't want anyone to know I'm in here." He flashed us a wild grin.

Riley and I stood next to each other, looking over Logan's shoulder. The strange symbols popping up on the screen meant nothing to me. Riley, though, frowned. Time to distract him.

"How about a tour?" I asked. "I've never actually been inside an upper's suite."

He turned his displeasure on me. "Really? But you've spied on them from above?"

For a moment, I wished for the goofy Riley. The one who mussed my hair and communicated telepathically with stuffed sheep. "I don't spy on anyone. I avoid the living areas, they're too dangerous. The places I've been on level four are the storeroom and Karla's office." And the holding cells, but I didn't think it would be wise to tell him. I pointed to a half-open door on the opposite wall. "Is that a bedroom?"

Still unhappy, Riley showed me his room. The tiny interior had two beds with a table between them and two desks. A few metal sculptures were propped against the light blue walls, and circuit boards littered the one desk, the other was neat. Same with the beds, one was made, the other was heaped with blankets.

He followed my gaze. "I share the room with my father. He's always harping on me to make the bed and clean up my stuff."

No other items decorated the space. "Where's Dada Sheepy?" I asked.

A half smile flicked on his lips before sadness dragged it down. "With my brother." Turning away, he strode into the living room and opened the door next to Logan. "Standard bathroom." He waved at the remaining door. "Suite entrance."

Except for the small peephole and extra locks, it mirrored the other two.

"There. That's the grand tour," he said.

"That's it?" Surprise tainted my voice.

"Yep."

"But I thought the uppers lived in apartments with lots of rooms."

"The admiral's and vice admiral's families do, but most have suites like mine. If my mom were still alive, we would have two bedrooms and a small kitchenette. But since it's just us, we get this and a refrigerator."

The rumors about the uppers' living quarters had been exaggerated. I wondered what else had been blown out of proportion. "What happens if you...want a family?"

"If I find a mate, my father would be reassigned to share a suite with another single man, and if he finds a mate then I would move."

"Does he want another mate?"

"No."

The whole mate thing was odd to me. Scrubs hooked up with others and stayed together for as long as they desired then moved on. Any children from the pair went to the care facility. A few couples never parted. The Pop Cops tracked the pairings, and would separate them if their bloodlines were too close.

Logan whooped with joy. "I'm in!"

Riley stood behind him and watched the screen.

"Do the uppers mate for life?" I asked Riley, hoping to pull his attention away from the computer.

"Most do, but if a union isn't working then they'll split."

"What do you do for fun?"

Riley glared at me. His stiff posture radiating his ire. "Trella, I know what you're doing. You haven't asked questions about the uppers unless it was directly related to your *mission*. You have a very strong opinion about the uppers, and you haven't shown any interest in us before. But I do know the systems your friend is accessing can only be seen by people with ten-degree security clearance. So unless he's a rear admiral, he's neck-deep in serious trouble—"

"Only if I get caught," Logan said. "Don't worry, I'm ghosting."

"Ghosting? What the hell is that?" Riley demanded.

"Not leaving a traceable trail," I explained. Coming here was a bad idea. I hoped Logan would finish soon.

Riley's anger flared. "You didn't tell me the whole story. Time to talk, Trella. What *exactly* is this man looking for?"

"Well…" To tell him we were looking for Gateway might have ruined whatever credibility I had left with him. He knew Domotor had been trying to find ways around the Controllers to seize control of the computer for the rest of the upper families.

He studied my face and when I opened my mouth he said, "Don't lie." His words growled and I knew I trod on dangerous ground.

"Got it!" Logan whooped.

"Got what?" Riley asked.

Before I could say anything, Logan, who hadn't listened to anything we'd said, proclaimed with pride, "The coordinates to Gateway."

"Yes!" I jumped and slapped Logan on the back. Cogon was going to be ecstatic and very smug. I could already hear his I told you so. But my jubilation died when a strangled sound escaped Riley's throat. The anger drained from his face. His flushed cheeks and red-tipped ears turned white, and I suddenly wished I could ghost back to the lower levels.

"Hold on," Logan said. His attention returned to the screen. "No…no…you lousy unrecyclable…"

"What's wrong?" I asked.

"It requires a password."

"But you just said you got it."

"I have the file. To open the file we need a password. Any ideas?"

I wanted to shake the screen until it surrendered and let

us read the file. To come all this way and to put so much at risk… I shoved my crushing disappointment aside and concentrated.

"How about *Gateway?*"

"Nope."

"Inside? Outside?" I looked at Riley for help. He just shook his head. A horrified fascination settled on his face.

"No and no. Wait!" Logan sat up straighter. "There's always a fail-safe."

"A what?" I asked.

"People forget things. It's part of being human. You don't want to risk someone discovering your password by writing it down, so the computer has a way to help you remember your password." He typed for a while.

"How?"

"It will ask you a question and the answer is the password."

"What if we don't know the answer?"

"Then we don't get the coordinates and we have to guess again. Except…" He leaned forward. "There's a limit on the number of guesses. After ten, the computer notifies the Controllers someone is trying to access the file."

"Not good." Horrible in fact.

"No." The clicking keys filled the silence. "Okay. I found the question."

"And?" I prompted.

"I don't know the answer," Logan said.

I reached out but managed to stop my hands from wrapping around his neck. "What *is* the question?"

"Oh. *It's the end and the beginning. What is it?*"

14

"A CIRCLE?" RILEY SUGGESTED. HE HAD RECOVERED
from his shock about Gateway, and was now intrigued by the
mystery question. "A circle doesn't have an end or a beginning."

Logan moved his hands over the keyboard.

"Wait," I said. "How many other passwords have you tried?"

"Three so we have seven guesses before the computer
shuts down."

"A circle is good, but let's think this through logically." I
swiped hair from my face and tucked it behind my ear. "The
question has to refer to something about Inside. We know
it is an object or place and not a person's name."

"We do?" Logan asked.

"Yes, the question contains the word *it* and *what. It's* the
end and the beginning. *What* is *it?* A person would be *who,*
and a place would be *where.*"

Riley sat in the remaining chair, and covered his eyes
with a hand as if blocking out all distractions. "Everything
in here is squares, rectangles and cubes. No circles."

I settled on the couch. The living room was too small to pace. Searching my memory for circles, I tried to find a connection. "If you think about it, everything in here is a circle. The air circulates throughout Inside, going through the filters and purifiers. Same with the water and sewage. Reused and recycled, nothing wasted."

"Should I try circle?" Logan's fingers hovered over the keyboard.

"Yes." I held my breath.

"Nope. Try again."

Damn. I repeated the question in my mind. It sounded familiar as if I read it or heard it before. Maybe when I was living in the care facility. But there had been so many weeks of lessons in math, biology, science.... "Water?"

"How does it fit?" Riley asked.

"It has a cycle. Evaporation, condensation, freezing and melting as it changes from a gas to a liquid to a solid. Water is a vital resource for Inside, without it we couldn't exist."

"So is air and food." He considered. "Air has a cycle. We breathe in oxygen and breathe out carbon dioxide. The plants in hydroponics absorb the carbon dioxide and release oxygen. Growing food is also a circle with eating and producing. Think of the sheep."

"Sheepy?" I wished he were there. "Would Sheepy know the answer?" I joked.

He removed his hand and shot me a smile. "No. Sheep eat grass and vegetables and produce manure which fertilizes the grass and plants in hydroponics. Another cycle."

Logan tried, *water, air* and *food.* "No. Three guesses left."

Thinking along those lines, I realized a hundred different aspects of our life were cycles, including people. Perhaps the answer wasn't a representation of a circle, but more a concrete object or mathematical symbol. "Zero is circular. Isn't the symbol for infinity a sideways eight?"

"That's assuming the answer is a circle of some kind," Riley said.

"Can you think of another answer?"

"No, but to try and connect it to a mathematical number or concept…" He threw his hands up. "There could be a million different possibilities. I wouldn't—"

"Stop!" One of his words triggered a memory. I replayed the incident in my mind, searching for reasons why it wouldn't work. Certainty bloomed in my chest. I knew the answer.

Logan and Riley stared at me, waiting.

"The millionth week. That's the answer." I remembered the assembly and the old man's words: *the millionth week isn't the end, it's the beginning.*

Riley groaned and the hope dimmed in Logan's eyes.

"That's just a myth to scare people. Week one million will be like all the others. Its importance doesn't exist," Riley said.

"People said the same thing about Gateway." I gestured to Logan. "Yet we're one password away from the location."

Logan met my gaze. "How should I type it? *Week one million* or *the millionth week?*"

"Try both."

Unable to remain seated, Riley and I joined Logan at the computer. I held on to the back of his chair as he typed *the millionth week* and hit Enter. The words disappeared and the password prompt returned. This time he entered *week one million.*

"Are you sure?" Logan's finger was poised over the key.

I let go of the chair and clutched Riley's arm. "Yes." I

wanted to turn away, but I watched the screen. It turned black then lines of text raced across, matching my heart's rhythm. I couldn't read the words; they kept jumping up as more white lines streaked on the screen.

"Logan?" I didn't care if I used his name.

"Yes! Got it!"

I wrapped my arms around Logan's neck and kissed him on the cheek, then turned and hugged Riley. Caught up in the excitement, he leaned back and picked me off the floor, spinning me around.

Logan rattled off a bunch of numbers.

"How do I find it?" I asked, still dizzy and thrilled Riley's arms supported me.

"Oh, right." Furious typing and a crude schematic of Inside appeared, showing a cube with a pulsing dot near the bottom of one side. "It's along the west wall in Quad G1. That's hydroponics."

"You'd think the workers would notice it," Riley said.

"Maybe it's one of those near-invisible hatches Trella found," Logan said.

"Near-invisible?" Riley looked down at me.

He held me close. Tall and with his strong arms wrapped around me, I knew I should extricate myself from his embrace, but a part of me wanted to stay. "Some doors are hard to see. Perhaps the vines have grown over it," I said.

"Oh, yeah. Lots of vines," Logan said.

Annoyed, Riley's muscles tightened. "Your friend's a lousy liar. What are you hiding?" When I hesitated, he moved his hands to my shoulders and pushed me back so he could see me better. "Enough. The location...the existence of Gateway is huge. No. It's way bigger than that…it's a whole other phenomenon. The repercussions are going to be unimaginable if it is really there and it works. I need to know everything right now, or I'm going to…"

"To what? Report me? You risk being implicated."

"No. I'm going to follow you. Yes, even through those vents until I know the whole story."

Logan eyed him. "You'll get stuck."

"It's ridiculous. He's not going to do it," I said.

"Then I won't let you leave until you tell me." Riley straightened, trying to look bigger.

"Two against one," I said. "And I'm armed." I rested my hand on my tool belt.

He deflated and dropped his hands, but, by the gleam in his eyes, I knew he hadn't given up.

"How about in exchange for Sheepy?"

"Really? You'd give me Sheepy?" I called his bluff.

"Yes."

He meant it, and my reaction surprised me. I would have loved to have the little sheep. "No. Sheepy stays with his mama." I put my hand up to stop Riley. "Just let me think."

As Riley had said, discovering Gateway's existence was a whole other realm of problems and possibilities. If caught right now, Riley would be recycled just for knowing about it. Too late to save him. Remembering his lecture about choices and sacrifices didn't make me feel any better.

"You'd better sit down," I said. "It's a long story."

"So Gateway wouldn't be on the wall in hydroponics, but on the *real* outer Wall?" Riley asked.

"Yes," I said.

"And no one knows about this except the three of us?"

"As far as I know. I've never seen anyone in the Gap, but it's possible high-ranking uppers could know or find it in the computer."

"Complete and detailed diagrams and blueprints of Inside have been deleted," Logan said. He had been searching through the computer, trying to gather as much information as he could about the Controllers.

"Are you sure? Wouldn't the engineers need them?" Riley asked.

"Each system—water, air, electrical and heating—has its own blueprints. Let's see…if I put them…together." Logan typed. "Still not showing Trella's Gap or Gateway. Lot's of other stuff's missing, too. Historical records and logs have been wiped clean up until…week 132,076."

Almost one hundred and fifty centiweeks ago.

"The first log is written by Admiral Peter Trava. He mentions saboteurs wielding magnets and trying to destroy Inside. He says they were stopped with no loss of life, but with major damage to the computer, causing data loss." Logan scrolled through a few more pages. "Something's wrong. The deletion was too clean for a magnet."

"Do you know when the files were deleted?" I asked.

"The same week Admiral Pete's entry was written, which was only fifteen centiweeks ago. Whoa! It's bogus."

"What happened that week?" I asked.

"Could have been when a few of the uppers tried to get into protected files on the system," Riley said. "My dad told me about it. Maybe they got too close to the truth, and the Travas decided to delete all the data prior to their takeover and write the bogus entry to explain it."

"Not all the data," Logan said. "There are about ten hidden and protected files in the system. I bet the Controllers don't know about them. The location of Gateway was one of them. Maybe the dissenters buried these files. They're all password protected." He clucked and hummed like a child with a brand-new toy.

"Could those be the files Domotor wanted?" Riley asked me.

"I don't know."

"Trella, what's your birth week?" An odd tone shook Logan's voice.

"It's 145,487. Why?"

"And the hour?"

"Why do you need to know?" I asked.

"Humor me."

"Hour four point fifteen."

He whistled.

"Logan, tell me."

"There's a file here named with your birth week and hour."

"What?" I moved closer to the monitor. He pointed.

"Why did you think it referred to me?"

"It says, 'For my daughter born on...' It's one of the ten files Domotor or whoever thought was important, so I just guessed it might have something to do with you."

"Can you open it?"

"Nope. Just like the others. The password question is 'Smile and show me your pearly teeth. How many do you have?'" He glanced at me. "Count your teeth."

"That's too easy, and what if I lost one?"

"Have you?"

"No, but I think it's referring to something else." The

words *pearly teeth* had jumped out at me. My sole possession. The comb with the pearls. The answer was the number of teeth on my comb.

"And it would be…"

"Something I don't have with me, so we can't answer the question anyway."

"It's getting late. The next shift starts in an hour," Riley said.

I looked at the clock in surprise. So engrossed in our puzzle, I hadn't kept track.

"I just need a couple minutes." Logan's fingers danced on the keyboard. "I want to put these files where I can get to them from the lower level computers."

Anxious to get moving, I fidgeted behind Logan.

Riley also had a worried look. "Are you sure all this time you spent on the computer hasn't been recorded or traced?"

"Yep. I'm ghosting. No port. No problem."

"What does that mean?" Riley asked.

"Uh…just that I can get into the system without a port." Logan was a bad liar, but his cry of alarm distracted us both.

"What now?" I really didn't want to know the answer.

"Gateway's going to suck a lot of energy when it opens. Plus it has a command to alert all of Inside's systems. We're going to need people in the network to cover the call," Logan said.

Yet another problem. Nothing was simple.

"I can cover electrical," Riley said, "but we'll need to recruit other uppers to help." He considered. "There are a number of uppers who supported Domotor and have been lying low since his capture. But if I tell them we found Gateway, they'll probably laugh in my face."

"But you believed us," I said.

"I saw Logan using level-ten clearance, and I saw the file. This is a huge risk for the uppers. They don't know me and they won't trust me. But they'll trust Domotor. Can you get him up here?"

He would probably do all right pulling himself through the air shaft, but he couldn't go between levels. "Only if we can use the lift."

"Too exposed. Domotor is too recognizable in the upper levels. His capture and punishment was discussed for weeks. He wouldn't be able to blend in up here, and I doubt we could get him from the lift to a room without being seen." Riley rubbed his face. "Also I'm not one hundred percent sure the people I'm thinking about are really supporters. My dad might know."

More problems. More people involved. To me, trusting uppers felt like the wrong thing to do, but we needed them. "Domotor would know who to trust. I can get the names from him and some kind of code word or something you can say to them to prove he's involved."

"That could work. But I'll need you here, too."

"Why?"

"To prove the scrubs are serious about opening Gateway," Riley said.

"And if I get into these hidden files," Logan said, "the uppers might have a way to bypass the Controllers and regain control."

"Sounds like a plan." Riley smiled.

Uneasiness swirled in my stomach as I steadied the ladder for Logan. I hated having to trust uppers. I trusted Riley, but he was different. Or was he?

"Thanks for your help," I said to Riley as Logan climbed the table.

"How soon can you get me those names?"

I needed to take Logan back, then go to Domotor's hideout. "Four hours give or take an hour."

"I'll meet you in our room during my break." Riley grasped my sore elbow to help me up the table.

I yelped and he let go.

"Sorry." Riley watched me rub the tender spot.

"Must have bumped it."

Logan called for help. His legs dangled from the vent. I pushed him into the air shaft. When his feet disappeared, I reached for the vent.

A click slide sounded.

"Get down," Riley ordered.

I didn't hesitate. He pulled the stepladder from the table, folded it and leaned it against the wall. In two strides he sat at the computer and whispered, "Stand behind me. Follow my lead." He rested his fingers on the keys.

The door opened as I reached Riley's chair. We both glanced at the man entering the room. He stopped short when he spotted us.

"Hi, Dad," Riley said. "You're back early."

15

THE SURPRISE ON RILEY'S FATHER'S FACE TRANSFORMED
into a smile. He had the same build as his son, but his
thinning hair was brown and cut short. Riley's blue eyes
must have been inherited from his mother. His father's
brown eyes and beak nose gave him a friendly and inquisi-
tive appearance.

"I see we have a visitor," he said as he stepped into the
room and closed the door.

"Dad, this is Ella, the student I've been training," Riley
said. "Ella, this is my father, Jacob."

"Hello, Ella, I've heard so much about you."

I shot Riley a look.

His father chuckled. "Don't worry. Nothing bad. Riley says
you're a quick learner and coming from him that's high praise."

"Thank you," I said.

"Something happen?" Riley asked his dad.

"No. I had to work through my breaks, so my supervisor
let me leave a little early." He glanced at the clock. "Shouldn't

you be reporting for duty? Or are you training Ella here?" He smiled broadly with a gleam in his eyes.

Riley stood. "No. We need to go. Just need to get...something." He strode into the bedroom.

Jacob stepped closer to me and whispered, "You're as beautiful as Riley claims. I hope you'll visit us again." He winked.

I smiled and wondered what the real Ella looked like. Riley returned.

His father spotted the ladder along the wall. "What's this?"

"Oh. Maintenance was testing air flow again. They must have forgotten it. I'll return it on my way to work." He grabbed the ladder and turned toward the door.

"Wait," his father said, staring at the ceiling. "They forgot to cover the vent, too. Hand me the ladder."

"I'll do it, Dad." Riley set the stepladder on the table.

"No. You're going to be late." He shooed us out.

Riley shrugged and opened the door. I hoped Logan had the sense to scoot away from the vent and to keep quiet. Jacob reached for the air shaft as Riley escorted me into the hallway. The door clicked shut.

"Let's hope Logan doesn't give himself away." He strode down the corridor. "Does he know where to go?"

I hurried to follow. "No. I'll have to go back and get him. Isn't this dangerous?" I swept my arm out, indicating the hallway.

"Not really. Just act like you belong here. Walk with confidence. No one knows who you are. Since you're wearing a student jumper, they'll assume you're from another sector."

"Don't you know everyone up here?" My vision of the upper levels as one big happy family was being shredded strip by strip.

He laughed. "No. Do you know all the scrubs?"

"There are ten times as many of us."

"Well, up here everyone keeps to themselves. I have a few aunts and uncles, some cousins, a friend or two and I know my fellow workers of course, but that's about it."

"What about the real Ella? What if she sees me?"

A few uppers walked toward us, and I braced for their cry of alarm. They nodded at us and continued past. Riley was right. I relaxed a bit and looked around. There wasn't much to see. Doors and plain white metal walls, the same as in the lower levels. The only difference was the thin strip of gray carpet on the floor.

When the uppers moved out of hearing range, Riley said, "You *are* Ella."

"I am?"

He gave me a don't-be-stupid look. "How do you think I justify all my time spent in our storeroom? My father likes to know what I'm doing during my off hours, so I tell him I'm training a student. Actually, his unexpected arrival helped me. Now he has met Ella and knows she's a real person. It should keep him happy for a while. Although…"

"What?"

"He might start bugging me to bring you around more."

Confused, I asked why.

Riley's stride slowed as he stared at me. "You really don't know anything about families do you?"

"Scrub, remember? We have care facilities not families." I believed I did a good job of keeping the bitterness from my voice, but he still frowned.

"Well, parents want their children to grow up, earn important positions and find mates. According to them, that's the key to happiness. My father, being no different, wants me to find a mate. It's the reason why he was grinning so much. He's hoping I have found someone."

I considered his explanation. In the lower levels, scrubs waited until after their tenure in the care facility to become couples. Care mates didn't hook up. It was frowned upon.

"Don't you already have someone? Another upper?" I asked.

"No."

"Why not?"

He stopped and searched my expression. I tried to let my genuine interest show. He had been right about my lack of curiosity and my assumptions of upper life. I was determined to learn more.

"I haven't met the right woman yet. Guess I'm waiting for someone to…surprise me." He continued walking.

"Surprise you how?"

"Oh, the usual way, I guess. Suddenly appear out of nowhere and completely change my life. You know, boring stuff."

He increased his stride so I couldn't see his expression, but I thought he might be joking with me.

"How about you?" he asked in a too-casual tone. "Anyone surprising?"

Domotor would qualify for appearing out of nowhere and changing my life, but I didn't think he was referring to him.

"No," I said.

"Why not?"

I huffed in annoyance.

"You have to answer," he said. "I answered you—it's only fair."

I bit back a sarcastic comment about fairness and sighed. "Would you bring a child into the scrubs' world? Add yet another body into an already overcrowded place? To be raised unloved and ignored as one of too many? I won't do it."

He remained silent for a while. "You don't have to have a child."

"But when you're intimate with someone, it's usually just a matter of time."

He slowed, glancing at me as if puzzled. Up ahead was a large intersection with many uppers grouped together, talking. A bunch of Pop Cops strode into view and turned toward us. Without thought I stepped back.

Riley grabbed my hand, pulling me beside him. "Confidence," he whispered. "You belong here." Riley squeezed my hand in encouragement.

Easy to say, harder to act. Especially when Lieutenant Arno was among them. I gazed at the floor, but realized it was a scrub reaction. Uppers made eye contact and nodded in greeting. With effort, I returned Arno's semidistracted nod and continued down the hall as if my heart wasn't trying to jump out of my body.

Riley kept my hand as he turned left at the intersection and increased his pace. He made another left into a smaller corridor without doors and which ended. He headed straight for the end.

I scanned the ceiling, looking for air vents. "Riley, where are we going?"

"Trust me."

Almost running now, I kept close to him. When we reached the end, he let go of my hand and stepped to the side, disappearing.

"Hey," I called and he poked his head out.

"Optical illusion. Pretty cool, isn't it?"

I felt around. The wall on the left side of the end was solid. The right side appeared to have a solid wall, but the wall was actually a meter past where it should have connected to the end. The corridor jigged to the right for a meter before going straight again, but it looked like another end. After I made the turn, I glanced back. The illusion worked from both sides.

However this hallway was only about two meters long and contained one door. Riley typed in a number sequence on the lock and the door opened into our storeroom. Relief coursed through me when we entered and I plopped on the couch. I couldn't believe I had just strolled through the upper level.

"That's why no one knows this room is here," he said.

It made sense. Unless you put your hands on the walls, you wouldn't discover the illusion. "How did you find it?"

"Lightbulb duty." When I didn't say anything, he continued, "During training, the newbies get assigned lightbulb duty. We go around changing lightbulbs in the corridors and public areas. Then we fix the broken filaments. A painstaking process." He waved his hand as if pushing away the memory. "Anyway, I was assigned this sector and the bulb at the end must have just burned out. It was still hot and I dropped it. The bulb landed on the rug and then rolled through the wall."

He grinned. "It's amazing, but that bulb has never burned out since I found this place." Riley pulled a drawer open. It was filled with lightbulbs.

After stashing the upper's training uniform under the couch with Zippy, I found Logan in the air shaft not far from

Riley's room. We returned to the lower levels and he raced to make his shift on time. The poor guy would be awake for thirty hours straight. Not fun, but doable. Having worked my shift, Anne-Jade would also be dragging. Perhaps the news of Gateway's existence would wake her up.

Gateway. I still couldn't wrap my mind around all the implications. But I did know actions and alliances needed to be made and I couldn't do it on my own. So I climbed into the heating vents to visit Domotor.

He sat in front of the computer, but turned an expectant expression toward me. I kept my face neutral, but couldn't maintain it for long.

"You found it!"

I smiled. "We know the location."

"Yes." He shouted and banged his chair's arms with his fists. "When are you going to open it?"

"It's not going to be easy." I explained what Logan had said about the alarms. "We need trustable uppers and we need to know more about Outside. Do you even know what's there?"

He played with the long strands of his hair. "Not really. I was hoping there would be more information in the computer system."

"Logan said there were about ten hidden and protected files. He moved them."

"Protected how?"

"With passwords."

"Passwords are the old security system. Those files are probably what I've been searching for. Did Logan move the files so we can access them down here?"

"Yes."

"Maybe I can find them now." Domotor returned his attention to the computer.

"Wait for Logan. He mentioned how the ports log your ID number every time you open a file."

"I've very familiar with the security system, Trella. I don't need Logan." His voice huffed.

I tried to reason with him. "I'd rather we all be together when you try to open those files. You only have ten guesses. The way we figured out the password for Gateway was by all of us bouncing ideas off each other."

"Fine. I'll wait. With nothing else to do, I've become an expert in waiting."

I ignored his snippy tone. "What about the uppers? Do you know who would be willing to help us?"

"I can give you the names of those who *said* they would support me. For security, I made sure no one knew who the others were. But one of them ratted me out, and once I was arrested and interrogated—" he shuddered with horror "—I couldn't hold out. I gave her a few names, hoping one of them was indeed her spy. Karla was a power-hungry lieutenant then, but she arrested all the people I named and recycled them all." A hitch caught his voice, and his eyes shone with grief. "At least I saved the others, and they wisely stopped looking for the files, keeping quiet."

"Why didn't they recycle you?"

"Karla suspected I knew more, but her superior officer was satisfied. I spent two centiweeks in the holding cells before the Travas released me. They claimed I was spared recycling for cooperating with them. I went back to my duties, but no one would talk to me or even look at me. The

rumors had spread, and everyone feared I was a Trava spy."
He huffed. "Ironic."

"When did all this happen?" I asked.

"About sixteen centiweeks ago. After I was released, I
played the game, acting timid and obedient. Eventually, the
Travas stopped monitoring me. I waited another three centiweeks before searching the network for the location of
those hidden files. Guess I didn't wait long enough." He
rubbed his back. "Karla hadn't forgotten about me."

I waited for the rest of his story.

"She suspected and had me interrogated again." He
closed his eyes and hugged his chest for a moment. "He
broke my back, but I didn't say a word about the disks I
hid. After I recovered, Karla sent me down here as punishment, but also to wait and see what I would do or who I
would contact."

"The spy?"

"I guessed wrong. I doubt Karla would kill her own, so he
or she is still spying for her." Domotor pulled out a wipe board
and wrote down five names. He handed the board to me.

I scanned the list. Most of them were women. One name
jumped out at me.

Domotor watched me. "Call me old-fashioned. When I
implicated my cohorts, I named mostly men."

"Who did you implicate?"

"Do you *really* want to know?"

"Yes." The word was a whisper.

Domotor gazed across the room, seeing into the past.
"There were ten of us." He huffed in sad amusement.
"Ten—the magic Inside number. Before I knew about the
Trava takeover, I always wondered why there were nine

major families. I learned later that Inside's original power structure had a voting system, which needed an odd number of voters." He paused. "I had supporters from each of the eight remaining families. A few were mates."

He returned his focus to me. "One of the couples was your parents."

I didn't care about my parents. To prove it, I imagined a thin coat of metal along my skin. So they tried to help Domotor. So what?

"After being tortured, I named your father, Nolan Garrard as an accomplice."

His name clanged on my defenses even though I already knew he had been recycled.

When Domotor didn't see any reaction he continued. "I also named Blas Sanchia and Shawn Lamont. Ramla Ashon was also recycled."

The other names didn't clang. "I thought the uppers all had two family names."

"The children do. Once you find a mate, then you pick one family to be a part of. If you don't find a mate, then you have the support of two families."

With this new knowledge, I read the names on the board again. Jacob Ashon was listed. "Is Ramla Ashon…?"

"Riley's mother."

"And…Kiana Garrard?"

"Your mother."

Her name stabbed through my metal defense. My parents had tried to change things, and my father had been recycled. But those events happened after I was born. No. I didn't care. I forced my metal skin to grow thicker.

"Do you want to know about your—"

"No." I read the list again. Kiana Garrard, Jacob Ashon, Hana Mineko, Takia Qadim and Breana Narelle. "Do you know which one of these uppers is the spy?"

"No. I thought it was Blas Sanchia."

How would I isolate the spy? My limited knowledge of the uppers once again hindered me. I trusted Riley, but could I trust his father? Perhaps Riley would have a few ideas or Logan could track the uppers' computer usage and see if one of them could access restricted Trava files.

"What about Gateway?" I asked.

"Find it underneath the foam. Dissolve the insulation and expose the door for now."

It was hour fifty-two. Eight hours remained before my next shift. I calculated the time needed to sleep, eat and get to the outer wall. Not enough, searching for Gateway would have to wait until my next break. Although, I had time for one errand.

I left Domotor and climbed to level four. Reaching my hidden cabinet, I removed the comb. It was a beautiful gift and should be used and displayed. After counting the teeth, I pocketed it in my tool belt and headed down.

Finding a warm spot to sleep, I dozed in the shaft. If I was Queen of the Pipes, I should request a better throne. Dreams of Outside swirled through my mind. The doorway hovered in front of me, but stayed the same distance away no matter how fast I ran.

My supervisor waited for me at the beginning of my shift. She scowled at me, and I knew it wouldn't be good. It wasn't. She yanked my arm out and slapped a red cuff around my left wrist. It bit into my skin.

"For failure to finish your shift. Explain," she ordered, "and don't try the broken troll excuse. Your troll was found in the air shaft in perfect condition, but no one could find you."

My thoughts raced. "I fell asleep."

"Where?"

"Air shaft seventeen."

"You're lying." She uncapped a marker and wrote the number ten on the cuff. "Report to Emek in solid-waste handling for ten hours extra duty. It can be broken into five-hour increments during your next two off-shifts."

"But that's—"

"Have Emek sign the cuff and return to me after assembly. Failure to comply will result in your permanent reassignment to Emek's team."

Her punishment was extreme for a first offense. "But—"

"*My* supervisor was not happy over your disappearance. Now *I'm* on notice. I'll be watching."

True to her word she stayed until I hefted the troll into the shaft, and she waited at each transition point during the next ten hours. I thought she would follow me down to the solid-waste plant in Sector H1, but she just made sure I headed in the right direction.

Emek smiled broadly when I arrived. Blood seeped from under the bright-colored cuff on my wrist. "Welcome to the crap cleaners. Grab a pair of overalls, a plunger and follow Rat. He'll be your partner."

"Rat?"

He pointed to a young scrub. Despite the name, Rat wore clean overalls and his brown hair was trimmed and tidy. His manner remained pleasant even when we un-clogged a bilious wad, reeking with the most horrible stench. My eyes watered and I almost lost the contents of my stomach.

To distract myself, I asked him, "How did you get the name Rat?"

"It's my nickname. My real name is Mark."

"Okay, so how'd you get your nickname?"

"Rats like me. I keep their population down and make sure the rest are healthy."

"Healthy rats?"

He laughed. "Most people don't want to know what goes on in solid-waste handling. All they want is clean water and fertilizer. Rats are important to our world. Bet you didn't know that."

"You're right."

"Bet you don't know about the bugs, either."

I held a hand up. "I don't, and I don't want to. For certain things, ignorance really is bliss."

My comment turned my thoughts to Gateway. What if I couldn't open it? What if I was caught and killed before seeing Outside? I berated myself. One minute I was convinced Gateway didn't exist, the next, I waxed maudlin over the possibility of not opening it. Just because we found a few coordinates in the computer, shouldn't make me an instant believer.

I forced that line of thought away. It wasn't helping, and I could what-if myself until I was reduced to a nervous mess. Instead, I followed Rat and tried not to breathe through my nose.

Shoveling black goo from the bottom of the incinerator was my last task.

"Isn't this maintenance's job?" I asked.

"Nope. This is good stuff." He dumped a shovelful into the bin. "That's it. Take the bin to the recycling plant and then you're done."

"Where are you going?"

"To the sheep's pen. Want to come? I'm good with sheep, too." He winked.

"No, thank you. Ignorance remember? Best I don't become an expert in waste management."

He waved as he left. And I realized he enjoyed his work. His job was used to punish other scrubs, but he didn't see it that way. He knew his job was vital to Inside and was content. Why couldn't the rest of the scrubs be content? Maybe they were, and I hadn't noticed.

"Trella? What are you doing here?" Logan asked as I pushed the bin through the sorting piles. Dark half circles hung under his eyes.

I waved the cuff in front of his bleary eyes. "I pissed my supervisor off. She assigned me extra duty."

"Anne-Jade will be glad. She's worried because she fell asleep in the air shaft, but she didn't see your supervisor, so she hoped it would be okay."

"She did fine. I'm glad you came over. Broken Man wants to open those files. When can you get the password questions?"

"My next off-shift."

"Great. Also can you—" I checked for Pop Cops "—get security information about the uppers?"

"Depends on what you want to know."

I'd already memorized the names Domotor had given me. Reciting the list of uppers to Logan, I asked, "Can you find out which one of these people is working undercover for the Travas?"

"If the information is listed in the computer system, but it's unlikely."

"Why?"

"Because someone could find it."

"Like Broken Man?"

"No. You need level-nine clearance...oh!"

I smiled as Logan realized only a few Travas had the required security clearance.

"It's still unwise to have such sensitive information listed," Logan said.

"I agree, but I'd bet the higher Pop Cop officers feel rather confident about their security network, believing no one, especially no *scrub* could breach it. So try not to bust their illusion."

"Oh, don't worry, I'm like a—"

"Ghost. I know." Two Pop Cops headed in our direction. "I better go. I can't miss any more shifts, but I'll stop by your barrack during one of my breaks."

Logan nodded and returned to work. I left the recycling plant and hurried to find Emek. Only five hours remained in my off time and I was determined to locate Gateway.

Emek issued orders to a couple scrubs. When they left, I pushed a marker into his hands. "Sign, please."

"Hold on, you still owe me five hours," he said.

I met his gaze. "Cogon's execution is in twenty-four hours. I don't have time."

Understanding softened his face; he signed the cuff. "Ever have a cuff before?"

"My first."

"Put a little sheep's oil on your wrist under the cuff before the Pop Cops remove it. Otherwise, the sucker tends to grab a hunk of skin when it's cut off."

"Thanks." I strode from solid-waste handling and headed to the right. My supervisor's voice called from behind me. She wasn't kidding about watching me. Suppressing a groan of annoyance, I turned.

My heart dropped into my stomach and ran laps. Lieutenant Commander Karla and three Pop Cops followed my supervisor. The LC's smug expression and the terrified fury on my supervisor's face told me all I needed to know.

Without hesitating, I ran.

16

MY SUPERVISOR'S SHRILL VOICE CALLED FOR ME TO
stop. One of the Pop Cops threatened to shoot me, but LC
Karla's calm order to stun me made my legs run faster. I
reached an intersection just as a sizzle slap sounded behind me.
Diving into the hallway on my left, I felt the pulse clip my legs.

I rolled along the floor. A burning pain danced along my
calves and left my muscles numb. Scrubs yelled and scattered.
The corridor filled with noise and confusion. Regaining my
feet proved difficult, I used my upper arms to balance on
numb legs. The quickest of Karla's Pop Cops reached the
intersection.

Pushing scrubs out of his way, he aimed his stun gun at
me. Without thinking, I grabbed a screwdriver from my belt
and flung it at him. The tool knocked into his arm. His shot
flew low, hitting me below the waist.

I fell over, landing on my back, feeling as if a million
needles jabbed through my uniform and into my thighs. The
Pop Cop stepped closer, raising his gun again.

He was bumped from behind. Cursing, he turned to stun the closest scrubs. I hurled my wire cutters at him. They grazed his head, so I lobbed my flashlight. A direct hit. His gun clattered to the floor with a satisfying crack. Surprised, he stared at me a moment, then glanced over his shoulder.

His buddies should be arriving any second, but sounds of a commotion reached us from the other hall.

Taking advantage of his hesitation, I rolled onto my stomach and pulled my body away from him—the benefits of having strong arm muscles. A heating vent beckoned from two meters away.

"Oh, no, you don't," he said.

Too much weight on me, I strained to a stop. He had latched onto my ankles.

"Don't you want to help your boss? Sounds like she's in trouble." I transferred my weight to my left elbow, turning my body sideways and freeing my right arm.

He paused. Karla's voice boomed through the sounds of panicked scrubs, ordering them to get out of her way. The sizzle slap of a stun gun increased the noise level.

"She can handle a couple of scrubs. You should worry about yourself." He reached for his handcuffs with his right hand. "You're under arrest for—"

I stabbed my needle-nose pliers into his left forearm. He yelled and let go. I continued, gaining another meter before he lunged for me. I managed to roll away, but he snaked an arm around my waist, pinning me down. He grinned as I searched for another tool.

"You're out, but I'm not." He pulled a knife.

The ruckus in the other hallway spilled into ours. The LC was caught in the middle of stampeding scrubs. It would have been comical if I didn't have an armed Pop Cop wrapped around me.

Taking advantage of the distraction, I grabbed the comb from my belt. I poked the teeth into his eyes as the crowd reached us. He let go of me, and I lost track of him as we were stepped on, kicked and crushed. The comb dropped from my hand, but all the while, I closed the distance to the heating vent. Removing the cover, I wormed inside, and replaced the metal grate.

I pulled my aching body through the semidark shaft until my arms shook with exhaustion. Laying my head down, I listened as the clamor from the hall died and the angry voice of LC Karla echoed.

Only a few of her words were coherent, but two stood out. Injured and blood. Then the grating sound of a metal cutter vibrated. I turned my head. In the faint light, a thin black trail shone. I wasn't in pain, but then again the lower half of my body remained numb. Running my hands along my skin, I stopped when my fingers encountered wetness.

The Pop Cop's knife had sliced a gash near my hip. I couldn't tell how deep, but I needed to stanch the blood. The rumble of the cutter stopped and a bright light glowed behind me.

The slide step rasp of a person in the shaft reached me. I continued, but I still left a blood trail. When I arrived at an intersection, I tore a part of my coveralls and made a make-shift bandage which became soaked in no time, alarming me.

Not much more I could do, so I kept moving. If LC Karla knew about me, she must know about the others. I wondered what had tipped her off. Concentrating on losing my tail, I glanced over my shoulder. I no longer left a smear of blood. Good. Next I needed to figure out where I was.

The light had changed from weak gray to blue. Bunks were visible through the slats. I had reached the scrubs' barracks. Trying not to make a sound, I removed a vent cover and slipped out of the shaft. I replaced the cover and peered around. It was hour seventy-six and most of the bunks were occupied with sleeping scrubs.

My legs remained numb, which, by the amount of blood pouring from the gash, was a good thing. I crawled across the barrack to another vent on the opposite side. This one would take me to Domotor's hideout. Once inside the shaft, I rested. My arm muscles burned with fatigue.

The trip to Domotor's room seemed unending. By the time I reached his vent, I didn't have the energy to remove the cover.

"Domotor," I called. No answer. I yelled louder.

"Trella? Where are you?" he asked.

"In the heating duct."

He rolled into view. "What's the matter?" He bent over and yanked the cover off.

I stayed in the duct. "LC Karla tried to arrest me. She knows."

"How much does she know?"

"I didn't hang around to find out."

Concern and fear filled his expression but not surprise. He had come from the right side of the room. "What have you been doing?" I asked.

Guilt flashed before he covered it. "Cleaning."

"You haven't tried to access those files?"

His gaze dropped to the floor. All the answer I needed. "Domotor, I told you to wait!"

"I was careful. There has to be another reason Karla's after you," he shot back.

"I doubt she'd bring along three Pop Cops if she wanted to follow up on my reprimand."

"You were reprimanded?" His voice held an accusatory tone.

"For failure to finish my shift. Which is pretty damn good, considering all the extracurricular activity I've been doing for you." This wasn't productive. I drew a breath. "If she knows where you are, she'll try and cut through the door. At least you'll have a warning. Once you're in custody, hold out for as long as you can before naming anyone. Give her Cog's and Roddie's names and then mine."

"Who is Roddie?"

"The man who was kill-zapped back when you first went missing. Hopefully, she'll be happy with those names."

"What are you going to do?"

"Warn my friends."

It was a good plan. Warn Logan then find Riley. However, the numbness wore off my legs. It was a bonus to have the use of my legs, and I switched from the heating system to the air shafts. But the sizzling pain shooting from my hip created a big problem.

After climbing to level two, I knew I wouldn't be able to find Logan. Light-headed and weak, I lay in the shaft, wishing for one of those pocket communicators the Pop Cops carried. A sudden memory flashed and I checked my tool belt.

Yes! I still carried the two listening devices Jacy had given me. Palming one, I toggled the On switch. I was supposed to plant it in air duct seventy-two, but hadn't gotten the opportunity. I chuckled wildly, thinking I could only break one rule at a time.

I wasn't sure if Jacy or his buddies would be monitoring the devices or even listening, but it was worth the effort.

Moving the device close to my mouth, I whispered, "Jacy, remember when you said to let you know if I needed anything? Well, I need your help." I paused, collecting my thoughts. To tell Jacy Logan's name could result in more danger for Logan. All Domotor knew about Logan was his physical description. My head spun and I realized I might not be conscious for too long. Better to tell Jacy then pass out.

I asked Jacy to warn Logan. "I also need you to *borrow* all the metal cutters, chisels and crowbars in the lower levels and hide them. The Pop Cops are going to want to cut a hole and the longer it takes them to complete this task, the better. Anything you can do to make the Pop Cops' lives difficult would be appreciated." I flipped off the device and returned it to my tool belt.

After the wave of dizziness passed, I decided to try to climb to the fourth level and warn Riley. Even if he wasn't in our room, I would leave him a note. And then what?

To distract myself from the pain and effort of climbing, I planned my next task. I could hide from the Pop Cops, but eventually they'd know about Gateway from Domotor. I had to get there first and open it. And then? No clue.

My progress slowed and I gasped for breath. Focusing all my energy into moving my body, my awareness shrank to pushing forward one foot at a time, to pulling with one arm then the other. Black and white dots swirled in my vision and I bit my lip to keep conscious.

A single goal propelled me forward, and the last thing I remember was the sensation of falling.

★ ★ ★

Sharpness jabbed my arm. I tried to jerk away, but my arm was stuck. My whole body ached and a hammer kept striking the back of my head. I retreated to the darkness, leaving all those annoyances behind.

The pricking and pulling around my hip demanded attention. I opened my eyes, but shut them against the harsh daylight. Two people stood over me.

"She's waking. Quick, more thiopental!"

Another painful prick on my arm, and fire raced through my veins. I welcomed the return of darkness.

Foggy thoughts floated sluggishly. Pain radiated from my hip, but only spiked when I moved, which proved difficult to do. My right arm was trapped. Squinting, I braced for the bright daylight, but sighed in relief. Soft bluelight glowed in the room.

The familiar shapes of our storeroom surrounded me. Reclined on the couch, I still couldn't comprehend why my right arm wouldn't move. I wore a soft robe. A liquid-filled bag hung above my head with a tube snaking down. I followed the tube and found the reason for my frozen arm. It was tied to a white board. The tube ended in a metal piece protruding from my skin.

Memories of being chased by Pop Cops sprang to life. They must have caught me and were using a drug to torture me. I struggled to sit up. Every muscle in my body hurt and I felt as if I'd been chewed by Chomper.

"Easy there," a woman's voice said. She knelt next to the couch and laid a cool hand on my shoulder. "You shouldn't move."

Panicked, I swatted at her hand with my free arm, but the effort was weak and she caught my wrist. The cuff was still in place around it.

"If you move, you might pull your stitches out and I'll have to sew you up again." She used the stern tone of a Care Mother.

Stopping, I peered at her clothes. An upper, but not a Pop Cop. Her words finally pushed through the fog of fear and I realized she worked in the infirmary. Yet I was in our store-room. Could the Pop Cops be waiting outside? "What…? Who…?" My throat burned.

"If you promise to lie still, I'll get you a drink and tell you what happened. Promise?"

I debated. Knowledge versus promising an upper. "Yes." But if she turned out to be a Pop Cop in disguise, then I could break my promise.

She moved away and returned with a cup of water. I grasped the heavy glass in my left hand, and she supported my head while I drank. The cold water felt wonderful going down, but turned my stomach.

"Sip it slowly," she said. "You just had surgery."

"Surgery? It was just a cut." I strained to sit up.

"Remember your promise."

I wilted. Who was I kidding anyway? I could barely lift a glass of water.

A fleeting smile crossed her lips. Her brown hair had been braided into a single long rope. The end reached her waist and she flicked it aside when she sat on the edge of the couch. In the bluelight, it was hard to see her eye color, but I guessed by the fine lines on her face she was around forty centiweeks old. Her thin fingers checked the metal thing stuck in my arm. She moved with a competent grace as if she did this all the time.

I winced when she touched my hip.

"Sorry, but I want to be sure you didn't pull a stitch." She pressed her fingertips through my robe and along my cut. "Feels fine."

"Okay, Doctor. Care to explain what's going on?" I asked.

"I was accosted by a very persistent young man who insisted I was needed for an emergency. Imagine my surprise when he led me here. You were on the couch, unconscious and bleeding. After an initial check, I determined you had a concussion and had been stabbed."

Which explained all the blood.

She watched my expression for a moment. "The young man would not let me take you to a proper surgical room, so we had to make do." The doctor fiddled with the tube. "I'm giving you an antibiotic, but the risk of infection is still very high."

"How deep?"

"The knife penetrated to your pelvic bone, damaging your large intestines and your ovary. I stitched you up as best I could, but you might have trouble conceiving a child."

Not a concern for me. "When will I be able to move?"

"You can walk around in a few hours, but it's going to take a week for you to regain your full strength."

A week! I'd be recycled in a week. Sooner if the doctor reported me to the Pop Cops.

"Now it's your turn. Care to tell me why you're here?"

"No."

"How about if I threaten to tell the authorities?"

I considered. The doctor could have reported me hours ago. "No."

She grinned. "You called my bluff. Good thing your

young man is a friend of mine." Then her smile dissolved as sadness pulled on her features. "I'm not an idiot, though. A rogue scrub wearing a red cuff has been reported to be in the air ducts and, although injured, is potentially dangerous. The uppers have been ordered to listen at vent covers and alert the authorities about any suspicious noise." She gazed at me as if memorizing my features. "Once the game is up, it never ends well."

Jacy's comment about results repeated in my mind. "Better to make an effort, than do nothing."

"When the effort fails, is it worth the cost?"

A tough question to answer. Failure meant Domotor, Logan, Anne-Jade, Riley and I would all be recycled along with Cog. Six people. A high cost. "No."

"Then why try at all?"

"Because there is a chance for success. Maybe not complete success, or even the hoped-for results, but maybe just planting a seed to grow long after I'm gone. It doesn't have to be a total failure." Logan already knew this. I understood his words about causing maximum damage on a deeper level.

"Good answer. It's the reason I'm here." She glanced at the clock. "Now that you're in stable condition, I need to report to the infirmary." Standing, she bustled about and gathered her supplies. "I'll be back later to check on you."

"Doctor?"

She turned.

"Thank you."

Flashing me a smile, she left. The bluelights remained on, and I wondered why her motion hadn't triggered the daylights. Perhaps Riley had turned off the sensor. Her comments about Riley as my young man made me laugh. Pain flared near my hip and I stopped.

I scanned the room for the fifth time. Nothing to do or see, I was alone with my thoughts. Funny how I had craved to be alone and now I wished for company. Wished to see Cog's happy face. I had been avoiding the clock, keeping my gaze away. If I didn't know the time, then Cog was still alive.

Instead, I reviewed my conversation with the doctor. This quest to find Gateway had started because I wanted to prove Broken Man wrong and save Cog the disappointment when his prophet disappeared without keeping his promises.

A simple task which had blown into a complicated mess, involving six—seven if I count the doctor—people. Actually, if I included Jacy and his group, the scrub who covered for me and the kitchen scrubs, I was well past twenty.

Not the actions of sheep at all. In fact, if I was honest with myself, I'd wanted to prove Broken Man wrong to save myself from hoping. To give myself permission to not care about the scrubs. So I could view them and treat them just like the Pop Cops did. As sheep.

Some Queen of the Pipes, I thought. I'd believed I was better than a mindless drone. But I was the mindless one, hiding away. Even now I referred to them as if I didn't belong. I had completely fallen for the Pop Cop propaganda. The computers in the care facility listed all the wonderful things the uppers did and their wonderful lives. Being a scrub was undesirable and hard work, living in crowded conditions with no privacy and just being one of many. Undistinguishable.

The propaganda was crafted to make scrubs distance themselves from other scrubs so they wouldn't be lumped into one universal category. Queen of the Pipes was better than being a scrub. I fell for it, but others hadn't. Cog, for one. He remembered names and treated everyone as if they were special. Rat in waste management. He was proud of his work, despite his job being considered even beneath a scrub.

Shame over my behavior pulsed in my chest. I dug deeper into my motivations for pursuing the location of Gateway and my entire body cringed. I covered my eyes with my free hand, yet the darkness didn't block the realization. *Selfish.* The word flashed in front of my eyes as if burned in the underside of my eyelids.

In my small metal heart, I'd wanted to find Gateway for me. So I could escape from being a scrub. I could try to rationalize it—my desire to help Cog was genuine—but my desire to help myself was stronger.

Disgust, self-loathing and guilt all rolled into a noxious mix, filling me until I acknowledged them and had wallowed in them for a while. Then I purged them. Gateway existed and the game wasn't over yet.

Maximum damage.

Unflinching, I looked at the clock. Hour ninety-six. Cog was still alive. I had three hours to… What? I couldn't even laugh without pain, and couldn't count on Riley's help. His shift lasted until hour hundred, and I assumed he would come straight here.

I scanned the room for ideas. My tool belt and bloodstained clothes lay tangled together in a heap by the desk. The tools were long gone, but I hoped the pouches still held Logan's decoder device and Jacy's microphone.

A small amount of liquid remained in the bag over my head. I wiggled into a sitting position, closing my eyes against a burst of pain and wave of dizziness. When my head stopped spinning, I examined my arm. My wrist had been turned to expose the underside of my arm. The top of the metal needle at the end of the tube had been taped to my skin on the opposite side of my elbow.

I pulled the tape off the tube. Each tug caused a pinching jab. When the tube was free, I tugged the needle out. Blood welled. Another round of dizziness claimed my attention for a few moments. Unwrapping the rest of the tape to remove the white board, I focused on the positive. There was less hair on the underside of my arm. If my wrist had been turned the other way, the sting from removing the tape would have been worse.

Once I was free, I paused to catch my breath before working the stiffness out of my arm. Bending over to retrieve my tool belt from the floor, I toppled. Bad idea. Daggers of pain robbed me of breath. On the upside, I landed near my tool belt. Sheer willpower kept me from passing out.

I found both Logan's and Jacy's devices close to the heating vent. My initial idea had been to bring Logan's decoder to Cog. He could unlock his cell door and escape. Pure fantasy. If the air shaft vent in the cells had been barred, it stood to reason that the heating vents would also be secured. Plus where would he go?

But I could do one thing for him. Determined, I found the student's uniform I had stashed under the couch. I wore nothing but a bandage under the robe. I wondered if Riley had helped the doctor. Heat flushed my face.

My line of thought wasn't conducive to my mission so I concentrated on getting dressed. I taped a small pillow to my wound before donning the uniform. Ignoring the pain, I crawled over to the heating vent and opened it.

Amazingly, the pillow did a decent job of cushioning my injury as I slithered/crawled through the duct. However, my battered muscles protested each movement and dizziness plagued my efforts. I paused often, and set little goals for myself.

Just make it to the bend, I willed, and I celebrated each one with a rest before setting the next. I had no idea how long I spent traveling to the holding cells. All that mattered was reaching Cog before they led him down to Chomper.

There was no mistaking the feeble light or the rancid stench of the holding cells. I peered through the bars, searching for Cog. Nothing but empty cells until I reached the third vent.

Cog sat on the edge of the bunk. Old black and yellow bruises painted his face, and the swelling around his eyes was gone. Bleeding cuts crisscrossed his legs and torso. He hugged his arms tight to his chest as if trying to stanch the blood. He rocked either in agitation or pain.

I called his name.

Cog jumped to his feet and looked around. "No, Trell, you shouldn't have!"

"Shouldn't have what?"

He cocked his head.

"I'm down here. In the heating vent."

He sagged back on the bunk. Keeping his voice low, he said, "Don't scare me like that."

"Sorry." I hated to see him so frazzled. "Cog, what shouldn't I have done?"

"I thought you had turned yourself in."

"Why?"

He gestured toward the door. "They came asking more questions about you. They found out Broken Man is still alive and you're involved."

"I know. Broken Man tipped them off."

"Really?"

"Yes. He used the computer, and then I was repri-manded for failing to finish my shift. Karla's suspected me all along, so the reprimand gave her enough reason to *try* to arrest me."

Cog smiled with glee. "That's my Trella, hiding in the pipes."

"You used to yell at me for it."

"You should have seen her. Bright red, sputtering with rage and I swear I saw fire coming out of her nostrils. That was worth every cut from Vinco's knife." He grew serious. "She said you were injured. Are you all right?"

"Fine." It was a good thing he couldn't see me. I thought about his earlier comment. "Why did you think I turned myself in?"

"Karla asked me stuff like what you knew, where you might be and who you were working with. I couldn't tell her anything. Then she said she would offer you a deal." He stopped.

"What kind of deal?"

"I'll only tell you if you promise *not* to take it."

I connected the clues. He didn't need to tell me Karla would offer to spare his life in exchange for me. "I'm not promising, Cog."

"You have to. Otherwise everything I suffered through will be for nothing."

"No, it wouldn't. You gave us time and freedom. We found Gateway."

He slid off the bunk and onto his knees as pure joy lit his face. "Did you open it?" The question was a reverent whisper.

"Not yet. I've been a little...busy."

"All the more reason to *not* take Karla's deal. *You* need to open it."

"Why can't I do both?"

"Not possible."

"Yes, it is. I can stall for time." But how much time? I needed to heal first if I planned to climb between levels. "Are you still scheduled for..." I couldn't speak the words.

"No. My appointment with Chomper has been delayed until further notice. I guess if they recycle me, the LC wouldn't have any bait for her trap." A tired resignation colored the tone of his voice. "How are you going to stall for time?"

"Don't worry about it. You just need to hold out for a little longer."

He huffed. "You have no idea. Do you?"

My thoughts raced. Communication with the LC would have to be through a third party, which would be time consuming. "I can make a few unreasonable demands, and by the time we negotiate Gateway will be open. And then..." I couldn't speculate any further.

"Everything changes," Cog said.

17

THE TRIP BACK TO THE STOREROOM PROGRESSED AT a much slower pace. No longer driven by the need to speak to Cog, I tended to stop often and lay my cheek against the cool metal of the duct. The warm air flowing through the shaft didn't help either. I dozed off a few times.

My sense of accomplishment on reaching the storeroom evaporated in an instant. Riley occupied the couch. I couldn't call it sitting. Every muscle was so taut he appeared as if welded in place. His furious expression matched his posture.

I concentrated on pulling my body from the vent. My adventure ended on the ground in a painful and exhausted heap. Wondering how I would find the energy to endure the inevitable recriminations and questions from Riley, I rested my head on the floor.

Instead, he gathered me in his arms and carried me to the couch. "This is the second time I've had to pick you up. At least, this time you're conscious." He knelt and set me down with care. All signs of his anger had dissipated.

"Good thing you don't weigh much, either." He fussed about, propping cushions.

I was half asleep when he said, "Let's see what damage you've done." He pulled back my uniform to expose my injury. "A pillow." He shook his head as he peeled off the tape.

Blood soaked the underside of the pillow. I closed my eyes against the sudden queasiness in my stomach. He probed the cut and I hissed in pain.

"Amazing. You didn't rip any stitches, but you need a new bandage."

I peeked at him. His tone was matter-of-fact and he moved with confident efficiency as if he changed bandages all the time.

"It's going to hurt." He gloated.

"You need to work on your bedside manner," I said.

"And you need to listen to your doctor. Now hold still."

I bit my lip as he removed the old dressing and replaced it with a clean one. He covered me with a blanket. Rummaging around his desk, he returned with a tool resembling bolt cutters but smaller.

"Cuff."

I held my arm out. "Any chance you have some sheep oil?" I asked as he tightened the clamp.

"Nope. And this *will* hurt." He grunted and the metal cuff buckled.

It broke with a crunch snap, gouging a hunk of skin in the process just like Emek had warned. Riley pulled the damaged cuff from my wrist and bandaged the bleeding gouge. He poured me a glass of water. Remembering the doctor's instructions, I sipped it.

Riley sat on the edge of the couch, and I knew the questions would start. He didn't disappoint me. "What was so important?"

I told him about Cog. About his strength, his sacrifice and his beliefs. "I couldn't let him be recycled without knowing about Gateway."

Riley listened without interruption. "Then we need to open Gateway before he's recycled." He glanced at the floor as if undecided, then met my gaze. "You said you didn't have a mate."

I almost laughed, but remembered the pain it caused. "I don't. Cogon is like…" I cast about for the right upper word. "A brother to me. You should know how that is, you have one."

"I saw him once, and then he was gone." He frowned. "I thought scrubs didn't have families."

"We don't. I was trying to match the feeling. Cog was my care mate. Which means we grew up together, looked after each other." I struggled to keep my eyes open.

"Get some rest, Trella." Riley smoothed a few hairs from my face and stroked my cheek.

"We need to plan."

"We'll make plans when you're stronger. Rest now. Doctor's orders."

This time I listened.

I woke to the ungentle prodding of the doctor.

She perched on the edge of the couch and held up the needle I had yanked from my arm. "I see you decided to stop your medicine. Are you feeling better?"

"Yes." The dizziness and nausea were gone. My stomach rumbled, and I had no energy. The doctor helped to prop me up, bending caused too many spikes of pain.

"Here." She handed me a warm bowl of tan-colored water and a spoon.

I sniffed the strange substance.

"It's broth. It'll help you recover." Amusement filled her voice. "If you keep that down, I'll give you a thicker soup."

Sipping a spoonful of broth, I waited for my stomach's reaction. My hunger strengthened, and I abandoned the spoon to drink right from the bowl.

"Enjoy being able to recover quickly. When you get past thirty-five centiweeks old, it's harder to heal." She handed me the soup. "In a few hours you can return to your normal diet." Rising, she glanced around the room. "Eventually, you're going to want to take a shower and sleep in a real bed." Her gaze returned to me. "You already have the student's uniform, and I have an extra bed in my rooms next to the infirmary you can use. It's supposed to be for an intern, but none of the current class has the skills needed, and I'm waiting for a few of the younger kids to grow older."

A generous and dangerous offer. She would be recycled if I was found in her rooms. "Wouldn't my presence be suspicious?"

"Not really. Students have more freedom and aren't tracked as closely until they choose a profession and are given a port. My supervisor would actually be happy to see I have selected an intern—he's been nagging me about it for weeks." She checked my pulse. "Strong. You should be fine."

Collecting a few medical items, she headed toward the door. Before she left, she looked at me. "Think about my suggestion, Ella. Riley knows where to find me."

Her offer was out of the question. Karla would not stop until she found me and I needed to confirm Gateway's location, talk to Logan about those files, open Gateway and turn myself in to the Pop Cops for Cog. Playing Ella the upper with a very nice lady wasn't included in my to-do list no matter how much I wished it was there.

Instead I reviewed each task. Confirming Gateway's location would require climbing through the shafts. Not possible right now, but could be accomplished in another ten hours or so I hoped. The concern was if Karla had gotten the coordinates from Domotor or Logan and beaten me to Gateway. What then? The Pop Cops would control it. I could tell the scrubs about its existence. I barked out a laugh. I'd be the new prophet, raving about Gateway for everyone's amusement. No. If Karla had Gateway, the game would be over.

If I found Gateway, I would need to learn more about Outside and how to open the door. Logan guessed the needed information hid in the old files. Opening the files required passwords and Logan. Again I needed to be able to climb to contact the Tech No. If Karla held Logan, or if we couldn't deduce the correct passwords, then it was game over.

Opening Gateway depended on the success of task two, plus we would need uppers to cover the computer alerts. I had a list of possible sympathizers, but one of them was a spy. Logan had planned to check the computer records of the uppers. If he couldn't discover who worked for Karla, we'd need to find another group via Riley, and hope we didn't contact another spy. If we did—game over.

The last task, turning myself in to Karla had the least problems. And once the game was over, it would be the only job left for me to do.

I needed to communicate with Karla somehow, and I really needed to find out what she knew and what she planned. Too bad I couldn't crawl through the heating vents again and maybe listen—

Jacy's device! I had planted one above Karla's office. If I could pick up the audio signal, I could listen in. I ignored the fact I had no idea how to do it. My whole future depended on so many ifs and hopes and assumptions and possibilities that I would consider it impossible right now if I thought about it too much.

I decided to think positive and impart maximum damage.

My tool belt was close enough to reach with a minimal amount of bending. I removed the microphone. Jacy might regret his offer to help.

I flipped it on and said, "Jacy, I need your help again. Lieutenant Commander Karla is offering me a deal and I need you to be my negotiator. Tell Karla that I will turn myself in if she promises to free Cogon so he can return to work in the lower levels and promises she won't recycle me. She won't accept those terms and she'll make a counteroffer. Tell her you'll communicate with me and let her know in twenty hours. Drag the negotiations out as long as possible. I don't care what the final terms are for me as long as Cogon stays alive and no one else is arrested. I'm trusting you."

"You don't care what the final terms are?" Riley asked. He closed the door and stood there holding a steaming bowl.

"No. As long as I cause problems and do maximum damage." I wondered how much he had heard.

"What about your friends? Don't you think they care?"

"But I would be helping them. And besides, it's my decision."

"Maybe they don't want you to help them. Did you ever think of that? Did you think about how *your* decision impacts others? Those you leave behind to deal with the gaping hole in their existence?"

Riley's agitation seemed excessive. He noticed my confusion. "I guess it must be a family thing. Something a scrub wouldn't understand. Although I wouldn't call me and my still-grieving father a family."

I remembered. Riley wasn't angry at me, but at his mother. Her name was on Domotor's recycled list. "I know you miss your mother—"

"You don't know. You're a *scrub*. You don't have a family."

Now I was livid. "Of course I do. The scrubs are my family. I have a Care Mother. I shared her with nine brothers and sisters, but she loves us all. And I have Cog, who I will give myself to Karla in order to save." My outburst surprised me, but not as much as the realization that I truly believed what I had said.

Riley couldn't keep the smugness from his voice. "Your description of life in the lower levels is completely different from how you described it to me when we first met. Perhaps uppers and lowers have more in common than you first thought." He tried to suppress a smirk and failed. "Come on, admit it."

"Did you come for a reason? I'm *supposed* to be resting."

He held the bowl up. "Admit it and I'll give you this stew." He blew over the top, sending a delicious smell my way.

"You're obnoxious."

"I've been called worse." He swept the food under my nose.

"All right. All right. Maybe I judged the uppers too soon."

"Nope. Not good enough for this wonderful meal. I want three words: *I, was, wrong.*" He held up three fingers and waggled them.

"You're mean. I'm injured and need nourishment to recover."

"The stew's getting cold."

"Fine. I was wrong. Happy?"

"Ecstatic." He gave me the bowl and a smile.

At least he didn't gloat. After scraping my spoon to retrieve the last bit, I decided the stew was worth my admission.

Riley hovered. I moved my legs so he could join me on the couch.

"You look better," he said. "Your face isn't as pale."

"I have you to thank. You risked a lot by fetching the doctor."

He shrugged. "Doctor Lamont is a friend of my father's." He pulled at a thread on the couch. "Considering the extent of your injury and blood loss, the doctor was amazed you made it up here."

"You know how stubborn I can be. I wanted to warn you about Domotor. Once they break him, he'll tell the Pop Cops about you and Logan." I looked at the clock. Hour twenty-one. Plenty of time for Vinco's knife to have done its job.

"They don't have him yet," Riley said.

I straightened, tugging my stitches. "What happened?"

"LC Karla knows he's been using his port, but her computer experts can't trace it back to an exact location. All she knows is he's on level one. She's been trying to search the entire level."

"Trying?"

He grinned. "The Pop Cops have been besieged with a run of bad luck. Malfunctioning equipment, missing tools, miscommunications and a broken water pipe."

Jacy had heeded my request, which meant he'd warned

Logan and probably received my most recent communication. I wondered if Logan was the reason for Karla's computer woes. "How do you know about her troubles?"

"One of the metal cutters overheated and injured an ensign. Doctor Lamont treated him. Nice, chatty fellow." He leaned forward. "Now we have a little time to find Gateway."

"Yes. But we'll need Logan and a bunch of uppers to help."

"We have me, my father and Doctor Lamont. I have a cousin in mechanical that I can trust. Who else did Domotor mention?"

"Kiana Garrard, Hana Mineko, Takia Qadim and Breana Narelle. But one of them works for the Trava family. Logan might be able to tell us which one."

Riley wound the couch's thread around his hand. "I've heard of Takia. She works in the Control Room. One of only two people who are not Travas. I've met Breana and Hana. They were part of my father's training group, but he hasn't visited with them in hundreds of weeks. I never heard of Kiana Garrard. Do you know which system she works in?"

"No. We need Logan."

"You're in no condition to bring him through the air shafts."

I agreed. LC Karla was occupied with locating Domotor. Perhaps Logan could take the lift. It would be a matter of timing, and Logan being able to find the Pop Cop uniform I had hidden. I shared my idea with Riley.

"It could work as long as his nerves don't give him away. How are you going to contact him?"

I showed Riley the listening device.

He whistled. "When you decide to break the law, you certainly don't skimp. Illegal technology *and* a stolen Pop Cop uniform."

"Borrowed. You're not exactly Mr. Law-and-Order. In fact…" I had an idea.

"Oh no. This can't be good."

"Is there any way you can pick up an audio signal?" I asked.

He took the device and examined it. "If I had the frequency, yes. Why?"

"There is one of these hidden in Karla's office. Knowing her plans will help us."

His surprise didn't last long. "Gee, I wonder how it got there," he said with a light sarcasm.

"No idea," I said, playing along. "Kids these weeks." I tsked. "Always getting into trouble. Not like me, I'm the soul of conformity."

He laughed. "We should make that your code name. Soul of Conformity or SOC for short."

After Riley left, I contacted Jacy through the device, telling him about our plans. "Send Logan up at hour twenty-six. He tends to get nervous so it would be a good time for another distraction. I also need the frequency of the bug in Karla's office."

If all went as planned at hour twenty-six, Logan would dress in the Pop Cop uniform and take the lift to level four where Riley would be waiting to escort him to our storeroom.

Realizing I'd used *our* instead of *Riley's*, I grunted with amusement. Storeroom also failed as a descriptor. Recent events had transformed the room into an infirmary, a hideout and a bedroom. Riley had ordered me to rest.

I wormed into a comfortable position, but my thoughts swirled with worries and my hip ached. Giving up, I scanned the room for something to distract me. Besides Riley's electrical sketches, nothing caught my eye. I could understand why Domotor hadn't waited for Logan. Boredom was worse than unclogging pipes for waste handling.

A little gray lump rested under the desk. Careful of my stitches, I eased to my feet and shuffled to pick up Sheepy. His mother was a few feet away. I carried them both to the couch. Small flecks of blood dotted their coats and I used the water in my drinking glass to clean them off.

I wondered about Riley's brother. From his comments, I guessed the boy died right after birth. So where was Dada Sheepy?

Eventually, I dozed, dreaming about sheep. I held a bleating lamb as I waded through a hallway filled with sheep. A wet crunching sound chased me. It grew louder as I stumbled over the animals, convinced Chomper's blades would soon bite me. I tripped. Rolling over, I pushed the lamb behind my back to face the threat, but Cog stood between me and darkness.

He offered his hand. I grasped it and he pulled me to my feet. Then he stepped aside and flung me toward the LC.

"Use her to ensure their cooperation," he said.

His laughter followed me as she dragged me away.

"Game's over, Tre… Trella. Trella. Wake up."

I squinted into the daylight. Riley stood next to a Pop Cop. Wide awake in an instant, I nearly tore my stitches sitting up before I recognized the face. "Anne-Jade? What happened?"

"Logan's being monitored," she said. "A Pop Cop noticed he was spending a lot of time on the computer."

"I thought they were all busy with the search," I said.

"Most are, but a few Pop Cops are convinced the missing scrub is being helped and are determined to be the one to find you and get a promotion. They've made life in the lower levels even more intolerable." Her gaze swept the room. "Although, I must say I'm disappointed by level four. Is level three any better?" Anne-Jade asked Riley.

"No. It's about the same."

"Pity."

"Anne-Jade, do you have any news?" I asked.

She settled on the couch, leaving Riley to sit on the floor. "The first thing I'm supposed to tell you is from Jacy." Her nose creased with distaste. "He says you owe him big and when this whole mess is over, you're his slave for a week."

Nice of him to be optimistic.

Riley's mouth opened in stunned outrage. "He doesn't mean—"

"No." I assured him. "Jacy'll have me planting his bugs all over Inside. Go on, Anne-Jade."

"Logan gave me a list of password questions to memorize. Do you have a wipe board?"

Riley rummaged through the desk, and wrote down the questions. All were vague yet had enough information to make them seem possible to answer. The third question mentioned a platitude about being unable to see. No quick answers jumped to mind.

"What about the uppers? Did Logan have time to check them?" I asked.

"Yes. He said he found one of the names mentioned as an informant in the security files. The rest had clean records."

"Which one?" I asked.

"Kiana Garrard."

Her name banged hard against my metal heart, sending

vibrations along my skin. I shouldn't be surprised. If she could abandon her child in the lower levels, she could rat out her husband and others.

"Anything else about the uppers?" Riley asked.

"Yes, Logan said Takia Qadim would be the best person to have on our side as she has access to multiple systems."

"How will she and the others know to trust us?"

I shuffled through all the information Domotor had told me. "This is going to sound hokey, but tell them the Force of Ten is back in action." Which was true. If I counted Logan, Anne-Jade, Riley, Doctor Lamont and myself the number was ten.

"I don't know if I can say that with a straight face," Riley said.

"Just think of the consequences if they don't help us."

"Good point."

Anne-Jade had been fidgeting with the top button on the Pop Cop uniform. Dipping her head down, she spoke to her chest. "Did it work?" Then she pressed a fingertip to her earring, cocking her head.

Riley and I exchanged a significant look. Had the pressure been too much for her?

"Okay. I'll give it to her. Thanks." Anne-Jade noticed our dubious expressions. "I can't keep playing messenger between you and the lower levels." She pulled the small blue earring from her earlobe. "Receiver." She dug into her pocket, and removed a strange metal device that resembled a rivet gun. She placed the earring in the gun and pressed it to my left earlobe. "Hold still."

Before I could protest, she squeezed and a loud pop sounded in my ear followed by a sharp pain. Anne-Jade batted my hand away as she finished, wiping my lobe with a medicinal-smelling cloth. It came away wet with my blood.

"Now you can hear Jacy." She yanked on her top button. It popped off with ease and revealed an identical button underneath. "Microphone. It's built into a standard issue button and attaches with ease. Go on, try it."

I clipped the metal microphone to my top button.

"She's on," Anne-Jade said.

"Trella?" Jacy asked.

I started and glanced around. His clear voice sounded as if he stood next to me.

"Trella, are you there?"

"Yes."

"No need to shout, I can hear you just fine. These devices of the Tech Nos are wonderful. Once they make more, we can coordinate our team's efforts."

"What team?"

Anne-Jade averted her gaze.

"The Gateway team of course." Jacy's matter-of-fact reply contrasted with his upsetting revelation.

"How did you—"

"He threatened to report us to the Pop Cops," Anne-Jade said in her defense.

Under normal circumstances, Jacy wouldn't interact with the Pop Cops.

"You fell for his bluff. How much did you tell him?" I asked her.

But Jacy answered. "Everything and you should have come to me right away instead of blundering around."

Riley's confusion increased as I talked to Jacy, but he kept quiet.

"Blundering? You would have done better?" I asked.

"Of course. I would have assigned people to cover your shift, to help smuggle food and to supply you with information."

"But I couldn't—"

"Trust anyone. I know."

I had planned to say "get you in trouble," but he was right, too. "You're helping now." With Jacy, we were the force of eleven. It didn't have the same cachet.

"Small consolation, considering the havoc down here." Yet a gleeful challenge spiked his tone as if he looked forward to the upcoming difficulties.

"What's the status?" I braced for his answer.

"Pop Cops everywhere, snooping around. It's only a matter of time before they do a full level-wide search, and there are certain…things I'd rather they not find."

"What about the negotiations with Karla?"

A pause. "There are none. Before you yell, hear me out."

I growled my assent.

"Karla offered every enticement possible to get the scrubs to rat you out. Failing that, she has announced Cogon's life could be spared if you turn yourself in. Wait! Since nothing has resulted from her efforts, she believes you're hiding in the ducts, wounded and close to expiring. The air shafts are filled with RATSS. And I don't want to bust her illusions."

"What about Cog?"

"He's been protecting you since we were toddlers, and the worst thing you can do for him is to undermine his efforts and turn yourself in. Besides, once you open Gateway, it'll be a whole new world."

"But what if—"

"Stop! Don't what-if me. Do your part and get Gateway

opened, and I'll do mine, making life miserable for the Pop Cops. Time to go. I'm needed elsewhere, but I'll keep a man monitoring this frequency."

His comment reminded me. "Jacy, what's the frequency for Karla's bug?"

"Ninety-eight megahertz."

"Thanks for your help."

He chuckled. "Don't worry, you *will* return the favor. And once the Tech Nos build more of those receivers, I'll contact you."

I turned off the button microphone, and filled Anne-Jade and Riley in on what Jacy had said.

"What's to stop the Travas from picking up the frequency?" I asked.

"Nothing, but with a large number of frequencies, the odds are small they would find it," Riley explained. He stood and brushed off his pants. "I'll escort Anne-Jade back to the lift." He handed me the board with the password questions. "You work on these, and I'll start recruiting uppers."

I couldn't help smiling at his bossy tone. "Who put you in charge?"

"Sheepy."

"Are we the Force of Sheep now?"

"No. We are the Force of Onaaaaae." He bleated the word as if he were a sheep.

18

I THREW A PILLOW AT RILEY FOR HIS AWFUL PUN. HE
ducked easily and escorted Anne-Jade from our storeroom.
Before he left, he poked his head back into the room and
said, "Byaaaaae."

My aim was off and the next pillow hit the closing door.
I debated the merits of standing to retrieve the cushions and
decided to stay on the couch and study the list of ten
password questions. We had solved the one to gain access to
Gateway's coordinates, and the other referred to the number
of teeth on my comb with the pearl handle—which I had
counted before losing it when the Pop Cop had attacked me.

Eight questions remained. I puzzled over them, but I
couldn't solve any of them with one answer. Number six
was, *What do you turn to get the outside in?*

The answer could be a doorknob, a handle, a lock or a
screw. With no one for me to bounce ideas off of, I wrote
down as many possible answers and tried another.

Your eyes can see, but mine don't work, yet I see what you can't.

What am I? And tried another. After a few hours, my head ached. I abandoned my task and rested. Hour thirty meant Riley had returned to work and it would be a while before my next meal. My empathy for Domotor increased with every passing hour. Those first seventy hours in his hideout had been rough. At least he had a washroom and kitchen. I calculated how long he could survive on the food stocked in his refrigerator. His continued freedom still amazed me.

I tried to sleep, but my empty stomach complained, and Doctor Lamont's offer of using her shower tempted me. The floor plans of the four levels of Inside matched for the most part. Quad C4 was dedicated to the power plant, and Sectors D4, E4 and F4 contained living areas. The biggest difference between level four and one was the water tanks.

Sectors B4 and H4 housed large water-storage tanks, while on level one those sectors held the laundry and the waste-water treatment plant. The infirmary for the scrubs was in Sector H2 along with the care facility.

I had limited my excursions to the upper levels to avoid being detected, but I remembered seeing the uppers' infirmary on level three Sector B. To gain access through the air shafts, I would need to climb into the Gap. My tender hip would be a problem.

I still wore the upper's student jumper. Could I stroll through the upper levels as if I belonged there? More importantly, would I? Anne-Jade had worn Jacy's listening device in plain sight. Zippy appeared to be a regular cleaning troll. Even the decoder had an ordinary disguise as a timer.

Was a shower worth getting caught? No. But it was worth testing if I could travel through the upper levels without being recognized. A thin rationalization. And the Pop Cops wouldn't think to look for me up here. Right? Decision made, I searched for a good spot to leave Riley a note, hoping he wouldn't be too upset.

Before leaving the storeroom, I combed my hair with my fingers and let it hang down past my shoulders to cover the earring. I used the water in my glass to wash my face and rinsed the dried blood from my hands. A tool belt around my waist would appear odd to the uppers. Funny how I felt improperly dressed without its comforting weight, but all I had left was the decoder. It fit into a long pocket in the uniform's pants. Once I tucked the wipe board of password questions inside the top of my jumper, I was, at least physically, ready to go.

I mapped the shortest route from the storeroom to the infirmary in my mind, drew in a steadying breath and left the room. After a quick peek around the optical illusion of the hallway to check for people, I strode with purpose as if I had an important message to deliver.

A few uppers met my gaze and nodded, others ignored me and the three Pop Cops I passed didn't show any signs they recognized me. With my heart somersaulting in my chest, I arrived at the infirmary. The possibility that Doctor Lamont wouldn't be there didn't occur to me until I pushed open the door. The rectangular room duplicated the scrub's infirmary, containing a row of beds against each long wall, with a narrow path between them. But the privacy curtains hanging from a U-shaped metal track on the ceiling above the beds weren't included in the scrubs' room. Two beds were occupied with sleeping patients. A high counter arched from the back right wall next to a wide entrance.

When I was halfway across the room, Doctor Lamont bustled from the entry, carrying a tray. A slight hitch in her step indicated her surprise, but she smiled.

She gestured toward the back room. "I'll be there in a minute. I need to give Izak his meds."

I aimed for the door. Shelves filled with medical supplies hid behind the high counter on the right. Through the entrance was an examination room. Stainless-steel instruments glinted in the harsh light. I balked at the threshold. The flat table covered with a black pad, straps and stirrups reminded me of my first medical examination.

Scrubs were required to have a complete physical at fourteen centiweeks. No part of my body had been left unexamined. I shivered at the memory of the cold probes. The Pop Cops claimed the exam ensured the scrub's heath and ability to perform the job they had been assigned.

I jumped when Doctor Lamont placed her cold hand on my back, guiding me into the room.

"The surgery is over there." She pointed to a wide door on the right. "And my office is back here."

We entered a small alcove in the back left corner, which opened into her workplace. A far friendlier place than the last. My gaze was drawn to the oversized quilt hanging on the wall. Small squares of color had been sewn together in a pattern. I squinted and stepped back, trying to discern it.

She noticed my gaze. "It's a stethoscope."

The shape of the long tubes and round bottom became clear.

"You're wondering why a stethoscope." Her thin eyebrows arched as if inviting me to speculate.

"No. It's one of the tools of your trade."

"But why not a thermometer or a scope or a scalpel?"

"It's your quilt. I think you would know the answer better than me."

She laughed. "Yes, but I want your opinion."

I hid my surprise by focusing on the quilt. All the doctor's instruments were important. Each played a role. A stethoscope listened to a patient's heart and lungs. I imagined working as a doctor as patient after patient came through the doors. After a while, I thought doctors would view their work as just another job. How would a doctor make a connection with so many different people?

"You picked the stethoscope because hearing a person's heart beating is a…" I moved my hands as if I could pull the right word from my throat. "Treasured part of being a doctor. No one else can hear it unless they're really close to the person. By letting you listen to their heart, they're trusting you."

She nodded her head as if impressed by my answer.

"Am I right?" I asked.

"There is no right or wrong answer. You could have said it was my favorite instrument, which is also true. One thing I like to do with my stethoscope is listen to Inside's heartbeat." Doctor Lamont pulled it from her neck and handed it to me. "Go ahead. Press it to the wall."

Curious, I placed the ends in my ears. My left lobe throbbed when the instrument brushed the earring. Touching the wall with the round sensor, I braced for an amplified Hum. Instead, a distinct rumble sounded, alternating from louder to softer. A series of knocks also repeated in a steady beat. I returned the device.

"Interesting, isn't it? Our ears can't discern all those mechanical noises. To us it's just the Hum. Unnoticed until we make an effort to hear it. I enjoy listening to the different components of Inside's heartbeat. It comforts me." She swept her hand out in a dismissing wave. "Silly, I know."

"It's not silly."

"Well, I'm sure you didn't come here to discuss my quilt. I'm guessing my offer sounded more inviting with time."

"Yes."

"Any trouble on the way over?" she asked.

"None at all."

A tired sadness filled her olive-colored eyes. "I'm not surprised. People have been afraid to get to know others who are outside their families. The halls are filled with strangers."

Sounded liked the scrubs. "Why?"

"When noticed by the Travas, the friendship is immediately a cause for suspicion. The Travas view any group of people as potential rebels. Also, people are afraid of being reported. If you don't have a friendship with another, then when they get mad at you, they can't call you a scrub-lover and have you arrested."

I stared at her. If I exchanged Trava for Pop Cop, she could be talking about the lower levels.

She shook her head. "You don't want to hear about this. Wait here, let me check to make sure my clothes aren't all over the floor." The doctor disappeared through another door.

This place reminded me of a maze. I glanced around the rest of the room. Her computer occupied the middle of her neat desk, and two big armchairs faced it. A basket of toys sat on the floor. I knelt next to it and rooted through the meager contents. When disappointment stabbed, I realized I had been searching for Dada Sheepy.

"For my younger patients," she said behind me. "The

shower is clean, but I want a peek at your incision before your stitches get wet."

She led me to her suite. Bigger than Riley's, it had two bedrooms, a sitting room, a small kitchen and a washroom. I peeled the uniform down and showed her the cut. In the brutal glare of the daylights, the bruises appeared purple, and black thread held together a swollen and angry red line. I swayed and rested against the wall.

"Healing nicely despite your adventures."

I gave her a dubious look.

"Trust the doctor." She sniffed and eyed my uniform. "Shower. I'll bring you a bowl of hot soup and a change of clothes."

I removed all the devices and decoder and hid them under a towel. The warm water felt wonderful despite the sting of the soap. When I finished, a steaming cup and a clean jumper waited for me as promised. I could get used to this attention.

Perhaps I could let Trella die in the air shafts so Ella could remain here.

"Better?" Doctor Lamont asked.

"Much."

"Your room's on the right. Get some sleep."

My room, I repeated in my mind. My room. With a narrow bed and single table with lamp, it wasn't elaborate or even special. But it was a rich luxury compared to sleeping in the barracks. The mattress springs creaked when I sat on the bed. Fun. I bounced, enjoying the feel. The bunks in the lower levels were cushioned with thin mats. Not that it mattered to me, I could sleep in an air shaft. But this was the first time I felt a real difference between the uppers and lowers.

If my parents hadn't abandoned me, would I be living in

a similar room? Would I be happy? I imagined my life before the whole mess with Domotor. Would I trade that life for this? Yes. But trade my life now? No way.

As I stretched out on the bed, I worried I would be spoiled and unable to sleep in the vents after spending time here. For once, I decided to enjoy the moment.

Riley's insistent voice roused me from a dreamless slumber.

"...need to speak with her."

I stepped from the room feeling stronger and followed the voices to the doctor's office. Riley sat on the edge of one of the armchairs, leaning forward as if ready to launch himself across the desk. He sprang to his feet as soon as he spotted me in the doorway.

"You *are* better. When I saw your note..." Riley glanced at the doctor.

"He thought your condition had worsened and you sought medical help." A glint shone in her eyes. "He didn't believe me."

"Do you know how long it took her to trust *me?*" he asked the doctor. "I couldn't imagine Ella risking so much for a shower."

He had a point. Normally, I would be very suspicious of the doctor's motives. But my regular instincts no longer felt right. All I thought I knew had been wrong.

"Not just a shower," Doctor Lamont said, "but a bowl of my famous soup. And I'm sure she's ready for another serving." She winked at me as she left the room.

An awkward silence descended.

"I'm sorry you worried," I said.

He smiled. "It's not all bad. At least now I know to offer you a shower and soup if I need you to trust me again."

With the tension broken, I settled into the other armchair. "You were talking about others when I first came in. Do you have any news?"

"They're being difficult. The near miss before has convinced most of them it won't work, but they're willing to at least listen to you." He paused in thought. "If the doctor is agreeable, I can have the others come to the infirmary at different times, complaining of a headache or something. You can talk to them here. It wouldn't draw as much suspicion and we can still keep our room a secret."

His plan made sense.

"And it avoids having the group members find out about each other, making it safer," Riley added.

Domotor had done the same thing, yet four people had been recycled. Keeping the others ignorant sounded logical, and my initial reaction was to agree. But the notion clanged. The atmosphere of the upper levels mirrored what the Pop Cops tried to do to the lower levels. Keep to yourself. Trust no one. Report your fellow to gain favor. I fell for it. From my ease in traveling in plain sight, I knew the uppers had fallen for it, too.

And so had the scrubs. Before.

Before what?

My thoughts raced over the last four weeks. They had kept my secret despite enticements and threats from Lieutenant Commander Karla. The kitchen scrubs worked together to stow the food for Domotor in the air shaft. Jacy and his buddies. Logan and Anne-Jade. They never would have risked themselves before.

Before...Broken Man and the promise of Gateway. He gave them a reason to join together and risk themselves for another.

"No," I said. "It will fail."

"What do you mean?" Riley asked.

The doctor came in carrying a bowl of soup, but I had her full attention. I wondered how much she had heard or what she suspected.

I answered his question regardless of the doctor. "Keeping everyone separate won't work. They all need to know who is in the group. They need to talk and make a connection." I looked at the doctor. "Hear each other's heartbeat, and know they're all risking themselves for the same reason. It's too easy to report a name. Or to give up when you don't know who you're letting down." I glanced between Riley and Doctor Lamont, willing them to understand.

"She's right," the doctor said. "If you don't hear a heartbeat, it's easy to send the body to be recycled."

"Full disclosure?" I could see Riley struggling with my complete reversal.

"Yes. And we can start with the doctor." I turned to her. "You saved my life and performed surgery in a storeroom because Riley asked you to. Why?"

Taken aback, she frowned. "He's the son of a friend."

"You know him."

"Right." She relaxed a bit.

"But you don't know me. You suspect I'm the missing scrub, so why not report me?"

"Again, for Riley."

"But you offered me a shower and a bed."

"Don't forget the soup," Riley said.

I shot him a look.

"What? I'm trying to help." He feigned innocence.

"Yes, and soup. Why?" I asked her.

"Curiosity mostly. Your strength is remarkable. The fact that you're up here instead of at the wrong end of a kill-zapper is impressive. I want to know why you're here. And, I wanted to get to know the person Riley would risk his life for."

"You wanted to hear my heartbeat?"

She smiled. "You're going to overuse that analogy, aren't you?"

"It works, though."

"Yes, it does and, yes, you're right."

I drew in a breath. "If I ask you for more help, would you be willing?"

She considered. "It depends on what you need."

"We need a meeting place and we think the infirmary would be ideal."

The doctor stiffened as a guarded expression blanketed her face. "What for?"

Time to slide down the chute. The scrubs needed Broken Man to rally around, and in order to be successful, the uppers would need someone, too.

Locking gazes with her, I said, "So we can coordinate our efforts in opening Gateway."

She gasped as all color flew from her face.

Riley elbowed me. "The whole heartbeat thing—does it work in reverse? 'Cause I think the doctor's heart has stopped."

"You…found it?" The doctor gripped the edge of her desk.

"I know where it is, but opening it is going to be difficult, hence the need for help. Are you willing?"

"Of course," she said without hesitating.

A meeting time was set and Riley planned to contact the uppers with the details. Before he left the infirmary, he gave me a narrow metal box as long as my hand. The number ninety-eight was on the digital readout.

"So you can listen to the bug in Karla's office," he explained. Then he paused as if struck by a notion. "It works the same as the receiver Anne-Jade made. With the batteries, that's the smallest space I could cram everything in." He touched the earring. "That's some serious tech. We have nothing like that up here. The Travas don't encourage invention."

"Then we have an advantage." I hoped it would be enough.

I kept Riley's device close by, but no sound emanated. Karla must be off-shift or elsewhere. I also worried because I hadn't heard from Jacy in a while. Feeling stronger, I paced around the infirmary.

Finally, Doctor Lamont said, "If you're going to be in the way, you might as well help me." She showed me the supply cabinet behind the high counter, and asked me to organize the contents. "In an emergency, it saves precious time."

The shelves bulged with various sizes of bandages, packages of sutures, tape, splints and packs of gauze all heaped together. As I worked to put order to chaos, uppers stopped in, seeking medical treatment or advice. Most ignored me. But on occasion, Doctor Lamont would ask me to help with a patient. If they asked, she introduced me as her new intern, Ella.

At one point, Lamont placed a bin full of clean bandages next to me. "Can you roll those when you have time?"

"Sure. With such exciting tasks as these, I'm surprised you don't have a ton of students volunteering to be your intern," I teased.

"Watch it or I'll have you scrubbing bedpans."

"Rolling bandages right now, Doctor." I saluted her, and exaggerated my enthusiasm for the task.

She laughed. I liked the sound of her laughter. Light and carefree and warm. She wasn't quick to laugh; grief clung to her skin like perfume but hadn't doused her empathy for others.

Around hour forty-five, my energy level dropped. A nap was more appealing than the last three shelves. I sat on the floor, resting my back when a shrill voice broke through my drowsiness.

"Doctor?" A woman's panicked voice.

I stood as Lamont rushed past. A very pregnant woman clung to the door. Her face ashen, she swayed on swollen feet. Bright blood stained her pants.

"My water broke," she said.

Lamont held her elbow and half carried her. I rushed to support the patient's other side.

"It's not supposed to be red, is it?" she asked.

"Where's your mate?" the doctor asked.

"Won't come. Too hard." The woman slurred her words. We reached the exam room.

"Surgery?" I asked.

"Not yet. I need to determine what's the matter."

Hoisting her onto the table, I grunted with pain, but soon forgot about my injury as the woman's condition worsened.

Lamont shouted orders to me and the patient. I fetched bandages and sterilized instruments.

The woman groaned and shuddered. "The baby wants to come out."

"Not yet. Hold on a little longer."

Doctor Lamont examined the patient and I held her hand. She squeezed my knuckles so hard, I thought she would crack my bones. The hand-crushing grip came every minute and was accompanied by moans from the woman.

"Contractions," the doctor said. "Flip that switch there." She pointed to a wall and I extracted my hand long enough to comply.

"Surgery now." Lamont pressed a pedal and the table sprouted wheels.

We rolled it into the surgery.

"Don't you need more help?" I asked.

"Called with the switch. He should be here soon." She launched into a flurry of instructions, leaving me no time to think.

The events blurred together. Another upper arrived and I had two people yelling orders at me. The woman's cries mixed with the loud bawl of a newborn. And somehow I ended up out in the exam room, holding a swaddled infant while the doctors attended to the woman in the surgery.

If Cog could see me now, he would be incapacitated with mirth. At least, the baby was asleep. Although I marveled that she could sleep after what had happened to get her out. The doctor had said the placenta blocked the birth canal and the woman needed an emergency C-section.

The baby weighed the same as Zippy, my small cleaning troll. More than I expected. I peered at her tiny face and wondered what name the woman would give her. Naming a person seemed a huge responsibility. In the lower levels, the scrubs handed their babies over and the Care Mothers assigned them names.

The male doctor bustled from surgery, peeling off bloody gloves. "She'll be fine. Thanks for your help." He came over and examined the baby. "The mother doesn't want to see her." He took a small bottle from his breast pocket. Unscrewing the strange rubber-topped lid, he withdrew a thin glass tube. "Hold her still," he instructed as he opened one of the baby's blue eyes. He squeezed the rubber and a drop of liquid splashed into her eye.

She startled and blinked. The doctor quickly doused her other eye, and retuned the bottle to his pocket. He held out his hands. "I'll take her now."

As he settled her in the crook of his arm, she opened both eyes wide and gazed at me with brown eyes. I almost stumbled. He had changed her eye color! Is that what Domotor meant when he had said I had been born with my father's blue eyes?

Doctor Lamont wheeled the woman from surgery, and I helped transfer the patient from the table to a bed. The woman cried in silence. Tears flowed down her temples and her mouth gathered into a tight grimace.

Lamont stroked the woman's head and squeezed her hand. "It'll be all right. The baby's healthy. She'll do fine."

Nothing the doctor said eased the woman's misery. When we returned to Lamont's office, she collapsed in a chair behind her desk and opened a drawer. Taking out a small glass and a bottle filled with an amber-colored liquid, she poured herself a drink. She considered, then reached for another glass and poured another albeit smaller portion.

"Sit down, Ella. Your performance in surgery was exemplary." She pushed the second glass toward me as I settled in the opposite chair. "Most people would faint on seeing so much blood, and to see the inside of a person's body."

I sniffed the contents of the glass. The fumes stung my

eyes. "I tried not to think about what it meant. Just followed orders."

The doctor sipped her drink. I copied her, and almost spat the burning liquid out. She chuckled. "Haven't had spirits before?"

"No. My friend did once, but he wouldn't let me try it." Good thing, too, or I would have yelled and brought unwelcome attention.

"It's an acquired taste. The burn down your throat and the numbing warmth in your stomach become a pleasant experience."

Knowing what to expect, I swallowed the second sip without choking. The doctor rested her head on the back of the chair, closing her eyes.

"I do have a question," I ventured.

Without opening her eyes, she raised her glass in a swirl. "Go ahead."

"Why is the woman so upset?"

Her eyes snapped open and she fixed me with an incredulous expression. "You don't know?" Seeing my evident confusion, she straightened. "Aren't the women in the lower levels upset when they give their babies away?"

"Some are, I guess. But this is the upper level. You have families."

Understanding smoothed her sharp features before lines of grief deepened. "Yes, we have families, but, up here the rule is one couple, one child. We don't have enough room for more people, so if a couple has an accident and conceives another child, the child is sent to the lower levels."

The unexpected information slogged through my brain. Had she just said the child was sent to be a scrub?

The doctor continued, "The woman is upset because the baby is her second, and the infant will be sent to a care facility in the lower levels."

19

ONCE I UNDERSTOOD, THE DOCTOR'S EXPLANATION
slammed into me, shattering my beliefs. "Uppers are only
allowed one child?" The foreign concept refused to find an
empty seat in my logic.

"Yes. We have limited space, so the Travas have made it a
law." The doctor peered at me in concern.

Perhaps if I broke down her information into manageable
bits. "You mentioned the couple having an accident. How
can getting pregnant be an accident? If you have sex, you're
bound to have a baby in time."

"We have birth control, Ella. Women can choose if they
want a baby or not. I'm guessing by your horrified surprise,
scrubs don't have that option."

The revelation made perfect sense and yet made no sense
at all. My mind grappled with it. It explained why Riley only
saw his brother once, why he had said you don't *have* to have
a child, and it meant perhaps my mother hadn't abandoned
me. I could have been a second or third child—an astound-

ing notion! Finally Domotor's comment about my blue eyes made sense.

"Those drops?" I asked.

"Drops?"

"In the baby's eyes."

"Oh. To change the color so the babies blend in with the scrubs and don't get teased for being different."

It didn't always work. I mulled over what she had said about birth control. Why not let the scrubs use birth control? With the overcrowded conditions getting worse every hour, why not limit the number of children born?

"Ella, are you all right?" Doctor Lamont stood beside me. She placed a cold hand on my forehead. "You lost all color in your cheeks. Take another sip of your drink."

I gulped the spirits, welcoming the harsh sting as it ripped down my throat. I asked Lamont why scrubs weren't offered birth control.

"Truthfully, I'm surprised they don't. The uppers have assumed scrubs don't cherish their offspring. That they keep having babies because they don't have to care for them. Basically, we all thought the crowding in the lower levels was your own fault." She returned to her seat. "Interesting how certain facts have been ignored in the computer. Or deleted."

I mulled over the ignorance on both sides. The results created two groups of people who distrusted each other, which would be ideal if you didn't want them to join forces. Again my contemplations looped back to why they let the scrubs grow in number.

We did the grunge work, but even if we limited births, there still would be plenty of scrubs to work. Another theory popped into mind. "Is the birth control hard to make? Or of limited quantity?"

"Not really. It's grown in hydroponics. You only need to ingest it when you're planning to be intimate." She jerked her head as if struck with a sudden thought. "You didn't seem concerned about your damaged ovary. Was it because you don't want children?"

"Yes. I'm not going to be intimate with anyone so that—" I waved toward the infirmary "—doesn't happen to me or to a child."

We discussed various reasons the Travas would allow the scrubs to increase in number, but we couldn't find a logical explanation.

"I'll ask LC Karla next time I see her," I joked.

But Doctor Lamont's demeanor turned to ice. "If that woman was injured, I would not save her life. In fact, I would happily feed her to Chomper myself." She stood and strode from the room, claiming she needed to check on her patients.

While I agreed with the doctor about Karla, I wondered what the LC had done to cause such a strong reaction from a caring individual.

The meeting with the uppers who'd agreed to help us convened in the doctor's sitting room at hour sixty. Riley and Doctor Lamont stood apart from the group, who talked among themselves in low whispers, getting acquainted and reminiscing about prior events. Riley's father, Jacob, kept peering at his son as if amazed the boy was there.

After learning about the uppers' birth control, I had wanted to discuss so much with Riley, but the group arrived and we had limited time.

Takia Qadim was the most vocal and spoke for the group. "Why will this attempt work when our first one failed?" Her sharp and intelligent gaze focused on me.

I willed my heart to stop its panicked thumping, and reminded myself about the need for full disclosure. "First we already know where Gateway is." A mixture of expressions spread over the four uppers. I waited for the information to sink in.

"Second, we have access to the other hidden files. One led us to the location, and I'm reasonably sure the others will tell us how to open Gateway and what to expect on the other side."

"Why do you need us?" Hana Mineko asked. Her black hair had been piled on top of her head in a pleasing twist of curls. She fiddled with a curl hanging by her ear, pulling it straight and releasing it. The hair sprang back each time.

"When Gateway is open, it will alert all the systems in Inside, and we need you to cover the alert so the Controllers and the Travas don't know. Once we know exactly what to expect on the other side of Gateway, then we can plan how to use it."

"Why don't you know what's in the rest of the files?" Takia asked.

"They're protected by passwords. We haven't figured out the rest of them yet." A rumble of alarm rolled through the uppers. "We have the password clues, and I hoped as a group we could deduce the answers."

"Let me get this straight," Jacob said. "Provided you open the files, we then have to hide your activity from the Trava family while you open Gateway." He looked around. "You're going to need to recruit more uppers."

"We have two scrubs willing to ghost through the

network and aid in hiding data. And don't forget Domotor."
As long as he listened to Logan's instructions.

Breana Narelle pulled her shirt down over her pregnant belly. "Four people were recycled last time because Domotor was caught. This time we all know who's involved. What if someone here is the person who ratted us out?"

"We know who spied for Karla and she hasn't been invited back. Obviously you don't say anything to anyone, but especially not to Kiana Garrard," I said, proud I didn't stutter over her name. It's possible she hadn't abandoned me, but she still caused much pain and suffering.

Most of the group nodded with understanding, but Jacob flashed the doctor a strange, pain-filled look, which she returned. I wondered if they both knew Kiana.

"Why should we risk our lives for the scrubs?" Breana asked. "They hate us and are jealous of us. They won't do anything to help us. Why should we help them?"

I counted to ten before answering her, reminding myself she has been fed lies about the scrubs all her life. Then I explained to the group just how much the scrubs had done to get me here. The ghosting through the network, Cog's sacrifice and Jacy's risks as well as the amazing fact that not one scrub has yet to provide information to the Pop Cops despite the fantastic rewards offered by the LC.

"The Travas are our mutual enemy. They have lied to you and to the scrubs to keep us from joining together. Think about it. The scrubs outnumber the uppers ten to one. But you have control of the systems keeping us alive, and the Travas have control of us both. Teaming up takes the Travas out of the equation. We can return to the times when each family had an equal say."

My speech worked and the uppers set about planning. They wanted to hear the password clues and I read them aloud. Two questions produced answers right away. Six left. I repeated the first question and everyone brainstormed.

During an unusual lull in the conversation, LC Karla spoke from my pocket. Terrified faces turned to me and I hurried to explain about the listening device and Riley's receiver. I retreated to my room to hear the conversation better.

"…another busted scanner? That's three this shift. Something's going on," the LC said. Her voice strained with frustration.

"It can't be sabotage. No scrub was allowed near them. They were guarded the entire time by my men," a man said. His voice sounded familiar.

"Eyes on the devices? Or an ensign stationed outside the supply cabinet?"

"Why would it matter?"

"The scrubs are using the air shafts to get around, you idiot!"

"Lieutenant Commander, no one is in the shafts. The RATSS have found no evidence."

"I saw her with my own eyes, *Commander.*" Karla's tone was even, but each word had a little kick to it as if she bit back her anger.

She was talking to Vinco, the knife-wielding bastard.

"I believe you. But she's not there now. She's hiding with this Broken Guy. We need to entice her out," Vinco said.

"I've tried. I promised to not recycle her friend if she turned herself in. It didn't work."

"Perhaps we need to find someone she cares for more," Vinco said.

"She has no other friends. The general opinion is she's

a loner and detests being among the scrubs. Not that I blame her."

"She might think you're bluffing about her friend. Schedule him for execution. Parade him down through the lower levels on his way to Chomper's Lair, take him inside and kill-zap him if she doesn't give herself up."

"And if she does?"

"Contact me and I start the interrogations." I shuddered at the delight in his voice.

"Then what should I do about her friend?"

"Keep him alive. He's fun to play with."

"What time should I schedule him?"

"Before the hundred-hour assembly."

"All right. Go spread the word, Commander."

The sound of a shutting door echoed through Riley's metal box. I stared at the clock. Hour sixty-two. Thirty-eight hours to turn myself in. Yet another countdown. I felt as if I had already grieved for Cog, either that or I felt more confident of our success.

I rejoined the others. They had answered another two questions. Four left.

"What's the one about turning something in?" Takia asked me.

"Oh. It's number six. It's *What do you turn to get the outside in?*"

A discussion ensued, producing the same answers I had. Riley sat in the midst of them, adding his own arguments to the debate. But Doctor Lamont kept her place along the wall. Her pale face appeared strained. I walked over to her.

"Do you feel all right?" I asked.

She gave me a wan smile. "Isn't that my line?"

"When you look as white as the lady sleeping in the infirmary, it's a valid question."

"Just tired." She pushed away from the wall. "I better check on her and make sure there's no internal bleeding." Doctor Lamont hurried from the room.

That's all the poor woman needed, I thought. She had lost so much blood; I hoped she wasn't bleeding on the inside.

Daylights flooded my mind. Of course, how stupid! I punched the wall. Everyone quieted and stared at me.

"I know the answer to number six!" I cried.

"Don't keep us in suspense," Riley said.

"Inside out! You turn the inside out to get the outside in."

The group worked another hour, then each left at different times. We had answers, or what we thought were the correct answers to six out of eight questions. Not bad. I turned on my button microphone and hoped someone was listening like Jacy had promised. I sent a message, asking Jacy to bring Logan to Domotor's hideout at hour eighty-one. His hidden room would be the best to access the network without interruption and without Pop Cops looking over his shoulder. I toggled off the microphone.

Riley returned to his workstation and Doctor Lamont rested in her room. Exhaustion pulled at me, but the doctor had asked me to watch over her patients while she slept.

They all appeared to be asleep, and I wasn't sure I would even know if they were in trouble. Watching them sure beat scrubbing air ducts. At one point the woman moaned and I rushed over. Lamont had left a few pain pills by the patient's bedside in case she needed more.

"Are you in pain?" I asked.

"Yes," she said. Her voice was thin and weak.

"The doctor has pills." I moved to get her a glass of water, but the woman grabbed my arm.

"A pill can't ease this kind of pain. Can you sit and talk to me?"

"Sure." I pulled a chair beside her bed. We sat in uncomfortable silence for a while.

"What's your name?" she asked.

"Ella."

A half smile played on her white lips. "That's it? No family names?"

"Oh. Ella Garrard Sanchia."

"Still no mate, then?"

"No. I'm Doctor Lamont's intern." I pulled on my sleeves, reminding myself to tread carefully and watch what I said.

"Did you... Did you see her?"

Only one possible "her." The baby. "Yes. She is beautiful."

"Really?" The woman bit her lip.

Instinct took over my voice box. "She has long dark eyelashes and already a full head of hair. Her face was a perfect oval, her chin came to a little point with a dimple. Skin so smooth and as soft as the underside of a sheep's ear." My surprise matched the woman's. I'd held the baby for minutes, yet I could form a lifelike picture of her in my mind's eye.

Unfortunately, my description caused the woman more pain. Tears flowed and her chest heaved in quiet sobs. Feeling terrible, I tried to ease her anguish. "Don't worry so much. She will be loved in the lower levels. The care facility is broken into units of ten children per Care Mother. The Mothers love all the children and she will grow up with care mates, who will look after her. I'm sure one of the older boys will become very protective, and she will fuss about his attention but be his staunchest supporter."

The woman stared at me as if I had sprouted wings. I didn't know what caused me to say so much. At least I didn't lie to her. Care mates could be very protective.

Instead of questioning me on how I knew so much, the upper sighed in relief. "What do you think they'll name her?"

"Hmm… She'll need a pretty name, but not too girly as I think she'll be a bit of a tomboy."

"Gillie? I always liked the name."

"A good choice."

We discussed Gillie's life, her toddler years, her schooling and her career.

"I think she might gravitate to working in the care facility. As a helper to start and then as a Care Mother," I said.

By this time, the upper's tears had dried. She smiled proudly. "Yes, I'm sure she will love the little ones and have enough patience for the active three-hundred-week-olds."

"And the nice man who works in recycling, you know, the one who made her those metal flowers?"

"Do you think he wants to be her mate?" she asked.

"There's not much time or material to make those petals for just anyone. He's interested."

We talked through Gillie's life from start to finish, including all her accomplishments and major life events. The woman fell asleep with a dreamy half smile still on her lips.

I remained by her bedside. Cog would be amused by my efforts to comfort an upper. No. Not amused. Proud. I liked Ella. She was a good sort, much nicer than Trella, and I hoped she managed to survive the next thirty hours.

Doctor Lamont woke me. I had been dozing in the chair. "Sorry," I said.

"No, I'm sorry. You had a hellish twenty hours and I left you to watch my patients."

"You need to sleep, too." Memories of the emergency replayed in my mind. "I don't know how you could be so rational with all the blood gushing, and being able to cut through her stomach...." My own stomach rolled and I had to put my head in my hands to stop the swirl of dots in front of my eyes.

"But you were fine during the crisis. I've had to step over interns who had passed out during surgery."

"Like I said, I didn't think about it."

Lamont pressed her fingers to the woman's wrist, checking her pulse. "Poor Doreen. She's in for a rough time. Losing a child..."

She stared at the wall, but her gaze peered into another world. "The loss lingers inside you, clinging like beads of moisture until rust forms and spreads. Eventually, the structure can't hold the weight and it collapses."

Her description had to come from experience. Not knowing what to say, I again let instinct guide my words. "I hope she finds another way to support the weight and keep the rust at bay. It would be a pity for her to live her life as an empty shell, when she has a mate and another child to care for."

The doctor snapped out of her reverie. "It would be, but words are easy. It's convincing the heart that's hard. Get some sleep, Ella."

I did as the doctor ordered and slept for the next eight hours. Feeling almost normal, I ate a large portion of a three-bean casserole Lamont had cooked. She had access to the same ingredients as the lower levels, but her concoctions tasted better.

After enduring a lecture to be careful, I climbed into the air shafts above level three. The tight duct was at once comforting and oppressive. An unfamiliar moment of panic washed over me. I ignored the flood of doubts and fears that soaked me. It was just like being in the surgery, if I stopped to think too much about what we planned to do, I would be unconscious.

The trip to Logan's barrack lasted twice as long as normal. My movements were slow and my muscles protested being used after such a long time. I paused every few minutes to listen and search for RATSS. The mechanical clicking of their metal rollers echoed through the vents and I managed to dodge two devices.

Logan waited for me by the heating vent near his bunk.

"What about your Pop Cop?" I asked.

"He thinks I'm sleeping." Logan grunted as he squeezed into the vent.

I led him to Domotor's room. It had been over a hundred hours since I'd been there and I hoped he was well.

Slumped on the couch, Domotor's drawn face relaxed a bit when he saw me sliding from the vent after Logan.

"Where have you been? What's going on? I'm a wreck, jumping at every noise."

Dark smudges under his eyes stood out in contrast to his pale face. His uncombed hair hung in greasy clumps. An overripe smell emanated from his body.

He noticed my expression. "I didn't want to be caught in the shower. I do have my dignity."

"Not to worry," Logan said. "I covered your computer trail just in time." He aimed for the computer and pulled a chair close to the keyboard. "Trella, what are the passwords?"

For a moment, I felt as if he talked to another person and I didn't respond.

"Passwords?"

As if waking from a dream, I cleared my head and repeated the ones we had figured out. "We still have three unanswered, but at least we'll get some information."

"What about the teeth one?" Logan asked.

"Forty-one."

"I'll plug in the others first and see what happens."

Domotor struggled into his chair and wheeled it over to watch Logan. The images and numbers on the screen meant nothing to me. Trusting Logan would extract the needed data, I checked Domotor's food supplies. Low. He would need more and soon. With so many RATSS I doubted the kitchen scrubs would risk discovery by filling the air shaft again.

Perhaps I could raid the pantry when everyone attended the hundred-hour assembly. But I remembered I would either be in LC Karla's custody by then or perhaps I would be Outside. The strange thought of being somewhere else kept slipping away. With nothing to compare to, I couldn't even imagine it. To me, Outside resembled Inside with no Pop Cops and with more space.

I planned to touch base with Riley, and coordinate the opening of Gateway during hour ninety-seven. But first, I needed to uncover it.

After cleaning Domotor's washroom and bedroom as best as I could, I joined them. Huddled over the keyboard,

Logan's eyes were lit with a childlike glee and even Domotor seemed thrilled. They turned to me with identical grins.

"What?"

"We know," Logan said.

"Outside. Look." Domotor pointed to the screen.

My stomach boiled as I peered at the image. Green and blue jumped out, but I blinked and the details became clearer.

"It's like hydroponics," Logan said. "But the plants are huge and the sheep's special grass is all over the place. Look at the ceiling, it's blue and goes on forever."

"Does anyone live there?" I asked.

"I don't quite know. The text states numbers and details for things like breathable air mixture, compatible food source, mineral deposits, drinkable ground water and some-thing called wildlife. Which, as far as I could tell, are animals without any real intelligence."

"In order to obtain the information, someone has been to Outside." Even though thrilled with the news, I wondered how long ago the data was collected. Everything changed with time. "Can you find out when?"

"No. The information was pulled from various files and dumped together. A few sentences are incomplete, and the topic changes abruptly. Some of the files are damaged and I can only read about half of what's in them."

"It doesn't matter when," Domotor said, dismissing my concern. "Most likely it was before the Travas took control. Perhaps after the scouting mission, the Travas panicked, thinking they would lose power in such a big place. We know it's safe to go to Outside."

"And we know the code to open Gateway." Logan

typed at the keyboard and numbers marched across the computer screen.

I committed the code to memory.

"Something else…" He pointed. "Colored buttons. Green to open. Red to close. Any ideas?"

"To get back to Inside," Domotor said. "There would have to be controls on Outside. Proof that no people live there or they would have opened the door by now."

He had a point.

Finally, Logan announced he had no more useful info. "Wish we had those last three passwords."

"What about the file with my birth week on it?" I asked.

Domotor glanced at me in surprise. "There's a file with your birth week on it?"

"And the hour of her birth. I forgot about that one." Logan's fingers flew and he hummed to himself. A white screen flashed and he paused for a second. "Uh…Trell, you'd better read this. It's from your mother."

I backed away. "She couldn't have… No way to know I would be involved… A trap?"

Domotor leaned closer to the screen. "No. She admits the chances of you finding this letter is little to none." He continued to read. "It's similar to a diary entry. Written more for herself than you, explaining what had happened. Interesting… A confession. Why didn't you tell me Kiana was the spy?"

I plopped on the couch. "A lot has happened since I last saw you."

"Do you want to know her reasons for—"

"No. Four people were recycled because of her. I've no desire to hear her pathetic excuses."

He frowned at me. "Someday you'll want to know."

"Then I will ask you. It's not important right now—she isn't one of the uppers who have agreed to help us."

Domotor brightened when he heard this, and I explained what I had been doing in the upper levels, but I didn't tell him Doctor Lamont's name or Riley's cousin. He knew of the others, but those two were new. Despite my conviction that Kiana was responsible for my father and Riley's mother's fates because she had spied for the Travas, Domotor had been the one to name them.

"Excellent news," he said when I finished updating him. "Just imagine, we'll open Gateway and usher out all the scrubs and uppers who want to go, leaving behind the Travas with no one to rule."

I laughed at the humorous picture.

After I escorted Logan back to his barrack, I borrowed a few supplies from maintenance, filled my tool belt and headed to the Gap. With visions of blue ceilings and grass rugs filling my mind, I didn't stop until I reached the outer wall near Quad G1—Gateway's location.

I removed my new flashlight and shone it on the insulation. The thick yellow foam rippled on the wall, and I couldn't see any marks indicating a doorway underneath. Starting at the southwest corner, I sprayed water from the floor to level two's support beams and worked my way to the left. Made from vegetable starch, the biodegradable foam dissolved and dripped. It didn't take long to realize two bottles of water wouldn't be enough. One meter thick foam had been sprayed onto the wall.

When the bottles were empty, I pulled the insulation off. The bottom layers were brittle and easy to break apart with my new screwdriver. Logan had said Gateway would be between three to four meters from the corner. I planned to clear at least five meters.

The air around me cooled as I worked. My breath made clouds, but the cold felt good against my sweaty skin. Foam piled on the ground, and I reveled in the effort.

Bits of foam clung to my student's uniform and hair. I stopped well past four meters. Panting in the icy air, I grabbed my light. The beam lit specks of floating insulation. My attention focused on the exposed wall as I swept the light across the surface.

Its appearance matched the interior walls—metal panels riveted together with support beams. No obvious doorway. I searched for a near-invisible hatch.

Nothing.

I drew in a deep breath. Once again, I scanned the wall, but this time I started from the corner and concentrated on each section in a systematic way.

Nothing.

Emotions soured, but I ignored them. We had coordinates and codes and pictures. I ripped another meter of insulation from the wall.

Nothing.

We had uppers willing to risk their lives and knew which colored buttons to use to return to Inside. Another meter piled on the floor. I choked on the dust, but pulled off another half meter convinced it would be here. It *had* to be. Otherwise, I would have made the worst mistake of my entire life. Believing before seeing. Another meter landed on the pile.

Nothing.

I lost track of how long I worked or of how many

meters of wall I exposed or of how many times I scanned the wall. My body transformed into a machine with one task: find Gateway.

Eventually the fuel was depleted and the machine broke down. It was unable to complete its task. There was nothing to find.

20

I HAD NO RECOLLECTION OF LEAVING THE GAP, OR
the trip back to Riley's storeroom. My body felt insubstan-
tial as if crushed into powder and reduced to a layer of dust
to be sucked up by a cleaning troll.

Rooting under the couch, I pulled Zippy from his hiding
place. Tufts of dust clung to his brushes. I hefted the troll,
cradling his weight. The hunt for Gateway had been a whirl-
wind. A thrill of risks, and I had been swept up by the excitement. I had allowed myself to believe in something that
didn't exist. Gateway.

Cog. I'd already decided to lie and tell him we found
Gateway. It would give him a moment of joy before Vinco
played with him again and the Pop Cops recycled him.

I resisted the urge to hide in the pipes. Instead, I sat in the
storeroom, savoring an ill humor with the hope I could build
up an immunity to it and form another metal layer around my
heart. The first one was ill-wrought and had cracked with ease.

"What happened?" Riley stood over me.

I stared at him in confusion.

"You were supposed to report back to the infirmary hours ago and tell us the content of those files."

The files. I almost laughed. We'd been duped. Domotor had to be a Pop Cop spy.

"Riley, forget about the files. Gateway doesn't exist. It's all a big con. The Pop Cops planted those files and sent Broken Man here to see who they could get to fall for it. It's just a matter of time before we are arrested."

He rocked back on his heels as if slapped in the face. "Wait. You didn't say you were going to Gateway."

"Logan showed me a picture of Outside and I was... excited." I could have substituted *stupid, naive* or *brainless.*

"Really? What did Outside look like?" Even knowing Gateway didn't exist, Riley couldn't contain the excitement in his voice.

"Doesn't exist, remember? It was just a picture."

He sat next to me on the couch. If he wondered why Zippy was in my lap, he didn't show it. "Are you sure about Gateway? Were you at the right location?"

"I cleared at least six meters of insulation off the west Wall outside Quad G1. From the floor to the next level."

"Those files are old. Perhaps the coordinates are wrong."

"The age of the files is all part of the scheme."

"What about Logan? Is he part of the ruse?"

If Domotor duped me with ease, so could the others. "I don't know anymore. I guess those who don't get arrested are in on it." Karla and the Pop Cops must be enjoying the show. I wondered when they would spring their trap on us.

Riley wrapped his arm around my shoulders and pulled me close. I sank against him, breathing in his warm scent.

"Let's not jump to conclusions," Riley said. "You're suspicious of everyone. Domotor would have had to be a heck of a liar to convince you to help him."

"Deep down I wanted to believe. I probably saw what I wanted instead of the truth."

He rubbed my arm. "I don't know. It's a pretty complicated setup. The Travas don't have the imagination for it. Unless someone else is involved or something else is going on."

I straightened. "The Controllers?"

He frowned. "It's possible."

"Do you know who they are?"

"No. When I think about them in a logical way, I believe they don't exist. The Travas desire control of all systems, and I don't see them obeying orders from mysterious Controllers. I'm sure they invented them to have someone to blame when things don't go well. However, when I access the computer network, I feel like I'm being watched. That every time I go into the system I lose a part of myself, and when I'm done I have a horrible headache. Sounds silly. My dad says the pain is from eye strain."

"It's not silly. I wish I knew why someone went to all this trouble. Maybe Karla will grant me a last request and explain it all to me." Doubtful, but a girl could try.

"Don't say that."

"Why not?"

"Because we'll figure it out."

I didn't share Riley's optimism. Instead I checked the clock. Hour ninety-four. Six hours until Cog's final walk, until I...

No. I wouldn't think those thoughts. At least, not yet. Riley's arm remained around me. I set Zippy on the floor and turned toward him. My sudden desire to be closer to

Riley drove out my scary future. Our lips met. A wave of heat rushed through my body as we kissed.

He pressed against me; his hot hands splayed on my back. Wherever our bodies met, tremors vibrated on my skin. I twined my fingers in his hair.

Too soon, Riley pulled away. "My break's over." Regret flashed in his eyes. "I need to get back." He stood. "Don't do anything rash. Don't go anywhere. Please. You're safe here." He hesitated as if he wanted to say more, but instead, squeezed my arm then hurried away.

When the door clicked shut all warmth fled my body. Reality returned and time continued. My dreamy thoughts solidified and I planned my next move. I would have to find the perfect spot to approach Karla.

My head throbbed. I stared at the opposite wall, counting rivets. Twenty for each sheet of metal. No more, no less. The builders of Inside had never deviated from their plans. No creativity. No surprises.

However, the Pop Cops had managed quite the surprise with a fair amount of creativity. Impressive.

Time marched like Pop Cops on patrol. I located my scrub uniform balled up in a corner of the room. The musty-smelling fabric was stiff with dried sweat and blood, but I pulled it on anyway. No need to dress up for the Pop Cops. I covered the large hole and biggest bloodstain by ripping a part off the student's uniform and tying it around my waist. My goal was to get as close as possible to Karla and Cog before some other overenthusiastic Pop Cop arrested me.

I debated about bringing the microphone and receiver. Should I tell Jacy the bad news? He could be working for the Pop Cops. Yanking the earring from my lobe, I set it on Riley's desk with the button. No sense letting the Pop Cops find the technology on me.

Hour ninety-nine. Time to go. I glanced around the room, memorizing the details, and decided to write Riley a quick note. The words refused to come. I scrawled an inappropriate thank-you and an "I'm sorry for causing so much trouble for nothing" message.

Back into the air shaft, I proceeded to the lower level not caring if RATSS spotted me. I reached the bottom without encountering a single one. Figures.

As I crawled through the duct, a strange droning noise vibrated the metal. It grew louder as I drew closer to the vent. Scrubs packed the hallway below. In a few places, scrubs stood three deep on each side, leaving a narrow space.

Pop Cops tried to get them to move, but stubbornness radiated from tight jaws and hard eyes. The hundred-hour assembly bell rang—a faint ring compared to the general murmuring. Again, Pop Cops demanded they report to their assembly locations, screaming and harassing the scrubs to no avail. I wondered how long it would be before they started stunning people. They seemed reluctant to pull their weapons. I wondered if they feared a panicked stampede if they started shooting.

I stayed in the duct until I found a location without Pop Cops. When I dropped to the floor, the closest scrubs jerked in surprise, but soon they beamed at me. The line of people shifted, creating an opening my size. Sliding into the spot, I swallowed, trying to push my heart back down to its proper place, but it refused to budge, choking me.

While waiting for a sign of Cog, my body felt as if it

held too much water. My nose dripped and tears blurred my vision. I concentrated on the floor, counting the lines of rivets. If I couldn't see and was barefoot, I could probably navigate through the hallways of Inside by feeling the little bumps. At least, Inside's predictability would benefit the blind.

The sudden jolt of insight felt as if I'd just connected two live wires in my brain. I had the answer to question number three, *Your eyes can see, but mine don't work, yet I see what you can't. What am I?* It was the reason I couldn't find Gateway.

The noise level rose to my left, and Cog's head bobbed through the crowd. I gasped when he came into view. New bruises covered his swollen face, patches of blood soaked his coveralls and his hands were cuffed behind his back.

But the most astonishing aspect was his smile. He grinned at everyone.

I leaned out past the scrubs. Four Pop Cops led the way, pushing back the edges of the crowd, and four were behind him. Lieutenant Commander Karla wasn't there. Instead, Lieutenant Arno followed the procession.

I turned to a woman on my right, and stood on my tiptoes so I could talk into her ear. "Can you take a message to Jacy for me?"

She nodded. Her face pale and serious. When I told her the message about Gateway she gazed at me in frank astonishment.

"It's very important," I said. "Promise?"

When she promised, I stepped into the middle of the corridor. An angry frown replaced Cog's smile as soon as he spotted me.

"I found it," I yelled over the buzz and babble of many voices.

I knew he couldn't stay mad. His whoop of joy rang through the hallway. Everyone stopped talking. The silence became an eerie almost living presence.

The Pop Cops in front finally noticed me. They shouted and pulled their stunners.

Maximum damage, I thought and rushed them. The element of surprise was the only reason I managed to knock one of the Pop Cops over. I yanked his gun from his hand and stunned him.

"No one recycles Cogon!" I yelled, pleased the ad hoc battle cry rhymed.

Then everyone moved as if my shout were a signal. Scrubs overwhelmed the rest of the Pop Cops, taking their weapons and knocking them down. A short and brutal attack. I gaped at the unexpected turn of events.

The chant rippled through the lower levels. *No one recycles Cogon*.

It didn't take long for the scrubs to overpower the Pop Cops. A few scrubs were stunned, and little blood was shed on both sides. Cuffed with their own handcuffs, the Pop Cops huddled in the middle of the dining room. All the tables had been pushed back and scrubs surrounded Cog, slapping him on the back.

Cog organized teams to secure entrances. Every resident of the lower two levels had come to level one for Cog.

Understanding ripped through me as I watched them look to Cog for answers, for plans on what they should do next and for praise.

Broken Man wasn't their prophet, Cogon was the true prophet of Inside.

Karla made a huge mistake in wanting to parade him

through the scrubs as an example. The Pop Cops had grown overconfident and now her lieutenant knelt with the rest.

After a few minutes, I pulled Cog aside.

"Can you believe this?" Cog gestured to scrubs nearby.

I had been surprised, but shouldn't have been. The signs had been there; I was too wrapped up in my own problems to notice.

"They think I know all the answers." He shook his head in amazement, then sobered. "We can't hold out for long. The uppers control everything but the food. All they need to do is send gas through the air shafts or shut off our air. Unless…" He shouted at one of the maintenance crew to install air filters in the ducts. "Now tell me everything about Gateway," he ordered me.

"Yes, sir." I dodged his playful swat, then told him how we discovered the location from the files. "I need to get a few supplies to be absolutely sure Gateway is there."

"I'll come along," Cog said.

"You can't fit through the shaft."

He laughed. "Trell, you're still thinking we need to sneak around. Hank," Cog yelled.

A large maintenance scrub hustled over to us. "What do you need, boss?"

"A hole."

Raiding a maintenance closet, we found the needed items and climbed through the air shaft. A huge section had been cut open, revealing the Gap above. Hank and his team muttered in amazement and wanted to ask questions, but the urge to hurry pulsed through my veins. The scrubs might have filters, but they wouldn't last without fresh air.

I raced through the Gap. Cogon kept pace despite his size. We stopped at the uncovered west Wall. I shone my flashlight over the exposed metal, counting to twenty.

Rows and columns of twenty rivets. Starting from the corner and moving right.

Twenty. Twenty. Twenty. Twenty. Twenty. No deviations. Twenty. Twenty. Twenty. No creativity.

Twenty. Twenty-two. I found the blind. A sheet of metal covering Gateway. I pointed and Cog pulled a chisel from his tool belt and removed twenty-two rivets from each side. The metal blind had been connected to the wall for so long, it remained in place despite the removal of the rivets. Inserting the edge of a crowbar Cog pulled with all his strength. Then moved to another spot.

The metal groaned and squealed and finally dropped down. A loud clang echoed throughout the Gap. We didn't care who heard it.

Behind the sheet was Gateway.

Wild joy shone on Cog's face. An ecstatic sizzle pumped through my veins. Gateway even appeared different than a regular door with its rounded corners and a black substance shoved into the crack between the door and the wall. The bulging substance ringed the entire door and was smooth and hard. When I tapped it with my fingernail, it didn't clang like metal but produced a solid thumping sound.

Cut from one piece of metal, the door also lacked a knob or latch. But a small computer screen had been installed next to it. I pressed my ear to Gateway. Nothing to hear, but the Hum. The icy surface sucked warmth from the side of my head.

I pulled away. Now I knew why Inside was always heated. Outside was cold.

"Do you know how to open it?" Cog asked with a reverent tone in his voice.

"I have a code. But the uppers will be alerted."

"Trell, there's been a rebellion in the lower levels. I think the uppers are probably a little busy helping the Pop Cops to restore order. Besides, I doubt we'll get another chance."

Good point. Steeling myself, I touched the screen. It grumbled and grunted as if I had woken it from a deep sleep, then it glowed. Squares with numbers shone from the display.

With my heart slamming, I typed in the number code and hit the enter button. For a moment, nothing happened.

Then a horrible sucking noise sounded and Gateway's door sunk in first before swinging to the side with a loud squeal of protest. Weak light emanated as a puff of stale air blew in our faces. We coughed.

Nothing jumped out. Water did not flood Inside. No unknown substance oozed through. No strange beings flew through. No voices called or cheered in welcome.

Only a small room waited within. I stepped in and flinched. Silence greeted me. I looked around. A light panel on the ceiling illuminated the empty, metal rectangle-shaped space, which had another Gateway. No screen was next to this new door, just a panel of oversize square keys lit from underneath with different colored lights. One red button remained unlit.

Cogon joined me. His face showed his disappointment until he spotted the other door. "Do you have another code?"

"No. Logan didn't mention this little surprise. We couldn't open all the files." One of the keys glowed green. "But he did say green to open and red to close, perhaps that was for this part." I pressed the green button. Nothing happened.

He stared at the lights. "Ten buttons with ten colors. Perhaps…" He pointed to the one on the far left. "This one is the number one. Assuming they're in numerical order, you can try the code for the outside door."

I pressed the first number/color and the light under it turned off. Then I inputted the rest of the numbers, noticing that none of the numbers repeated. Nothing except the remaining key lights turned off.

"Or maybe not," Cog said.

After a few seconds, the lights returned.

"Perhaps the numbers are in descending order." I tried again. Still nothing. "Or, the numbers start with zero and go to nine."

This time all the numbers darkened—except the green one.

"Green to open," Cog said, and pushed it.

The door behind us hissed closed. The green light pulsed. A sucking hydraulic noise sounded, but the other door remained shut. Cogon pushed on it to no avail.

I struggled to pull air into my lungs. No one knew the code to enter. We could be trapped in here. I felt light-headed and my insides bloated as if I had eaten too much.

Cog turned, leaning on the door. The panic on his face matched mine. He clamped his hands to the sides of his head as if holding his skull together.

Without a sound, the other Gateway opened. Pure black waited on the other side. A bone-killing cold reached us. White spots sparked from the blackness, but it was hard to know if they were real or not. Black and white spots swirled in my vision. My eyeballs felt as if they would burst.

My stomach dropped and spun as if I fell from a tall ladder. I glanced down to see my feet no longer touched the floor, but floated. Cog twisted and his body drifted past the door. He pointed.

The red key burned bright. Red to close. On the edge of unconsciousness, I reached for the button. But Cog was Outside. I needed to help him.

He gestured again, but I didn't press it.

Cog threw his hammer. It sailed toward me as he somersaulted backward. Then the darkness claimed me.

21

I WOULD LIKE TO HAVE SAID THAT I WENT TO A BETTER place. However, the skin-freezing cold woke me. Dumped onto the floor of the small room, I untangled my legs and stood. My skin felt stretched and saggy. I wanted to crawl under a heavy layer of blankets to press my body tight. Red fog tinted my vision.

The outer Gateway was closed, but the door to Inside was open. The panel of colored lights glowed brightly and I wanted to smash them into tiny bits. Cog wasn't with me and I doubted he'd made it through the door in time.

No way could he survive in that airless, weightless…void. But I had to try. No living with myself unless I tried. I punched in the first few numbers.

"Stop!" a most unwelcome voice ordered.

I ignored Lieutenant Commander Karla, getting in another two numbers before she stunned me. A wall of energy slammed into my body. My last thought was of Cog.

★ ★ ★

The next time I woke, my situation hadn't improved. Rows of black bars, the stench of unwashed bodies, excrement and fear and the hard metal bunk underneath me all clued me in. I was under arrest and incarcerated in the holding cells.

When Commander Vinco arrived with the LC at his heels, I wished I had floated away with Cog.

"Just so you don't think you'll be rescued by your scrub friends, we have secured the lower levels," LC Karla said. Her lips flattened into a pleased smile that didn't reach her eyes. "Do you want to know how?"

"No." The truth. The game had ended badly. Cog was gone. Outside didn't exist. Nothing was left that Trella cared for. Ella, on the other hand, planned to keep her mouth shut.

"You've been rather busy these past four weeks." Vinco sounded impressed. "A little scrub like you, causing so much trouble." He tsked. "Finding the portal and opening it. Of course you paid a price. I'm going to miss my stubborn sturdy friend." He pulled a knife from his belt. The edge gleamed in the sick yellow light.

My pulse reacted to the threat out of habit, but I remained in my reclined position.

"She had help," Karla said. "She couldn't have found the space around the levels, hidden Domotor, stolen from my office and stitched the knife wound on her hip by herself. She's not that smart."

"You underestimated me. Don't feel too bad—it's a common mistake." I waved my hand in a dismissive gesture.

Vinco crouched down to my eye level. "You *will* tell us where Domotor is and who helped you."

I couldn't believe they'd failed to find Domotor. The game might be over for me, but there were a few others still able to do damage. I repeated my vow to keep my mouth shut.

Vinco straightened. "Key?"

No keypads here. Bored inmates could find the code by trial and error.

He grabbed the ring of keys from Karla. The light jingle sent a vibration of dread up my spine. The snap of the cell door's lock increased the terror. By the time he stood next to me, my body shook.

A beeping sound emanated from Karla's belt. She cursed and toggled on her communicator. "What?"

Vinco paused and I hoped she would talk for a long time. But she flipped it shut and flashed me an annoyed frown. "I'm wanted elsewhere. Do you need me?" she asked him.

Yes, I thought. Need her.

"No. I'll show her what I can do first. Then we'll come back and ask questions."

"Fine." She turned on her heel and left.

The slam of the door echoed in the room. No blankets or pillows or anything soft to absorb the sound. I pushed up to a sitting position, thinking to fight or maybe even escape around him. Maximum damage.

But Vinco's reactions were as sharp as his knife. He grabbed my arms and pushed me back on the bunk. Using his weight to keep me down, he pulled my hands behind my head and through the bars.

The click slide of handcuffs snapped around my wrists, trapping my hands. Feeling completely vulnerable, I twisted. Fear pulsed through my veins, and I clamped down on a plea.

I would not give him the satisfaction of begging for mercy. I would not whimper or utter a word.

He smiled in anticipation and proceeded to demonstrate with the tip of his knife just how much pain he could cause—a considerable amount.

True to his promise, he never asked me a question. Instead he remained quiet, taking pleasure in my screams. Screaming and yelling weren't weeping or pleading—a difference I clung to with a tiny bit of pride.

I lost track of time. Moments of burning pain mixed with excruciating pain and gaps of dull throbbing pain. Karla came and went. Vinco's knife danced on my skin.

They asked questions and I refused to answer, and we all settled into a routine. I disconnected from the fear and terror. Growing a metal barrier in my mind, I kept my emotions walled off. The visits tapered and my screaming sessions were further apart. Something was happening to keep the Pop Cops busy. Karla's insistence on knowing who I worked with grew more frantic.

The clang of a door roused me from a mindless stupor. I glanced around, but no Vinco. Confused, I raised my head and peered into the other cells.

The Pop Cops had locked up another person.

Riley stared at me with horror-filled eyes. I groaned.

"Are you all right?" he asked.

"What do you think?" I couldn't suppress my sarcastic remark.

"I think you look like something Chomper has chewed on and spat back out."

"Such sweet sentiment, lying to me to avoid hurting my feelings."

"At least you still have your sense of humor."

I let my head drop back onto the bunk. "How many have been caught?"

The silence pressed on me, but I didn't have the energy to look and decipher Riley's expression.

"Do you mean from the scrubs' revolt? They've been confined to the barracks and are only allowed to leave in small groups supervised by well-armed Pop Cops. No one's been arrested yet. I believe Logan and Anne-Jade are hiding with Domotor. Cog is missing."

I avoided the inevitable conversation about Cog. The rest was nice to hear, but not what I wanted. "I mean of the uppers. You, obviously, have been caught, but what about Doctor Lamont and the others?"

"Oh! I'm here for talking back to a commanding officer. Ten hours extra duty and ten hours in the brig."

Relief flowed through my skin, helping to calm the angry welts.

He continued, "No upper has been implicated. Karla's people have been so busy in the lower levels it took me three smart remarks to three different officers to get punished."

Shame Vinco wasn't needed below. But then his comment sunk in. "You *wanted* to get arrested?"

"Since I don't fit through the vents, it's the only way to talk to you. Logan and Anne-Jade have been busy." He huffed with amusement. "Anne-Jade's been wearing the Pop Cop uniform and delivering these devices—little anti-stunners shaped like belt buckles. It deflects the energy from the stunner somehow."

I smiled at his awe-tinged voice, but couldn't share his en-thusiasm. Time to burst his bubble. "Riley, we opened Gateway. Outside is nothing. A great big black place of nothing. Cog is gone. He's out in the nothing. No reason to resist the Pop Cops. No escape from Inside."

Silence and more silence. Perhaps I shouldn't have been so blunt.

"Sorry to hear about Cog," Riley said. "I wish I could have met him. He sounded like a great guy."

"He was. The scrubs revolted because of him. Now they don't have him or Gateway."

"But they have you."

I tried to laugh, but it turned into a coughing fit. "So do Karla and Vinco. Don't think I can do anything for the scrubs, but keep my mouth shut and hope Vinco's knife slips." Slips into my neck and ends my time here. During our last session, I'd lost my grip on my metal barrier and almost told Vinco everything.

"You are the reason I'm here," Riley said. "If you remember, I didn't get involved to find Gateway. But to find a way to improve living conditions in the lower levels. I talked to Doctor Lamont and there is a way to even things out between uppers and lowers. The Force of Sheep is worried about being caught, but they're also motivated."

"Why?" I figured they would do what they had done before and lay low.

"Because of you."

"Me? You've got to be joking."

"You're right. I am. It's really because of Sheepy. How he risked his life for them, and how he showed them that scrubs are real human beings who care and want the same things in life. Opened their eyes to the fact the Travas are our mutual enemy."

"Sheepy's a great guy...er...sheep."

"He is. But he's going to be mutton chops soon if he doesn't fight back."

Energized I raised my head and glared at Riley. "Hard to fight back when I'm cuffed to the bars."

"Your legs don't work?"

"Vinco's built like a tank. Have you tried to resist him?" I demanded.

"Yes. If you remember, extra duty is being Vinco's sparring partner. Except he has a weapon and you don't." He rubbed his left forearm.

I remembered Riley's bloody sleeve. "Then you know how hard it is."

"I never said it would be easy. Giving up is easy."

I grumbled.

"Vinco isn't very smart. If you do decide to try resisting, there is a package for you in the heating duct right near the vent."

"Who—?"

"Logan rigged Zippy to deliver it to you."

"Hard to get it out with solid iron bars acting as a vent cover."

"Think about it," Riley said.

I grudgingly realized Logan would know about the bars and had probably packed the gift so I could pull it through. I wiggled my fingers. My hands felt swollen, and my wrists felt as if the metal cuffs had ripped off my skin.

"All you need to do is free yourself from those cuffs," he said as if commenting on the food in the cafeteria.

"The Force of Sheep don't really need me. You have

Logan for the computer stuff and Anne-Jade building anti-stunners. In fact, by staying here I'm keeping Vinco and Karla busy for you."

"That's mighty nice of you. But don't you think you've suffered enough? Or do you still feel guilty for Cog's loss?"

I sputtered, fuming. "You act like I can just saunter out of here. I didn't ask to be tortured. If it were up to me, I'd have been Chomper's dinner hours ago."

He sighed. "It's going to be hard to tell Sheepy that Trella has given up. To tell him that fierce, spunky scrub I first met is gone."

I refused to comment.

"Poor Sheepy will be sad. He'll miss his best friend."

"He's a toy, Riley. He'll get over it."

He remained quiet for a moment. "You're right. He will recover. But you've gotten a lot of other things wrong."

Now it was my turn to sigh. Here we go again. "I don't have the energy to argue anymore. My throat hurts." Every word burned and my dry tongue kept sticking to the roof of my mouth. I rested my head on the bunk and closed my eyes.

"Then just listen to me. I'll tell you all the things you're mistaken about. First, you're not going to be able to resist Vinco much longer. Cog eventually broke. He's the one who named you and told Karla that Domotor was still alive." He paused, probably to let the news sink in.

No wonder Cog had been so frantic when I had visited him the second time. But I couldn't blame Cog for anything. He suffered enough for me.

"Second, you're wrong about no one needing you. The Force of Sheep has been working to infiltrate the security systems, but they need motivation only you can provide. Doctor Lamont needs her intern back, and I need…"

I waited, but when he didn't continue, I looked up. He sat on the bunk in his cell with his face in his hands. We both startled when the heavy clang of metal sounded as the main doors to the holding cells were unlocked. For me, it meant Vinco returning for another dreaded session.

Riley jumped to his feet and stared at me through the bars. "Whatever I say to the commander about the scrubs and you is all a lie. Understand?"

A wedge of bright light grew between the doors.

"Yes." Before he could turn away, I asked, "What do you need?"

"I need you. I need to give you a proper kiss. I need you to be my mate." His words were a harsh whisper, but tenderness shone in his eyes. Nothing like the shock that must be in my own.

The door swung wide, slamming into the wall. Vinco eyed Riley with disgust. "What're you in for, boy?"

"Telling Lieutenant Arno to go screw himself, sir."

Vinco laughed. "That takes balls, boy."

"Well, I didn't know there was a scrub in the cells, sir. Otherwise I would have been nicer. Don't you think being so near one of them is cruel?"

I bit my lip, remembering Riley's words about lying.

"Worse than extra duty with me?"

"Yes, sir."

The commander chuckled again. "Okay, boy. You can work off the rest of your brig time. Ensign Hollis," he called, "release Mr. Ashon."

Another man entered and unlocked Riley's cell. Glad to

see him free, I watched him leave, but all pleasant thoughts disappeared when the door shut and I was alone with Vinco.

He entered my cell and began his work. Jabbing me with the tip of his knife, I recoiled. With my pain-addled mind, I was surprised when a plan to escape formed. Not a great one, but better than being Vinco's playmate.

During a particularly intense bout, I shouted, "Enough. I'll talk." I tried to ignore the satisfied smirk as he drew back.

"I'm listening," he said.

"I'll show you where Domotor is hiding on level two. It's all I know, honest."

A doubtful, but interested expression creased his ugly face. "Tell me."

"Can't. The entrance is hidden. It's easier if I show you. You'll need to bring bolt cutters."

He considered and I tried to appear pathetic and weak. Not hard to do, considering I was pathetic and weak.

"Okay." Vinco unlocked my cuffs.

Burning pain shot through my arms as I moved them, sitting up turned into an effort of will. I rubbed my hands together, avoiding my blood-soaked sleeves.

"Come on." He jerked me to my feet.

I swayed and stumbled against him. He shoved me away in disgust. As I fell I grabbed his stunner from his weapon belt. Aimed for his chest. Pulled the trigger. A grunt of surprise and he collapsed on the floor with a wonderful thud.

The effort left me winded. After a few huffs of air, I stepped over Vinco's unconscious form and knelt by the heating vent. Nothing visible through the bars, I slid my hand inside. My fingers brushed cloth and I pulled a narrow bag from the duct. Tied with string, the sack contained a number of useful items—a sparkly metal cutter, Logan's decoder, bandages, a bladder of water and a handful of protein nuggets.

I ate the nuggets and downed the water. My stomach rebelled for a moment, but I kept the food down by pure force of will. I would need the energy.

Pulling off my mangled uniform, I wrapped the bandages around my arms, legs and torso. I stole Vinco's shirt. It fell to my knees. I also snatched his knife and stunner, leaving the kill-zapper on his belt.

Coated with diamond dust, the metal cutter sawed through the bars. I worked as fast as I could, but it still felt as if hours had passed. Every sound caused me to jump. Finally I finished the last bar and slid into the vent. Making sure I didn't leave a bloody trail, I hurried to…where?

Only one place to go—Doctor Lamont's. The warm air inside the shaft sucked at my energy. I used our storeroom on level four to switch to the air shafts and then to the Gap. The space between levels felt as it always did, hollow and un-occupied. I thought the Travas would have it filled with Pop Cops by now.

I dropped into Doctor Lamont's office, thumping hard on the ground. She showed little surprise when she came to in-vestigate.

She bent over me. "Can you walk to the treatment table?"

Now that I had arrived, all my cuts throbbed and burned for attention. I nodded and she helped me stand, keeping a hand on my elbow as I wobbled to the table and collapsed on top of it.

Starting with my legs, the doctor unwound the bandages.

She clucked and tsked and cleaned the cuts. I, in turn, cringed and winced and hissed in pain.

"Four need stitches, and that's just your legs." She crossed to her supply table and filled a metal tray with various instruments, including a needle and thread. "This first." Handing me a glass of water and a small white pill, she gestured for me to swallow it.

"What's it for?" I asked.

"Sleep. Unless you want to be awake when I stitch your injuries?"

I popped the pill into my mouth, wasting no time. After all the hours spent with Vinco's knife, I had no desire to feel metal sliding through my skin ever again.

It didn't take long for the room to soften and for shadows to gather in the corners of my vision. Soon a blanket of black settled over me as I slipped into a dreamless heavy sleep.

LC Karla's voice woke me. I nearly groaned aloud. My escape had just been a dream! But through slits in my eyelids, I discovered I still lay on the exam table. However, I had been wheeled into surgery. A sheet covered my body up to my neck. Blood stained the cover in the area around my midsection, and a mask rested over my nose and mouth. Some kind of soft cap held my hair.

Doctor Lamont argued with the LC beyond the double doors. "You can*not* go in there," she said. "You are not sterile and could cause a horrible infection."

"We have a dangerous scrub on the loose and you're worried about an infection?" Karla asked in amazement.

"I haven't seen this scrub. I told you no one is here but me and my patients. And Ella, of course."

"Why is she in surgery?" Karla demanded.

"Appendicitis. In fact, if I don't finish the surgery soon, she could die."

"Then you should want to cooperate fully with our search." The surgery doors banged open and Karla's voice sounded right next to me. "I'll be quick, Doctor, so you can return to your patient."

22

I LAY STILL AND KEPT MY EYES CLOSED. KARLA'S HEAVY
footsteps sounded all around me followed by the clang of
metal hitting metal.

Doctor Lamont pressed her fingers into my neck as if
checking my pulse. "Do you want to search the *incision,* Karla?"

The sheet near my hips bunched as if she gripped it. I held
my breath, terrified Karla would call Lamont's bluff, but at
the same time impressed by the doctor's courage.

"I'm not amused. You should be offering your assistance
to find this scrub. Remember your history, *Doctor.* Cooperation saves lives."

"Why should I cooperate? I don't have a child for you to
hold over me anymore. You've seen to that."

Interesting. It explained why Lamont hated the LC so much.

"I'm sure I can find another you care for. Your intern
perhaps? How long can she survive with a burst appendix?"

"Get out." Lamont's icy voice sliced as sharp as a scalpel.

"I've hit a nerve. Kiana, you're way too caring of others.

No one will miss a few of them. We have plenty more below."

I wasn't sure of Lamont's reply because my thoughts reeled over Karla calling the doctor Kiana. But I was sure there had to be more than one person named Kiana in the upper levels. The lower levels had a number of scrubs with the same name. Plus the coincidence would be too great.

Of course the clues all added up. The doctor's queasy expression when I named the spy during the first Force of Sheep meeting. Her pointed glance with Riley's father. The fact she was a friend of Jacob's from their training days. But the odds I would be the one climbing around the pipes and getting involved in the search for Gateway and that I would find Riley were huge. Unless…

It wasn't a coincidence. Domotor had sought me out, claiming my reputation as Queen of the Pipes drew his notice. It had been a setup from the start.

I had lost track of Karla and the doctor. The room remained quiet and I risked a peek. No one. I waited and soon enough Lamont entered. Her flushed face and tight grimace softened once she saw me.

"Karla and her cops are gone. How long have you been awake?"

I pulled the mask from my mouth and sat. "Long enough, *Kiana*. Were you going to rat us all out at once or wait until I'd healed enough for Vinco to have fresh skin to gouge?" Wrapping the sheet around me, I tried to slide from the table.

She blocked my way, pushing me back. "Oh, no, you don't."

"You can't stop me." I struggled to sit up.

Kiana jabbed me with a needle. "Yes, I *can* stop you."

Liquid fire coursed through my veins, erasing all desire to fight. I wilted and dropped into oblivion.

I knew I hated examination tables for a reason. When I woke from my drug-induced sleep, I was strapped to the table and unable to move. A few of the cuts on my body pulsed with pain, but otherwise I felt all right. For now.

Voices murmured in the infirmary, and I wondered if I should call for help. Knowing my luck, it would be Karla and Vinco so I kept my mouth shut.

I turned my head at the sound of footsteps and was shocked by Riley's arrival. He looked ill at ease, tugging his shirt and glancing everywhere but at me. I closed my eyes to keep from crying. How many times have I been wrong? You would think I'd cease to be surprised.

"Ella, are you all right?" he asked.

"My name is Trella. My friends…" I swallowed. Yes, I had friends, damn it. "Call me Trell. How long have you been planning this?"

"Ah… She just contacted us. Doctor Lamont said she needed us to help you understand. Understand what?" he asked.

My eyes flew open and I gaped at him.

He gasped. "Is it about your eyes?"

"What's wrong with my eyes?"

"They're blue."

Alarmed, I asked "What the hell is going on?"

"I don't know!"

"He is owed an explanation, too," Jacob said as he entered the room with Doctor…Kiana following.

"So why isn't he strapped to a table?" Sarcasm rendered my voice sharp.

"Because he isn't full of new stitches," she said.

"What did you do to my eyes?" I demanded.

"I returned them to their original color to help disguise you. Riley said you might be an upper sibling. Since the reversal drops worked, you must be."

"Why would you bother? Is it going to make you feel better when you betray us?" I asked.

"Dad, what's going on?"

Riley's father sighed. "You both know about the Force of Ten and Domotor. What you don't know is exactly how the group was betrayed nearly eighteen hundred weeks ago."

"Nolan…my mate…" A hitch interrupted the doctor's words before she continued. "Nolan grew too confident. He had discovered the information about Gateway and Outside and was putting it into protected files when the Travas found out. He was…arrested and tortured but refused to name anyone else as an accomplice even when the Travas threatened me and our daughter."

I turned my head to stare at the wall, bracing for the rest of the story.

"I wasn't so strong. Lieutenant Commander Karla, who was an ambitious lieutenant back then, merely threatened to recycle my daughter and I blabbed. Told her about Domotor and agreed to spy for them to keep my mate and daughter alive. When the arrests were made, they…"

Silence. Then Jacob picked up the story. "Karla didn't keep her bargain. Father and child were recycled as well as three others. Riley, you should know Domotor named me as a member, but your mother convinced the Travas she'd used my port and was working alone."

"Why didn't you tell me?" Riley asked.

"She made me promise to keep you safe and to not put crazy ideas into your head. Ramla didn't want you to know." He huffed in tired amusement. "She knew any more attempts by the uppers would fail. Yet look at what has happened from a chance encounter."

I glanced at Jacob. He looked hopeful.

"Why don't you call yourself Doctor Garrard?" Riley asked.

"The name is too painful for me. After Karla recycled Nolan, I returned to my mother's family and used her name." She met my gaze. "I'm trying to amend my past deeds by helping you. I knew once you heard my real name, you wouldn't listen to me. That's why I invited Riley and Jacob here."

I mulled over their story, searching for hints of deceit. "I'm not so sure about the chance encounter. Domotor did seek me out in the lower levels."

"That's because you knew how to travel through the pipes," Riley said.

The others nodded as if this explained everything.

They didn't know I was Kiana's daughter. They didn't know I was alive. Still, the story seemed too pat. "But what about the loose vent cover in the storeroom? Someone had to sabotage it."

Riley flushed. "That's my fault."

We all stared at him and his cheeks reddened.

"Uh…I wanted to meet one of the cleaning scrubs, so I… I did push the couch underneath, but even though you missed it you didn't get hurt…well, not too bad, and…" At a loss for words, he finally stopped.

I glanced at them. But couldn't decide whether to trust them or not. Not like I had any other options at the moment. Although I planned to keep the information about my birth parents to myself. Even with my eyes blue, Kiana hadn't recognized me. For once I knew something the rest did not.

When I had healed enough for the doctor's approval, I entered the air shafts and headed toward Domotor's room. I brought as much food as Lamont could smuggle without raising any suspicions. The duct was free of RATSS because the scrubs kept the Pop Cops busy with small revolts.

Jacy relayed the details of the resistance to me through the earring/receiver. Interesting how the Pop Cops generated more problems when they clamped down harder on the scrubs. The scrubs also stopped working and cleaning. Dirty laundry spilled over bins in Sector B1, piles of fertilizer and items to be recycled grew into large mounds.

I arrived at Domotor's room without any trouble. The prophet sat on the couch surrounded by bits of metal. Anne-Jade and Logan worked together at the table. They all stared at me as if seeing a ghost.

Logan whooped and ran over to me. "You escaped!" He hugged me.

"Easy," I said as his arms brushed several healing cuts.

"We thought you didn't. What took you so long?" Anne-Jade asked.

"Overprotective doctor." I tried to explain about the uppers and the Force of Sheep, but they already knew more than I did. "What's been going on?"

"I'm getting good at traveling through the ducts," Logan

said, "and Anne-Jade's been wearing the Pop Cop uniform so much the others are calling her Ensign Mineko." His brow creased. "They keep close track of the scrubs, it would make sense that they would keep even closer track of their own people."

"They're glad to have the extra help," Anne-Jade said. "Besides, just because the Travas have control of Inside doesn't mean they are smart enough to know all their weaknesses." She smiled with a predatory glint in her eye. "Weaknesses we can exploit to the fullest."

"But don't get too cocky," I said, thinking of my father. "The Pop Cops have, and see what's happening?"

"But it's all noise," Domotor said. "Travas control the computer systems. Despite these anti-stunners—" he flourished the metal piece in his hand "—another outright revolt will fail again. Although this time they might use poison gas instead of sleeping gas to subdue us."

"Won't happen," I said. "They need us."

"But what's to stop them from putting us all to sleep and then going around and kill-zapping the troublemakers?" Domotor asked.

Nothing. "Then we'd better get control of the computer systems. Logan?"

"It's going to take a coordinated effort from both uppers and lowers, but it's doable." He met my gaze. "And we'll need to get into the Control Room."

"Impossible," Domotor said.

"Why? We have one upper who works there," I said.

"All the overrides are there. One person isn't enough," Logan said.

I considered. All the high-ranking officers work there and

they were all armed. Probably had extra guards, too. No way to walk through the door. Air duct seventy-two was the best way in, but we could be picked off as we dropped down.

"Logan, do you have any anti-kill-zappers?"

"No, but I have Zippy." He hunted under the table and pulled Zippy from a pile of metal. "I've added another feature. Toggle this switch—" he pointed "—and Zippy will emit a pulse that should knock out their weapons."

"Should?" I raised my eyebrows.

"I haven't fully tested it yet. And he only has a short range."

"What about the computer systems?" Domotor asked.

"They'll be fine."

A full-out rebellion would take a major amount of luck and coordination. The Tech Nos and Domotor looked at me, waiting. No one else would be able to organize both sides. I drew in a deep breath. We had the technology, the intelligence and the people—put enough sheep together and you have a herd, a force to be reckoned with. We needed a leader.

"Anne-Jade, how many of those listening and receiving devices do we have?" I asked.

"Four."

"We're going to need seven more all on the same frequency, plus all the anti-stunners you can make."

"We'll need more supplies," Logan said.

"Make a list, I'll contact Jacy." He should be able to find a few skinny scrubs willing to make deliveries through the air shafts.

I made my own mental list of all the steps we would need to take. A daunting effort. Sadness gripped my heart. I wished Cog were here to help. He would be able to motivate the scrubs.

Maximum damage. It was the beginning of the end. Either we would fail or not. At least we could say we tried.

The Force of Sheep planned to declare war on the Travas during week 147,006 at hour sixty-six. After eighty hours of planning, of secret meetings, of setting distractions and false trails and of assembling illegal technological devices, we were ready.

At hour sixty-five, I crouched in air duct seventy-two with Zippy, waiting for the signal. Takia worked at her station. Even through the vent I could feel her nervous energy, and I willed her to stop looking over her shoulder. The atmosphere throughout Inside had been charged. Those who didn't know what was about to occur, still sensed the keyed-up feeling of expectation. The Travas had tripled the number of Pop Cops on patrol.

Twice as many Travas had assembled in the Control Room. Both the fleet admiral and the admiral studied maps over the conference table in the far corner. I knew to expect one admiral, but not both. Surrounded by computers, the captain occupied the center of the room. I checked Zippy for the hundredth time. So much rested on the little cleaning troll.

Various stations called in their readiness. Riley and the rest of the uppers had changed their shift times and managed to be at their workstations. Domotor and Logan ghosted in the network. Doctor Lamont prepped for casualties. Anne-Jade, Jacy and his gang waited to overpower the Pop Cops on the lower levels and I prepared to spring a surprise on the Control Room.

Jacy's voice sounded in my ear. "We go."

Warning lights flashed in the Control Room's panels.

Banks of computers lined three walls of the room, and uppers sat before them, leaving an open space in the middle for the captain's station.

"Call for help from Commander Vinco, sir," an upper called. "Scrubs are revolting."

The fleet admiral strode over to the captain. "Time to weed out the troublemakers, Captain," he said.

"Send reinforcements, alert the air controllers to prepare the poison gas canisters," the captain ordered. He typed on his keypad. "I've had it with these bothersome scrubs."

A spinning feeling of panic grew in my stomach.

"Sir? The air controller on duty just told me to blow the gas out my ass." Shock whitened the upper's face.

I suppressed a chuckle. Logan's voice sounded. "We're in."

All I needed to hear. I finished loosening the screws on the vent cover and pulled the cover inside the duct. No need to mask my noise as the upper workers reported one by one to the captain that the mechanical systems failed to respond.

"What do you mean not responding?" the captain demanded.

I lowered Zippy a few inches into the room and flipped the switch. No hum or spark, according to Logan the pulse would be silent. Still I would have felt better to at least see a flash. Trusting the technology, I yanked Zippy back.

The captain pounded on his computer. "Damn thing."

"Engage the override, we'll control the systems from here," the fleet admiral ordered.

My turn. I dropped down onto the fleet admiral. A few cries of alarm had alerted him, but all he had time to do was look up. We landed together in a heap. The stun guns from all the Travas aimed at us, but none of them worked. I wore one of Anne-Jade's anti-stunners just in case. Yanking my protected stunner from my belt, I neutralized the fleet admiral, the captain and the uppers working near the override controls.

It didn't take long for a flaw in my plan to become obvious. I needed more time to aim and shoot than I expected. The other uppers left their seats to join in the fray, grabbing for me. Takia remained at her post.

Outnumbered, it was a matter of time before I was unarmed. Stunned bodies littered the ground and a few uppers moved awkwardly with half-stunned body parts. Two men held my arms with tight grips. Not part of the plan. I was supposed to stun everyone and open the Control Room door from the inside.

The admiral remained by his station. He glanced at his stun gun in his hand, then tossed it aside. "Report," he ordered his team.

Except for the two holding me, the uppers returned to their posts.

"Override engaged, sir," an upper said.

"Lieutenant Commander Karla is at the door," Takia reported.

I suppressed a grin of triumph. The override would be knocked out as soon as the door opened and Anne-Jade, Jacy and his group stormed the room.

"Let them in," the admiral said.

Preparing to join in the fray, I braced for action. The double metal doors slid aside with a hissing noise.

My heart shattered and the men beside me grunted and supported me as my legs turned to liquid.

Lieutenant Commander Karla Trava stood at the door with Commander Vinco on her right side and Doctor Lamont, or rather Kiana Garrard on her left.

23

SPEECHLESS, I STARED AT MY MOTHER. DOCTOR LAMONT'S
expression fluctuated between fear and hope as she scanned
the faces in the room with a frantic intensity. She clutched
something with both hands. When she met my gaze, guilty
pain flared for a moment. I marveled at my own stupidity.
Even when we knew she had betrayed the last group of
rebels, she had conned us again.

Karla swaggered into the Control Room with a smug
smirk. Vinco followed with ten Pop Cops behind him. One
of them pushed Doctor Lamont into the room. The door
hissed shut with a thump that crushed the remains of my heart.

"Report, Lieutenant Commander," the admiral said.

"The lower levels are secured, sir."

"Excellent work. How did you manage it so quick?"

Karla glanced at Doctor Lamont. "We had a few hours'
notice."

"Well done. Braydon, send instructions to our men below
and have them separate the leaders."

"Yes, sir," an upper called, typing at his computer.

Takia remained at her post. Her fingers rested on her keyboard, and I hoped she countered the admiral's order.

The admiral pulled his kill-zapper from his belt and advanced on me. "I'm going to enjoy weeding out the first troublemaker."

I shrank against my captors, but they held me tight. My heart trembled when he pressed the nozzle to my chest. Hell of a way to find out if Zippy worked and neutralized the kill-zapper.

"Stop," Doctor Lamont shouted.

The Admiral paused. He frowned, turning toward the doctor. "Why?"

"She's the leader of this whole thing. She knows everyone involved. If you recycle her before you question her, you might miss a few troublemakers."

"Trella's proven resistant to torture," Karla said. "If you keep her alive, the scrubs will have someone to rally around." She scowled at Vinco. "Or she might escape into the pipes again."

He hunched his shoulders and ducked his head.

"She might become a martyr and you'll have more scrubs revolting," the doctor said.

"I don't care," the admiral said. His focus returned to me. "Clear." The men holding me let go. He pulled the trigger and I screamed. Nothing else happened. I swayed with relief.

My relief was short-lived. The admiral scowled, threw his weapon down and gestured for Karla's kill-zapper. She hadn't been here when Zippy had knocked the other weapons out. Hers would work.

Before he could press it against me, I smiled. "Go ahead. That one won't work either."

"She's bluffing," Vinco said. "If she's so confident, why did she scream before?"

I shrugged. "I was having a little fun." My voice remained steady despite my muscles turning to mush.

Vinco flashed his knife. "This will work." He grinned in delight.

Breathing was difficult, I sucked in air through my tight throat, trying not to gasp.

The admiral considered then returned Karla's kill-zapper. "It's too messy. Take her to the brig, Commander. Find out what she knows, but if you don't learn anything new, feed her to Chomper."

"Yes, sir!" Vinco snapped to action, striding toward me.

"Wait," Doctor Lamont said.

"Now what?" Annoyance creased the admiral's face.

She turned to Karla. "What about our bargain? You said *she* would be here."

"And she is." A nasty glee sparked in Karla's eyes. She pointed at me. "Meet your daughter, Kiana. Trella, or should I call you by your birth name, Sadie?" She rubbed her chin as if deep in thought. "I liked the name Trella. Guess I'm partial to *TR*s and *A*s." She shrugged. "Anyway, Trella, meet your mother."

Horror gripped Doctor Lamont's face, but she shook her head. "You're lying, Karla. It's too big of a coincidence." She uncurled her fingers. My pearl-handled comb lay across her palms. "I fell for it, too." The faint words just audible.

"Troublemakers tend to breed more troublemakers," Karla said. "Although, I must admit I was a bit surprised when I went digging into Trella's records. I knew keeping your child alive would come in handy sometime—she's your weakness.

I suspect Domotor also did a little digging into the computer files and recruited her to his cause."

"No. I don't believe it. She looks nothing like me or Nolan," the doctor said.

"Really?" Karla cocked her hip, studying me. "With her new blue eyes wide with fear, she looks exactly like Nolan did right before we fed him to Chomper."

A murmur ran through the Control Room as the others either agreed or disagreed.

"Touching as all this is, there is much work to be done." The admiral issued orders for the Pop Cops to carry the stunned officers to the infirmary. "Doctor, please make sure they are comfortable. Commander, take this scrub from my sight."

As Vinco's hand wrapped around my upper arm, I said, "This is just the beginning." It was a delay tactic, but the truth of the words knitted my heart together. Even though our rebellion failed, and we had been betrayed, I stood in the Control Room. A future effort might bring the scrubs even further.

I laughed. "You can try and weed out the troublemakers, Admiral, but you'll miss one or two and they'll multiply. Think about it. How do you think we managed to get this far? If I can take advantage of Karla's incompetence, then it's only a matter of time before others do the same."

The lieutenant commander yanked her kill-zapper and shoved it into my ribs. "Let's see if my weapon works."

Vinco released his grip.

"Hold on, Karla," the admiral said. "What do you mean by incompetence, scrub?"

"Look at what we accomplished. Domotor disappeared. We opened Gateway. I escaped the brig and have been living in the upper levels for a week. We infiltrated the computer system. And I'm in your Control Room and your captain is stunned. It was ridiculously easy to break into her office. The list of her incompetence is endless." I tsked.

She dropped the kill-zapper—the upside of my taunt. And wrapped her hands around my neck—the downside.

"I'm going to feed you to Chomper myself," she said, and then squeezed.

She cut off my air and I feared she would crush my windpipe. Groping for her belt, I found her stunner and pulled the trigger. A jolt ringed my neck, but her fingers kept the pressure on my throat. I dropped the stunner and pried them from my numb skin, I shoved her back into the admiral and they fell to the floor together.

Now I would go to Chomper happy.

I almost jumped a meter when Logan's chuckle vibrated in my ear. "*That* must have felt good," he said. "Wish I could have been there."

Jacy added, "We have regained control of levels one and two."

"Trell, stay with us," Riley said. "Once Takia can open the Control Room door, we'll send a rescue party."

Distracted by their voices, I had lost track of events in the Control Room. After a quick scan, my mind raced to plan a way to delay the inevitable. The admiral's red face failed to encourage me. Vinco helped him to his feet.

"Messy or not, silence the scrub," the admiral ordered.

Vinco advanced on me with his knife in hand.

"Overconfidence, Commander, will be your downfall," I said. Weak, but all I could come up with.

"And a sharp blade through your heart will be yours," Vinco replied.

Why didn't I hold on to Karla's stunner? I thought fast. "Actually time is against me right now."

"Time?"

The admiral answered. "She doesn't have any left. Finish the job."

Vinco raised the blade to slice my throat. Movement across the room caught my attention for a second.

"The admiral's wrong," I said. "What I meant by time was I didn't think I had enough of it to distract you. But I did. So I guess I was wrong, too."

Armed scrubs streamed into the room. Before the room erupted into chaos, a number of uppers had been stunned.

Vinco managed to dodge the initial blasts. With his knife still aimed at my throat, he lunged at me. I kicked him in the chest. Instead of cutting deep into the skin, his slash skimmed my neck.

Single-minded, he stepped closer. My back hit a wall, trapping me. He grinned with satisfaction as he pressed his blade under my chin. The steel bit into my jaw. Then strong arms yanked him from me and spun him around.

Riley gave him a mocking salute.

Vinco was amused. "Okay, boy. You first, then the scrub." He pounced.

Riley twisted his hips to avoid the knife thrust and knocked Vinco's arm aside with his hand. Vinco tried again and this time Riley grabbed Vinco's wrist, pulled him off balance and pressed a palm to his elbow, forcing him to the ground.

"Thanks for all those lessons, Commander," Riley said. "They've really paid off."

★ ★ ★

After the takeover of the Control Room, events blurred together. Lack of sleep and the stress of the previous eighty hours caught up to me. With my body aching from Vinco's attack, I blindly followed Riley back to the infirmary to have the cuts on my neck stitched. At this rate, I would use up all the thread.

The male doctor who had helped with Doreen was pressed into service while the others decided what to do with Doctor Lamont.

I woke hours later in the infirmary's extra bedroom. Searching, I found the doctor bustling about the infirmary, tending the others wounded in the fight.

"Go back to bed, Ella," he ordered.

I didn't bother to correct him. Trella, Ella or Sadie—at this point I didn't care. Instead I said, "Every bed is full. You'll need my help."

He scanned the room. "Nothing serious, thank air. And only a few Pop Cops were recycled. You need your rest. Once things settle down, it's going to be…interesting around here."

I shuffled back to my room, thinking my task was complete and I'd leave the others to figure out the rest.

The second time I woke, Riley sat on the edge of my bed. He beamed as if he knew something I didn't.

"What?" I asked.

"You look much better." He smoothed a strand of hair from my face.

"I'm sure you didn't come here to tell me that."

"No, but it's nice to see. Especially after…you know… Vinco."

I shuddered at the memory of his wicked knife. Touching the tender area on my throat, I remembered how it could have been worse. "Thanks for saving me."

"Anytime." He flashed me another overly bright smile.

I pushed to a sitting position. "Okay, Riley, tell me what's going on."

"I found my brother."

"Wonderful. How—no, let me guess. You went to the lower levels with Mama Sheepy and found the man who still had Dada Sheepy."

"Yep. The Sheepy family is whole again. His name is Blake and he works in the kitchen." He beamed.

I squinted. "You have more news."

This time, he shot me a nervous smile. "I was hoping—" he pulled a necklace from his pocket "—we could make a commitment."

A brief pulse of fear shot through me. "You mean be mates?"

"No. At least, not yet. Our tradition is to give a gift as the first step. Sort of a symbol that we plan to see how well we get along." He laid the necklace in my palm.

A silver pendant swung from a thin chain. "A sheep?" I asked.

"I thought it appropriate, considering what has happened."

So much had happened, and Inside would no longer be the same. But the thought of Riley by my side sent a comforting pulse through my body.

"How do I accept?" I asked.

"You wear the necklace."

I marveled at the detail of the sheep. "Are you sure? You don't know everything about me—"

"I do know I felt as if my heart had been shredded when I found you in our storeroom, unconscious and bleeding. And leaving you with Vinco in the holding cells was the hardest thing I've ever done." He wrapped an arm around me and pulled me close. "We can take it slow. We have plenty of time."

He kissed me. A sizzle traveled through me that didn't stop when he drew back. My mouth tingled.

"Your answer?" he asked.

I kissed him, enjoying the sensation of happiness blooming inside me for the first time. Too soon, we parted.

"I'll take that as a yes." Riley unhooked the clasp of the necklace. "Another one of our traditions is for me to make the pendant myself, but I had help from Logan and Anne-Jade." He looped it around my neck then secured it, sweeping my hair out of the way.

I fingered the sheep. "Logan and Anne-Jade? Is it one of their gadgets?"

"Yes, but," he hurriedly added, "it's inactive. If you ever get into trouble and need help, you can squeeze the pendant and it will send a signal. We can trace the signal to your location and send reinforcements."

I laughed. "Do you really think it's necessary now?"

"I may not know everything about you, but I do know that if there is trouble, you'll be in the middle of it."

He stifled my squawk of protest with another kiss. After a while, I forgot to be mad.

The transition from the Travas controlling Inside to a more democratic method wasn't smooth. Even though each family elected a representative and each scrub "family" had a person attending organization meetings, many uppers still viewed the scrubs with suspicion and the scrubs in turn made planning difficult with their distrust and bitterness.

I had hoped to avoid all the political wrangling, but, since I understood both sides, I attended all the meetings to smooth relations. Even so, we had a long way to go. Overcrowding remained a problem, and a few people resisted the change in their lifestyles. Violence erupted on occasion, and Anne-Jade organized a security detail with members of all the families to keep the peace.

Being able to walk the hallways of the upper levels without worry felt liberating. Domotor also enjoyed his freedom from the hideout. He was busy preaching to everyone to be patient and understanding. All the Travas had been incarcerated for now. The Committee would decide their eventual fate. Doctor Lamont had been confined, too.

It was week 147,007, and I had received a message to meet Logan in the Control Room at hour ten. He had been camped out there since the takeover, using the computers to harvest lost information.

He hunched over a keyboard, muttering and humming to himself. I touched his arm and he almost jumped from his seat.

"Don't scare me like that," he said, waving a hand in front of his face.

"I'm sorry. Should I have bowed and announced my presence first? Have they coronated you fleet admiral yet?"

"Go ahead and be sarcastic." He swiveled back to the screen. "I'm not going to tell you—ow! Let go of my ear, I'll tell you."

I released his lobe. He rubbed it.

"Logan?"

"All right. I found the answers to those final three files and accessed the information. Outside is something called Outer Space. It's an airless and pressureless environment unable to support life."

Sorrow and guilt welled. If we just had waited, Cog wouldn't be floating out there. "Thanks for the reminder."

"Sorry. Ah…well, we are actually traveling *through* it. Seems it is so vast that it takes an incredibly long time to get from one planet to another."

"Planet?"

"As far as I can tell, a planet is the *real* Outside." He typed on the keyboard. The picture of the blue ceiling and greenery filled the computer's screen. "This is our destination. We've been heading there for the past 147,000 weeks."

"When are we scheduled to arrive?" But the answer popped into my mind. *It's the end and the beginning. What is it?* I looked at Logan.

"Week one million," we said together.

I groped for a chair. We had 853,000 weeks to go! My head spun as I sat. Eight thousand generations of people would be born, live and end in this metal cube before reaching the true Outside.

"There's so much to learn about our past and why we're here," Logan said. "I've just scratched the surface. The Travas tried deleting all the files, but they were protected by the system's safety guards and buried."

"The system's guards? What about the Controllers?"

Logan flipped his hand as if dismissing an underling. "No evidence of them. At least no indication that the Controllers are actual people. It's the system's operating parameters and fail-safes. Also certain directives have been programmed into it, which were set by the original designers."

"What directives?"

"Like the one about our population. Once we reach Outside, the designers wanted to make sure we had enough people to survive. These directives couldn't be changed or altered, so the Travas must have thought they were a divine message." Logan chuckled. "Anyway, it's amazing Domotor found those buried files, and was able to copy parts of them."

"It wasn't Domotor. He was the leader of the group, but Nolan Garrard was the first to find them."

"Then Garrard was a genius." Logan tapped a finger on his chair. "Speaking of Garrard, did you want to read your file?"

My file? It took me a moment to remember the file marked with my birth week and hour. "No."

"But it's important. Your mother explains her actions. You *need* to forgive her."

I glared at him. "She betrayed you, too. We almost lost."

"Almost. She didn't tell them *everything* about our plans. How do you think we rallied?"

"I don't care. She told them enough. Besides, Karla could have planted the information about my birth parents in the computer. It could be a complete hoax and she's not related to me at all."

"There's a way to prove or disprove the relationship," Logan said.

"How?"

"With your blood. Those vampire boxes do more than test for pregnancy."

★ ★ ★

Logan had overwhelmed me with information. I wandered around in a daze until I was needed for yet another Committee meeting. The uppers and lowers squabbled like children and I wished to be back in the infirmary, helping the doctor. Or better yet, to be with Riley in our room.

As I let the discord roll over me, I decided I needed to be the Queen of the Pipes for a little while and not worry about blood tests and overcrowding.

Returning to the air shafts, I felt light and free. I explored more of the upper levels. With the constant threat of being caught by the Pop Cops, I had limited my forays above level four. Now, I climbed into the Gap and investigated the space between the pipes and the ceiling of Inside.

I felt as if there was a missing element. Air shafts and water pipes crisscrossed above the level. No laundry chutes or waste pipes—understandable since both of them go down to level one.

Climbing over a duct, I bumped my head on the ceiling and realized the missing element was foam. There was no insulating foam. I sat until the pain subsided.

Why wasn't there any foam? I shone my light on the metal panels, counting rivets. I lost track of time, but I didn't care, planning to search the entire ceiling.

In the northeast corner, I found a hatch. It resembled the near-invisible hatches that accessed the Gap, but it had a black rubber seal around it.

No keypad. No handle.

My body hummed with nervous energy. This door was different than Gateway. I should leave it alone and tell the Committee I had found another hatch. I *should* didn't mean

I *would*. Gateway had another inner door, and I couldn't leave without seeing if this one did, too.

I pushed with my hands. Nothing. Putting more force into it, I tried again. A crackling sounded. I bent over and pressed my shoulders to the hatch, using my legs for added strength.

A slow sucking noise grew louder as I kept the pressure on. Then it popped free. I staggered with surprise. The hatch banged down off to the side as darkness spilled from the opening.

I braced for the ice-cold nothing to rob me of air, but only the stale smell of dust reached me. I straightened, poking my head into the space past the doorway.

The semi-darkness stretched up to an impossible height and disappeared into black. It felt like Outer Space, but with stale air and walls. Faint bluelight climbed the sides. I hoisted myself onto the floor constructed of metal sheets riveted together just like the rest of Inside.

I walked along, shining my light. It was a huge empty space. At least, it was empty until my light lit stacks of metal sheets, pipes, equipment, barrels and I-beams. An amazing array of supplies.

In the far southwest corner, were gigantic shelves. The shelves appeared to be half-completed levels. I counted them. Six. The space had room for six more levels!

No. A huge expanse loomed above the sixth one.

I knelt on the floor as understanding sucked my breath away. The builders of Inside knew the journey would be long and our population would grow. Above me was plenty of room for us to expand. No more overcrowding. No more restrictions on the number of children. We could have large families and privacy. I could have a family.

I pressed my forehead to the cold metal floor, trying not to pass out. My shaky hand found the pendant. I squeezed the sheep, sending the signal.

Riley, I thought, *bring reinforcements, we're going to need them.*

★ ★ ★ ★ ★

Acknowledgements

My thank-yous always start with my husband, Rodney. His support is critical to my writing and essential when I'm flying all over the place to attend book events. My children, Luke and Jenna, also get a thank-you for inspiring me and for not making me feel too guilty when I'm running around for my other job.

The entire story for this book came to me in a dream, including characters, plot twists and ending. That hadn't happened to me before and hasn't since. However, dream novels still need to be written, and I'd like to thank a group of Seton Hill University critiquers who looked at the first chapter and said, "You may have something here."

Thanks to Dr. Michael Arnzen, Venessa Giunta, Johanna Gribble, Sara Lyon, Kathryn Martin, Heidi Ruby Miller, Darren Moore, Sabrina Naples, Rachael Pruitt and Shara Saunsaucie.

A special thank-you to the original Tricky (the good one), Mike Mehalek, who came up with the cool title!

A big thank-you to those who read the first draft and helped with revisions—my editor Mary-Theresa Hussey, my agent Robert Mecoy, my critique partner Kimberly Howe, and Elizabeth Mazer. Also to all those at MIRA who helped the book along the way (too many to count, let alone list), thank you all so much! The cover is dead-on perfect—a heartfelt thanks to the art department and all the talented artists and designers who helped with the cover.

No acknowledgements are ever complete without thanking my mounting army of Book Commandos. They are spreading the word about my books in bookstores, in book groups, in libraries, in line at the grocery stores, throughout their families and online. You guys rock! A special thank-you for those who went that extra mile: Amberkatze, Lorri Amsden, Deborah Beamer, Linda Childs, Allison Leigh Davis, Michelle Deschene-Warren, David Hankerson, Michelle Haring, Kristy Kalin, Lexie, Holly Nelson, Lora Negrito, Rosemary Potter, Lee Ann Ray, Christina Russo, Rachel Smith, Michelle Staffa, Jenny Sweedler and Diana Teeter. Trella will want to recruit you all to the Force of Sheep.

Are YOU ready for

OUTSIDE IN

It's coming soon…

INSIDE

SURVIVAL GUIDE

Also known as:
TRELLA'S GUIDE TO
SURVIVING INSIDE

First rule of survival

DO NOT get noticed by the Population Control Police (Pop Cops). Being noticed is dangerous! You need to blend in with your fellow Scrubs.

Here are a few ways to blend in:

○ Make sure your voice isn't louder than the general hum

○ Don't wear anything other than standard-issue uniforms and jumpsuits

○ For women—pull your hair into a ponytail or single braid. For men—keep your hair short like the Pop Cops. Don't put anything flashy and/or colourful in your hair

○ Keep your expression neutral— angry, upset and/or happy faces draw unwanted attention

○ Sit in the middle of the dining room

○ Don't ever be the first person or the last person to arrive for assemblies

○ Don't laugh

○ Make sure you have plenty of acquaintances and don't hang out with the same people all the time

○ Always be on time for your work shift

○ Don't show any spark of intelligence or personality

○ Don't show any gumption or inventiveness

○ Don't express your opinion and/or complain

○ Repeat Pop Cop propaganda during casual conversations

○ Remember Scrubs are sheep—act accordingly

If you should attract the attention of the Pop Cops, follow these guidelines:

○ Don't make eye contact—keep your gaze on the floor at all times

○ Be polite

○ Keep your expression neutral and your voice steady

○ Answer the questions that are asked and don't elaborate unless requested

○ Don't run or resist arrest

○ Don't cry

○ Don't volunteer ANY information

Second rule of survival

DO NOT trust anyone. That's right—ANYONE!! Not your Care Mother, not your best friend (which you shouldn't have—see rule No. 1), not your Care Mates, not your supervisor, not your lover, not your doctor, and not your birth mother or father (if you even know who they are). Anyone of these people can be a spy for the Pop Cops.

Third rule of survival

DO NOT break any of the Pop Cop's laws.

Fourth rule...

I can't do this any more! Surviving *isn't* living, so… If you happen to break all these rules like I did, then follow this advice:

- ○ Always have an escape route planned
- ○ Find good hiding spots
- ○ Gather a group of intelligent cohorts, including Tech Nos
- ○ Trust your friends
- ○ Don't hesitate to run
- ○ Be prepared for surprises
- ○ Aim for maximum damage
- ○ Remember Scrubs are sheep. They outnumber the shepherds—act accordingly!

Fifth rule

ANYTHING is possible.

Choose:
A Quick Death
Or Slow Poison

Meet Yelena Zaltana, prisoner, food-taster—and a girl about
to discover her own extraordinary magical powers.

The Kingdom of Ixia needs a heroine…

POISON STUDY
by
Maria V. Snyder

"A woman? The next prisoner to be executed is a woman?" His voice was icy. My body trembled on hearing the word *executed* aloud. The calm I'd established earlier fled me. I would have sunk sobbing to the floor if the guards weren't with me. The guards tormented anyone who showed any weakness.

The man tugged at the black ringlets of his hair. "I should have taken the time to reread your dossier." He shooed the guards away. "You're dismissed."

When they were gone, he motioned me to the chair in front of his desk. The chains clanged as I perched on the edge.

He opened a folder on his desk and scanned the pages. "Yelena, today may be your lucky day," he said.

I swallowed a sarcastic reply. An important lesson I had mastered during my dungeon stay was never to talk back. I bowed my head instead, avoiding eye contact.

The man was quiet for a while. "Well-behaved and respect-ful. You're starting to look like a good candidate."

Despite the clutter of the room, the desk was neat. In addition to my folder and some writing implements, the only other items on the desk were two small, black statues glittering with streaks of silver—a set of panthers carved to lifelike perfection.

"You've been tried and found guilty of murdering General Brazell's only son, Reyad." He paused, stroking his temple with his fingers. "That explains why Brazell's here this week, and why he has been unusually interested in the execution schedule." The man spoke more to himself than to me.

Upon hearing Brazell's name, fear coiled in my stomach. I steadied myself with a reminder that I was soon to be out of his reach forever.

The Territory of Ixia's military had come to power only a generation ago, but the rule had produced strict laws called the Code of Behavior. During peacetime—most of the time, strangely enough for the military—proper conduct didn't allow the taking of a human life. If someone committed murder, the punishment was execution. Self-preservation or an accidental death were not considered acceptable excuses. Once found guilty, the murderer was sent to the Commander's dungeon to await a public hanging.

"I suppose you're going to protest the conviction. Say you were framed or you killed out of self-defense." He leaned back in his chair, waiting with a weary patience.

"No, sir," I whispered, all I could manage from unused vocal cords. "I killed him."

The man in black straightened in his chair, shooting me a hard look. Then he laughed aloud. "This may work out better than I'd planned. Yelena, I'm offering you a choice. You can either be executed, or you can be Commander Ambrose's new food taster. His last taster died recently, and we need to fill the position."

I gaped at him, my heart dancing. He had to be joking. He was probably amusing himself. Great way to get a laugh. Watch hope and joy shine on the prisoner's face, then smash it by sending the accused to the noose.

I played along. "A fool would refuse the job." My voice rasped louder this time.

"Well, it's a lifetime position. The training can be lethal. After all, how can you identify poisons in the Commander's food if you don't know what they taste like?" He tidied the papers in the folder.

"You'll get a room in the castle to sleep, but most of the day you'll be with the Commander. No days off. No husband or children. Some prisoners have chosen execution instead. At least then they know exactly when they're going to die, rather than guessing if it's going to come with the next bite." He clicked his teeth together, a feral grin on his face.

He was serious. My whole body shook. A chance to live! Service to the Commander was better than the dungeon and infinitely better than the noose. Questions raced through my mind: I'm a convicted killer, how can they trust me? What would prevent me from killing the Commander or escaping?

"Who tastes the Commander's food now?" I asked instead, afraid if I asked the other questions he'd realize his mistake and send me to the gallows.

"I do. So I'm anxious to find a replacement. Also the Code of Behavior states that someone whose life is forfeit must be offered the job."

No longer able to sit still, I stood and paced around the

room, dragging my chains with me. The maps on the walls showed strategic military positions. Book titles dealt with security and spying techniques. The condition and amount of candles suggested someone who worked late into the night.

I looked back at the man in the adviser's uniform. He had to be Valek, the Commander's personal security chief and leader of the vast intelligence network for the Territory of Ixia.

"What shall I tell the executioner?" Valek asked.

"I am not a fool."

CHOOSE:
A QUICK DEATH...
OR A SLOW POISON...

About to be executed for murder, Yelena is offered the chance to become a food taster. She'll eat the best meals, have rooms in the palace – and risk assassination by anyone trying to kill the Commander of Ixia.

But disasters keep mounting as rebels plot to seize Ixia and Yelena develops magical powers she can't control. Her life is threatened again and choices must be made. But this time the outcomes aren't so clear...

www.mirabooks.co.uk

MIRA

UNTRAINED. UNTESTED. UNLEASHED.

When the Stormdancer clan needs help, Opal's knowledge and unique magical abilities make her the perfect choice – until the mission goes awry.

Now Opal must deal with plotters out to destroy the Stormdancer clan, as well as a traitor in their midst.

With danger and deception rising around her, will Opal's untested abilities destroy her – or save them all?

www.mirabooks.co.uk

Something is wrong with Kaylee Cavanaugh...

She can sense when someone near her is about to die. And when that happens, an uncontrollable force compels her to scream bloody murder. Literally.

Kaylee just wants to enjoy having caught the attention of the hottest boy in school. But when classmates start dropping dead for no reason and only Kaylee knows who'll be next, finding a boyfriend is the least of her worries!

Book one in the Soul Screamers *series.*

Available 1st January 2011

www.mirabooks.co.uk

Meghan Chase has a secret destiny...

Meghan has never quite fitted in at school…or at home. But she could never have guessed that she is the daughter of a mythical faery king and a pawn in a deadly war.

Now Meghan will learn just how far she'll go to save someone she cares about…and to find love with a prince who might rather see her dead than let her touch his icy heart.

First in the stunning *Iron Fey* series

Available 21st January 2011
www.mirabooks.co.uk

There's something different about the new guy at Crossroads High…

With four undead souls living inside him, Aden's about to discover just how different he is. Helped by his new friends, Mary Ann, a human teenager with powers, werewolf shapeshifter Riley and especially vampire princess Victoria, Aden enters a dark and dangerous underworld.

When one of the souls in Aden's head foretells his death, Aden must uncover his own supernatural skills if he hopes to survive.

www.mirabooks.co.uk